THE BEASTS OF

by the same author
Disappearer
Colin Cleveland and the End of the World
Girl's Rock
The Eternal Prisoner
Rogue Males

Mark Hunter series
Beautiful Chaos
Sixty-Six Curses
Trouble at School
Mysterious Girlfriend
The Beasts of Bellend
Countdown to Zero

frontis. Trina Truelove's t-shirt *(chap.16)*

The Beasts of Bellend

Chris Johnson

Samurai West

Published by Samurai West
disappearer007@gmail.com

Story and Art © Chris Johnson 2023
All rights reserved

This paperback edition published 2025
ISBN-13: 9798293401956

Prologue

'You wanted to see me, sir?'

'Yes, but it's nothing urgent. Just a query a routine check of the personnel files has thrown up. Take a pew.'

'Thank you. Is it something in my file then?'

'Yes. It's about your home address: it's down on the file as "Bellend Close." Must be an input error that somehow slipped through the net. So, what is it really? Bellenden, I suppose.'

'No sir, it's not Bellenden.'

'Bellen*dean*?'

'No, it's Bellendean either. Just Bellend.'

'Would that be "Belle," as in French for beautiful, hyphen "End"?'

'No sir, just Bellend.'

'Just Bellend…? As in Bee ee double-ell ee en dee…?'

'Yessir, Bellend, exactly as it's written in the file. Bellend Close; it's on the edge of Bellend Wood.'

'Bellend Close on the edge of Bellend Wood…'

'Yessir.'

'You don't have to look so anguished about it, man. So, you've got a silly sounding address: it's not your fault, is it? Don't let it get you down.'

'Oh, it's not the address, sir. To be honest, it had never occurred to me until you brought it up just now. I've just been feeling a little under the weather recently.'

'Oh! Well, I'm sorry to hear about it. What's up? Is it anything in particular?'

'No… I'm just feeling a bit rundown… Out of sorts, you know…'

'No, I don't know. What's making you feel rundown? Is it overwork? If you need some time off—'

'No, no, I'm fine. Really…'

'Look, you're obviously not fine, David. Have you had a

check-up recen—wait a minute: your wife's a GP, isn't she? Hasn't she been able to help you?'

'My *wife*? She's the last person I can—she's one of *them*.'

'One of them? What are you talking about? One of whom?'

'*Them*. The *women*.'

REAL LIVE CAVEMEN SEEN WITH THEIR CLUBS OUT!

Yes, it's true! An eyewitness reports seeing these brawny brutes in their birthday suits just outside the town of Strepford, Surrey, in a place called (wait for it) Bellend Wood! 'They were all big and hairy and they weren't wearing anything!' exclaims the goggle-eyed eyewitness. 'And they had these really big muscles!' Whether this 'big' description included the stripped-off stone-age studs' *love* muscles, the eyewitness, Luke Gosling, age 7, of Sycamore Street, Strepford, is too young to say!

from an article in *The Sun* newspaper, 26th July 202-

Chapter One
Doctor's Orders

The woman lies on the examination couch with skirt hitched up and legs spread wide. The doctor, hunkered down, performs a careful inspection of the exposed genitalia.

'No... No, I don't see anything wrong here at all...' she says.

'But do you *smell* anything wrong?' asks the patient.

'No, not a thing. The odour is quite normal.'

'Yes, but is it *excessive*?'

'Not at all.'

'It doesn't repel you?'

'Not at all. Quite the reverse, in fact.'

'Really? Are you absolutely sure?'

'Absolutely. Allow me to demonstrate.'

The demonstration that follows is not in accordance with strict medical practice, but is swiftly and skilfully brought to a successful climax. While the satisfied patient adjusts her clothes, the equally-satisfied doctor, a pink tongue-tip gathering up the dewy fruits of her malpractice, walks to the window and raises the blind, admitting the daylight into the ground floor office. The doctor's name is Mhambi Khoza and she holds the respected position of senior practitioner here at Main Street surgery, in the small town of Strepford. A tall woman, ebony-skinned, her tight-curled hair close shorn, she wears her doctor's white coat unbuttoned over a patterned summer dress, belted at the waist, and a pair of low-heeled sandals on her feet. Approaching forty, she possesses a stately beauty, the features of her face regal and composed.

Turning from the window, Mhambi now reseats herself at her desk, and her patient, clothes adjusted, sits facing her. The patient's name is Ramona, and as well as being her registered GP, Mhambi Khoza is also her next-door neighbour and close friend. (Very close, as we've just seen.)

Of Indian ethnicity, Ramona is about the same age as her friend, and nearly as tall but not quite. Her hair is, long, loose and abundant, its raven hue just beginning to be threaded with the odd strand of silver. (Silver being the nice way of saying grey.) Possessed of a calm, gentle beauty, her features are patrician (especially the nose), and her eyes heavily-lidded. She wears a front-buttoned denim dress and strappy gladiator sandals.

'So, there is no cause for concern,' says Mhambi, assuming a professional tone. 'I can give you a clean bill of health. You have no venereal ailments or diseases, and you are not suffering from excessive odour due to neglect of personal hygiene.'

'Then why does my husband keep complaining that he can smell it from across the room?'

'Because your husband is a neurotic,' is the firm answer. 'He is neurotic and hypersensitive, and his condition is deteriorating rapidly. You told me he's also started complaining about the noise you make when you chew your food, yes? Well, that's another classic symptom of neurosis.'

'So, what should I do?'

'Be blunt with him. Tell him the truth. Tell him that your vagina smells the same as it's always smelt and that you chew your food the same way you've always chewed it. The problem is entirely with him, and you have to let him know that.'

'He won't like hearing that…'

'He doesn't have to like it, does he? You've always been far too indulgent with your husband; always letting him get his own way. It's time to rein him in a bit.'

'I don't like to. He's very sensitive…'

'*Hyper*-sensitive. That's what he is.'

'Yes, but perhaps I could make *some* concessions…'

'Like what?'

'I thought perhaps I could try using one of those vaginal deodorants…'

Mhambi snorts. 'If it was me, I'd stop washing down there altogether.'

'But I don't want to antagonise him…!'

'Why not? If you can't get along with him, then you might as well just enjoy yourself *not* getting along with him. Try baiting him and ridiculing him. You've coddled him so much in the past, it's the last thing he'll be expecting. It'll completely knock him off-balance. Think of all the fun you can have.'

'Mhambi! I can't do that! It would be cruel!'

'So what if it is? *Be* cruel. He's no good for you in bed anymore, so you might as well get some use out of him. It's what I do with my husband.'

'With David? Really? You treat him like that?'

'Yes, we're at daggers drawn, we.'

'But you always seem so friendly when I see you together…!'

'Oh, that's just keeping up appearances. But behind closed doors it's open warfare, and I've never had so much fun in my life.'

'Really? Is it that enjoyable?'

'It is. Especially when you're the one who's winning. So I recommend you give it a try yourself. Consider it your doctor's prescribed course of treatment.'

A smile slowly spreads itself across Ramona's face. Yes… Yes… Why hadn't she thought of this before? That husband of hers! That arrogant, pretentious, demanding, and altogether completely childish husband of hers! Why had she put up with him so long? Why has she always placated, conceded, conciliated? Why had she always put his feelings before her own?

The answer is obvious: because she's such a nice person. And now at last the solution is equally obvious: to *stop* being such a nice person!

'You're starting to get it, aren't you?' says Mhambi.

'Oh, Mhambi!' gushes Ramona. 'You are perfect! You are a queen! No: a goddess! The goddess of all goddesses! The woman divine made flesh! You have shown me the true path! Oh, thank you, thank you, thank you!'

Yes, it's time to start fighting back! Energised, Ramona springs from her chair, takes Mhambi's hand in both of her own, pumps it vigorously, and exits the room, fleet of foot and light as air.

Alone, Mhambi settles back in her chair, experiencing a sense of job satisfaction rare to most general practitioners in the NHS. She checks her appointments on her computer screen. Good. Just one more appointment, and then it's time for the morning coffee break, that relaxing interlude where the physicians gather together to stoke up on caffeine, smoke 'em if they've got 'em, and exchange amusing anecdotes about their patients' ailments.

That one more appointment now arrives in the form of Patricia Pinecone, another resident of Bellend Close. A flurried-looking female with a mass of manic wavy hair, and overzealous eyes magnified by spectacles, she erupts into the room, clutching a large framed photograph to her chest. This, upon taking her seat, she deposits on Mhambi's desk, positioning it so that the subject of the photograph faces herself. The image is the portrait of a rather underwhelming man of middle-aged who has the appearance of a travelling salesman, and funnily enough *is* a travelling salesman. This man is Patricia Pinecone's beloved husband, and whenever he is absent, she carries his image around with her wherever she goes.

(Perhaps I should also have mentioned, having described the ethnicities of our first two characters, that Patricia is Caucasian? Or shall we just proceed on the usual understanding that 'all characters appearing in this novel are white unless otherwise specified'?)

'And what can I help you with today?' asks Mhambi,

after greetings have been exchanged. A reasonable question, and one generally asked by GPs upon receiving a patient—but in the present situation it appears to touch a raw nerve, because Patricia's response to this simple inquiry is to burst into a flood of tears.

Mhambi sighs. 'Look, Patricia, I understand that you miss your husband when he's out of town, but I am not a counsellor and short of prescribing you some anti-depressants, which as I've said before, I really do not recommend, there's not much I can—'

'No, no! It's not that!' sobs Patricia, when, having noisily blown her nose, regains the power of speech. 'It's not that at all! You see, I... I... Oh! I don't know how I can even look him in the eye!'

And upon doing just that, she bursts into renewed floods of tears.

'What have you done that makes you say you can't look your husband in the eye?' asks Mhambi.

'I've... I've been... *unfaithful* to him!' blubbers Patricia.

Another weary sigh. 'Look, Patricia, I thought we'd already agreed—'

'Oh, I don't mean *that!*' elucidates Patricia. 'I know *that* doesn't count! But I mean that this time, I've been with a... a man! An actual and identifiable man! Oh, I'm despicable! I've basely betrayed my darling husband! The man to whom I swore eternal fidelity!'

And she has recourse to her handkerchief again, blowing her nose violently.

'I see...' says Mhambi, surprised at the news but doing her best to conceal the fact. 'You mean you've started an affair? Or was it just a one-night stand?'

'Well, neither really,' is the reply. 'We haven't actually got to the stage of actually... you know... *sleeping* together...'

'Then what are you upset about?' demands Mhambi, annoyed. 'If you haven't slept with this man, then you haven't actually been unfaithful yet, have you?'

'Oh, haven't I?' retorts Patricia warmly.

'Of course not! If you haven't actually, physically—'

'That's hardly the point, is it?' insists Patricia.

'But if—'

'Look; do you know what someone once said?'

'No, I don't know what someone once said.'

'Well, I'll tell you what they said: they said that you are unfaithful to your spouse the moment you even *think* about being unfaithful to them. And I *have* thought about it! Therefore, in my own eyes, I am guilty. I cannot deny it. I have developed *feelings* for this man! And what's even worse is, I've promised him that tonight is going to be the night I surrender myself to him!'

'I see. So where did you actually meet this man…?'

'Meet him? I didn't *meet* him: I've known him for years. He lives in the close.'

Hearing this, a look of enlightenment settles on the doctor's features. 'We wouldn't happen to be talking about Gerald Banbury, would we?'

Two wide eyes open even wider. 'Yes, it *is* Gerald! How on earth did you gue—Oh, of course! Process of elimination! He's the only unmarried man in the close. Silly me!'

A thin smile crosses Mhambi's full lips. 'Being married has never stopped most men from making moves on their neighbour's wives,' she says. 'But even if it did, I'd still have known it was Gerald for the very good reason he once tried the same thing with *me*.'

'With *you*?'

'Yes, me and, to the best of my knowledge, every other woman living in Bellend Close.'

'What?' thunders Patricia, outrage emerging from her stupefaction. 'Every woman in the… That-that Casanova! That Don Juan! That Lothario! That Lovelace!' (pronouncing the latter incorrectly.) 'I thought that he *loved* me! The way he would roughly handle my buttocks and whisper obscene suggestions in my ear… And it was all an act! A put-on! He just wanted to make me another notch in his belt! And I thought he was a poor, lonely bachelor who had fallen desperately in love; and I was all set to break my sacred marriage vows and let him have his way with me! The wretch!'

'Well, for what it's worth, he would have been a major disappointment to you,' says Mhambi, consolingly.

'Oh… You mean… is he… impotent?'

Mhambi pulls a face. 'Well, you could put it that way, but technically, to be impotent you need to have something to be impotent *with*.'

'Oh, I see. At least I think I do. You mean his… equipment… is a bit on the small side…'

'You could put it like that.'

Patricia sniffs. 'Well, in other circumstances I might have felt sorry for him. But after what you've told me… Every wife in the Close… That means he left *me* till last! As though I'm the least desirable! Well, I'm *glad* he's got a small one! And the moment I get home I'm going to ring him up and let him know in no uncertain terms that tonight is definitely *off*! Off forever!'

'I think that is a wise plan of action,' concurs Mhambi.

Patricia takes up her husband's photograph in loving hands. 'Oh, Malcolm! I can look you in the eye once more! I know I am not entirely guiltless, but I am as much victim as wrongdoer: I was tricked by a trickster! And never will I allow such a thing to happen again! I shall be strong! I shall be resolute in my undying fidelity to you, my one and only!'

And she plants a sloppy kiss on the protective glass.

Rising to her feet: 'Well, thank you, Mhambi, for your timely warning. Now I shall go home and I shall send Mr Gerald Banbury about his business!'

Patricia marches for the door. She stops and marches back again. 'Oh! I almost forgot!'

'Forgot what?' inquires Mhambi, who had just started to relax and think of coffee and biscuits.

'The new people who are moving in today: I've found out who they are!'

'Who?' asks Mhambi, interested.

'You'll never guess!'

'How could I guess? Is it someone I know?'

'It's someone everyone knows! Celebrities!'

'It's time for my coffee break, Patricia. Can you just tell me, please?'

'It's Dodo Dupont and Mayumi Takahashi!'

'What?' flabbergasted.

'Yes! Dodo Dupont, the woman who does all those fascinating television documentaries! And Mayumi Takahashi is her partner! She's the photographer who takes all those naughty pictures! Who would've thought *they* would be moving to Strepford!'

'Who indeed…' murmurs Mhambi, frowning.

'It… it's not going to be a problem, is it?' asks Patricia.

Mhambi looks at her. 'A problem?'

'Yes, I… I thought maybe with those two being a… you know, *same-sex* couple, it might cause a problem… You know, disrupt the atmosphere, or something…'

'Oh, no. *That* won't be a problem,' Mhambi assures her.

The problem, thinks Mhambi when Patricia has departed, is that aside from her writing and documentary filmmaking, Dodo Dupont also sometimes works as a spy, assisting her friend Mark Hunter of MI5. Not many people know this fact about Dodo, but Mhambi knows it because Mark Hunter also happens to be her husband's boss.

The expression on Mhambi's face does not bode well for her husband.

Chapter Two
Slayve the Barbarian!

Abigail is pursuing her solitary way through Bellend Wood when she discovers Fat Tulip sitting under a tree at the edge of the clearing. Fat Tulip is so-called because her given name is Tulip and she is indeed what is politely referred to as full-figured. Abigail is only nine, while Fat Tulip is fourteen, so Abigail knows Fat Tulip only by name and appearance, while Fat Tulip, who doesn't generally pay much attention to other people, doesn't know Abigail at all.

Fat Tulip is annoyed when she first catches sight of the skinny little primary school girl, thinking she is only the vanguard of an invasion of skinny little primary school girls, disturbing her in her solitary possession of the clearing. Fat Tulip considers this clearing to be *her* clearing and the advent of any uninvited intruders is an act of desecration. When it becomes apparent that the skinny girl is in fact alone, Fat Tulip is somewhat mollified, not to mention surprised. In her experience, little kids are usually always very social, as well as very noisy, creatures, and that the solitary habits connected with personality disorders usually only start to manifest themselves during adolescence (case in point: Fat Tulip herself); and clearly the pig-tailed stick-insect in the white dress and flip-flops standing before her now has yet to reach that stage.

In fact, Fat Tulip considers not just this particular clearing, but the whole of Bellend Wood to be her own particular domain, but she does graciously tolerate the presence of others within its leafy precincts. As long as they stick to the footpaths. And especially as long as they find their way to this particular spot.

For a minute or two the girls subject each other to silent scrutiny. Abigail is the first to speak.

'Hello,' she says, lively.

'Hello,' responds Fat Tulip, flat.
'What are you doing?' asks Abigail.
'Sitting under a tree,' replies Fat Tulip. 'What are *you* doing?'
'Talking to you!'

Abigail laughs, because she thinks her reply is a funny one.

Fat Tulip doesn't laugh. 'How did you find this place?'
'The woods? I've always known the woods were here!'
'Not the whole woods; I mean just this clearing.'
'Oh! I didn't know about this clearing until I found it just now.'
'Well, I found it before you,' says Fat Tulip. 'This is *my* clearing. So you better not tell anyone else about it.'
'I won't tell anyone,' says Abigail readily.
'Promise?'
'Promise!'
'Good. Cuz if you *do* tell anyone, I'll know about it and I'll put a curse on you.'
'Can you do spells then?'
'Yes I can, because I'm a witch.'
'Ooh! I like witches!'

The girl sitting beneath the tree doesn't look much like a witch. Fat Tulip is, as advertised, inclined to obesity, she wears glasses, has her dark, unruly hair cut in a chin-length bob, and is dressed in a baggy t-shirt, faded jeans and neglected trainers. To look at her, you would have her pegged as the indoor type, an avid gamer. But nevertheless, she has just announced herself to be a witch, and Abigail, while wise enough to doubt some of the statements made to her by her peers, is still of that age when she accepts as truthful anything told to her by her elders and betters.

And in the case of this particular assertion, there is also an additional readiness to believe what she's just been told—because as she has just said, Abigail likes witches.

'What kind of witch are you?' she asks. 'A good one

or a bad one?'

'I'm a Wiccan witch.'

'A wicked witch?'

'A *Wiccan* witch!'

'What's a Wiccan witch? Is that a good one or bad one?'

'A good one.'

'But you still put spells on people, don't you?'

'I only put spells on bad people who break promises and tell people about other people's clearings.'

'Oh, I won't do that!'

'Good. What's your name?'

'Abigail,' says Abigail. 'And your name's Fat Tulip.'

'It's just *Tulip*. And how did you know?'

'Just do. You live near here, don't you? Bellend Close.'

'Yes. Where do you live?'

'Over on Silver Street. Can I stay here with you? I *like* witches.'

Fat Tulip thinks about this. 'Alright then,' she decides. 'You can stay. You can be my assistant witch.'

This proposal sends Abigail into ecstasies, whooping and jumping up and down clapping her hands.

'Come and sit here,' says Fat Tulip, patting the ground beside her. 'And don't call me Fat Tulip again, either.'

Abigail sits down beside her. Fat Tulip has a bag by her other side, and from this she produces a plastic bottle filled with water. Uncapping it, she takes a long drink, then offers the bottle to Abigail.

'Want some?'

'Yes, please.' She takes the bottle, hesitates. 'Should I wipe the top first...?'

'Nah. Witches don't have to do that.'

Abigail now drinks from the bottle. (In Japan they would call this receiving an 'indirect kiss.')

The bottle returned to the bag, Fat Tulip now produces a comic magazine from the same receptacle. It is the latest issue of *Slayve the Barbarian*, a somewhat notorious publication aimed at middle-grade schoolchildren. The lurid cover shows an impossibly-muscular warrior wearing bearskin briefs and very little else and brandishing a huge battleaxe.

'What do you think of that?' says Fat Tulip proudly. 'Pretty cool, yeah?'

'Wo-ow!' says Abigail, suitably impressed.

'I've got every issue,' announces Fat Tulip. 'This one just came out today. I've already read it once, but we can read it together if you want.'

'Yes, let's!' enthuses Abigail.

'Okay,' says Fat Tulip; 'but I better explain the premise before we start.'

'Explain the… what?'

'The premise. That means what it's about.'

'Okay. What's it about, then?'

'Well, Slayve the Barbarian—this is him on the cover—is a Celtic warrior king—'

'He plays for Celtic?'

'No, stupid! *Celtic*, with a ku. The Celts were people from ancient pagan times—'

'When was that?'

'A really long time ago. Anyway, Slayve got brought forward to the present day by Cassie, the New Age Dryad. She's the heroine of the comic; you'll see her in a minute.'

'What's she called again?'

'Cassie, the New Age Dryad. A dryad's a tree spirit, so she lives in a tree.'

'In a treehouse?'

'No, actually inside the tree. She's got all these witch powers and she like controls Slayve and sends him out on his missions. The woman's in charge, you see? That's how it's supposed to be.'

'But women aren't in charge of everything…'

'I said that's how it's *supposed* to be,' snaps Fat Tulip, 'not how it actually *is*. Everything's all wrong in the world at the moment.'

'Why is ev—?'

'Look, let's just talk about the comic for now, okay? Now, you've got the main characters, right? There's Slayve the Barbarian and there's Cassie the New Age Dryad. And there's also one more main character, and that's Groob the Goblin Squire. He's this little goblin who's Slayve's sidekick.'

'He sounds funny!'

'He is. Now, let's start reading the comic. You hold this end, and I'll hold this end. Tell you what: I'll read it out loud to you, so you've just got to look at the pictures. Okay?'

'Yeah! Let's do it that way!'

'Okay, here we go. Here's the first page; it's called a splash page when it's just one big panel like this. Here's what's happening: they want to build this new motorway going right across the countryside, and these protesters have come there to protest about it. See? They've got their protest banners. 'No More Roads!' 'Save the Countryside!' And look, here's the riot cops with their shields and riot sticks, advancing menacingly towards them. And see that woman with the loudspeaker? The leader of the protesters? That's Cassie!'

'That's Cassie? But she just looks like a normal woman!'

'That's cuz she's in her civilian clothes right now. She turns into her New Age Dryad clothes when it's time for action. But look at her: she's pretty, isn't she?'

'Yeah, she's very pretty!'

'"Turn back!" says Cassie through her loudspeaker. "This road must not be built! This is sacred ground!" "Disperse immediately or we will be compelled to use force!" replies the chief riot cop. "This is your last warning!" "You must not use force!" replies Cassie, through her loudspeaker. "This is a peaceful protest!" "Right! That was your final warning!" says the chief cop, grinning nastily. "Now, we'll get you, you neopagan cow and your hippy friends! Charge, men!" And the riot cops charge at the protesters, the protesters try to fight back, but they're unarmed and the cops start clubbing them with their sticks! BLAM! "Take this, hippy scum!" POW! "Have some of this, you heavily-pregnant scruffy-looking bitch!" THWACK! "This is for you, four-eyed pacifist trash!" CRUNCH! "In your face, New Model Army t-shirt wearing bastard!" Things are looking bad for the protesters; but then, there's a flash of light and SPARKLE! SPARKLE! it's Cassie transformed into her New Age Dryad action costume!'

'What costume? She's not wearing anything!'

'What are you on about? Look: she's wearing her special tiara, and she's got necklaces, bracelets, anklets, and there's a leather belt round her hips, and leather straps on her thighs and arms; and look at that: that's her magic staff she's holding! That's what she summons Slayve with!'

'Cool! And she can fly as well!'

'Well, no… she can't really fly; she just sort of floats in the air like that sometimes, when she's doing her incantations.'

'Her incan—?'

'Her magic spells. And here she goes! "Slayve the Barbarian: I summon thee!" And WHAM! Slayve appears in a blaze of light! "I am Slayve the Barbarian!" cries Slayve (cuz he always introduces himself.) "What task do you require of me, O Cassandra?" (He always calls her that, even though she keeps telling him she prefers "Cassie.") "Slayve! These peaceful protesters are being assailed by these brutal minions of patriarchal law! You must aid them in their hour of need! And get a bloody move on!" "Groob, my Goblin Squire! Bring forth my trusty battleaxe!" says Slayve. And here's Groob! See, he's tiny and he's got these long pointy ears and a big bald head, and he's dragging the axe along the ground, cuz it's way too big and heavy for him to hold it! "Groob do this, Groob do that!" he grumbles. "And just when I was having my afternoon nap!"'

'That's *funny!*'

'I told you he was funny, didn't I? Now Slayve takes his axe and holds it aloft. "Stand aside, peaceful protesters! I, Slayve the Barbarian, shall deal with your foes!" And he charges at the riot cops! HACK! SLICE! THRUST! But look: now the bloodlust is on him! And when that happens, he goes into Berserker Mode! See; his face is getting more and more angry! "Slayve!" cries Cassie, still floating in mid-air. "Transform to Berserker Mode! I command you!" And here's Groob, all arms folded and cynical. "Yeah, like he could stop transforming now, even if he wanted to!" And here it is! "BERSERKER MODE!" roars Slayve! And he charges into the riot cops like a human whirlwind! He's swinging his axe so fast you can't even see it! Dismembered arms and legs flying everywhere!'

'Wow!'

'And he doesn't stop until he's cut down every last one of them! And then, flexing his huge muscles and throwing his head back he goes "RRRAAAAARRRRHHH!" He always does this at the end of a battle; it's his primal scream and it makes him feel better. But look at all the riot cops! Slayve, in his berserker rampage has somehow only sliced off their arms and legs! They're heads are still on, so they're still alive! "Behold!" cries Cassie. "A miracle! The lives of our foes have been spared!" "Not for long," says Groob. "In case you hadn't noticed, they're all bleeding to death." "Yes, but in an act of clemency, I shall cast a magic spell which will heal the wounds of our vanquished enemies!" And Cassie waves her magic staff and ZAP! But hang on: it looks like nothing's changed! "I thought your spell was going to put our arms and legs back on!" cries the still quadriplegic chief riot cop. "Alas I cannot do that, but my spell has healed your wounds, so now you won't bleed to death! Nice one, eh?" And here's the last page! The protesters are having a celebration party; they're dancing and making merry! And they're even letting the quadriplegic riot cops join the dance!

See, they're throwing them up in the air!'

'Great! They don't look very happy, though. And what's Slayve doing there lying on top of Cassie?'

'Oh, he's worshipping Cassie. You see, Cassie's a goddess to Slayve, and that's how he worships her. You know, like when you go to church. So, what do you think? Best comic in the world, right?'

'Yeah!' enthuses Abigail.

'Good!' says Fat Tulip, closing the comic. 'That means you've passed your first test as my assistant witch. You can't be a proper witch if you don't like Slayve the Barbarian.'

'Oooh! What's that on the back page?'

Fat Tulip shows her. It's an advert featuring the image of a spinning disc being thrown by a trio of happy youngsters. The explosive lettering proudly announces:

FREE! WITH NEXT WEEK'S ISSUE!
YOUR VERY OWN SLAYVE THE BARBARIAN
FRISBEE!
WATCH IT FLY!
A MUST FOR ALL SLAYVE FANS!
ORDER YOUR COPY TODAY!

Chapter Three
At *The Woodsman's Chopper*

Gerald doesn't like Mike Grimsby. He doesn't like him at all. He'd just dropped in on his local for a lunchtime pint and a chat with whoever might be around, and this idiot he's never set eyes on before in his life comes and sits down at his table without so much as a by-your-leave! Still, the place is pretty dead today, and as the guy is obviously an idiot, and equally obviously is trying to pump him for information, he might as well get some fun out of him now that's here.

'So you live round the corner in Bellend Close, do you? Heard there's some pretty funny stuff going on around there,' says Grimsby, pausing for a drink from his pint, depositing a moustache on his moustache in the process. He wipes it off with his sleeve.

Grimsby, a jowly and paunchy fellow, small of stature, looks like someone who's enjoyed many pints in his time, someone who hasn't done much to compensate for his alcohol intake by way of exercise and healthy eating.

'Seedy' is a word that was coined for people like Grimsby, thinks Gerald. There is a distinct aura of seediness about the man—and the bright colours of his baseball cap and Hawaiian shirt in no way compensate for this seediness.

By comparison, Gerald Banbury is immaculate. Tall and well-groomed, scented and smartly-dressed, an athletic frame, strong jawline and a full head of hair sculpted to perfection, to any looker on (of whom there aren't many at present, the pub being so quiet) Gerald's stylish appearance only further emphasises the other man's grubby, perspiring seediness.

And in fact, deep down Grimsby is all too aware of how he suffers by comparison with his new acquaintance—and quietly hates him for it.

'Funny stuff?' echoes Gerald. 'Nothing of the kind, old man. We're a very quiet, respectable community, us Bellend Closers.'

'Not what I've heard,' insists Grimsby, affecting a knowing smile.

Gerald persists in knowing nothing. 'Then you've heard wrong. Nothing's going on in the close. Everything just ticking along the way it always has.'

'Not what I've heard,' repeats Grimsby.

'Then what *have* you heard?'

'Them housewifes,' he says, ungrammatically. 'Up to something, aren't they? When the cat's away…'

He chuckles conspiratorially.

'Housewives?' echoes Gerald. 'Bellend Close, old man, is a solid middle-class, *professional* class, community. Most of the women have jobs, careers; they don't just sit around at home all day. And as most of us are also getting on a bit, approaching those middle years, you won't find any young homemakers with squalling brats on the close.'

'I know that,' Grimsby assures him easily. 'But that's just when they can start getting a bit itchy, ain't it? The women, I mean. When they're getting on for forty, the big four oh. And a lot of them work from home, don't they? Eh? When the cat's away…' Another chuckle.

'You seem to be very well-informed for a newcomer to these parts, Mr Grimsby,' observes Gerald.

'Call me Mike,' says Grimsby. 'Friends call me Mike. As for knowing a thing or two; well, it's my job, ain't it?'

'You're a journalist, then?' hazards Gerald, wondering if Grimsby ever gets addressed as Mike.

'No, I'm a reporter,' is the ingenuous reply. 'Local newspaper.'

'I see,' replies Gerald. He refrains from asking the man for his credentials, suspecting he wouldn't be able to produce any. 'So, you're doing a story about Bellend Close? Well, I'm not sure that there *is* a story. I mean, where's your evidence?'

'I've got my sources,' says Grimsby. 'Heard that the husbands are all looking a bit under the weather, and the wives, they're just the opposite: all chipper an' cheerful and on top of the world.'

Gerald laughs. 'And from *that* you've deduced that the wives are all having extra-marital affairs?'

'Well… Got to be something in it, ain't there? They say it makes 'em glow, doesn't it? The ladies. When they're getting more than their usual allowance. An' then there's *you*, ain't there? Only man there who's not married, and only man who's not looking all tired an' rundown.'

'And how would you know that I'm unmarried, Mr

Grimsby?' inquires Gerald smoothly. 'I haven't mentioned that fact since we've been talking. I've only told you my name and where I live.'

A sheepish Grimsby grin. 'Oops. Let the cat out of the bag, ain't I? Yeah, I knew who you were. That's why I wanted to talk to you. Thought you might know something.'

'About what?'

'About what the wives are up to.'

'And why would *I* know?'

'Well, you're the only bachelor on the estate. Handsome fellow. Don't commute to work, do you? When the cat's away…'

Another conspiratorial grin.

And then it hits Gerald. He realises what's going through Grimsby's grubby little mind. 'You think that I—?' He bursts into laughter.

Grimsby laughs too. 'See? Now am I right or am I right?'

'No, Mr Grimsby, you're hilariously wrong!' More laughter. 'Good God, man! Do you know how many women there are in the close? If I was devoting my days to servicing each and every one of them in turn, *I'd* be the one who was looking tired and rundown, not their cuckold husbands!'

Grimsby's face falls, as much it can be said to fall, bolstered by those substantial chins of his. 'Ah… Off the mark, am I?'

'Way off, old son.'

Grimsby ruminates. 'Still… *Something's* going on…' A thought occurs to him; he perks up. 'What about that story in the papers?'

'What about what story?'

'That kid. Saw a bunch of cavemen in Bellend Woods.'

'You don't believe *that*, do you?' incredulous. 'That story was in *The Sun*, for heaven's sake. Not the most reliable of sources.'

Grimsby shrugs. 'One newspaper's as good as another.'

The Sun… Yes, if Grimsby really *is* a reporter, it will be

for a rag like that, not the local paper… Yes, the fellow's got tabloid sleazebag written all over him, written in tabloid font.

'And how do you connect *that* with what you think might be going on in Close?'

'Well, happened in Bellend Woods, didn't it? Bellend Woods starts at the end of the close.'

'Well, yes it does, but then it runs along all of this end of Strepford, not just Bellend Close. And I still don't see how an alleged sighting of prehistoric men can have any bearing on the situation.'

'Yeah, but what if the kid only *thought* he saw cavemen? What if what he really saw was just *men* men?'

'Oh, I get it! Orgies in the woods: that's what you're thinking of!'

'Well, the woods are handy, ain't they? Nice an' quiet an' private.'

'Well… It's a nice idea, Grimsby. Better than your last one, anyway. But all I can say is, I haven't noticed any of my female neighbours heading into the woods in large parties.'

'I reckon they'd make sure they *weren't* noticed, eh?'

'True, true,' concedes Gerald. He drains his pint. 'Look, I'll tell you what, Grimsby. I like you.' (His biggest lie of the day so far.) 'So, I'll tell you what I'll do: I'll keep my eyes open whenever I'm out and about, and the moment I see anything suspicious, I'll let you know about it. How does that sound?'

'I'd say that sounds like a deal, Mr Banbury!' producing a smartphone from a Hawaiian shirt pocket. 'What say we swap numbers?'

'Unfortunately, I don't have mine on me.'

'Not a problem! I'll just scribble my number down for you.' From another Hawaiian pocket he extracts notebook and pen, opens the latter, holds pen poised; then, realising he doesn't have his own number committed to memory, reaches for his smartphone again.

Chapter Four
For External Use Only

Mhambi's suspicions were confirmed the moment her husband walked in through the door. He looked pleased with himself, instead of looking like the downtrodden, nervous wreck he by all rights ought to be looking like.

And as she sits regarding her enemy, across the neutral territory of the dining room table, he still looks pleased with himself. And Mhambi knows that there is only one thing that could make her husband look pleased with himself, and this would be when he thinks he's got one up on her.

'The new people at number twelve moved in today,' remarks Mhambi casually.

'Really?' sipping his wine. 'What sort of people are they? Have you been round to say hello?'

'No, I haven't been round to say hello yet. And as for what sort of people they are, I think you would know a lot more about that than I would, David dear, wouldn't you?'

'Me? How would I know?'

'Because, darling, our new neighbours happen to be Dodo Dupont and Mayumi Takahashi.'

David pauses, fork halfway to his mouth. 'What? You don't mean Professor Dodo Dupont, pop psychologist and media celebrity, and Mayumi Takahashi, her erotic photographer girlfriend?'

'Yes, darling, I *do* mean Professor Dodo Dupont, pop psychologist and media celebrity, and Mayumi Takahashi, her erotic photographer girlfriend.'

'And they're our new neighbours? Well, that's a turn-up for the books! But dearest, what makes you say I would have already known something about it?'

'Because of the coincidence, darling. Because of the fact that Dodo Dupont is a close friend of Mark Hunter, the man you happen to work for, and that she has been known to help him on his assignments.'

'Has she? Whoever told you that, dearest?'

'*You* did, darling.'

David pauses to think. 'No… I don't think I would've told you anything like that. Official Secrets Act, you know. Not allowed to talk about that sort of thing.'

'Look, don't bullshit me, darling. I always talk to you about my patients and you always talk to me about your job. You squealed, didn't you? You squealed to your boss Mark Hunter, and now he's sent those women here to snoop around! *That's* what's happened!'

'Darling! Dearest! How could you think such a thing? That I would traduce my own wife? I'm hurt. You ought to know me better than that. Really, you need to dismiss these paranoid ideas. I can assure you I have said nothing against you, and if my boss's friends Dodo Dupont and Mayumi Takahashi have decided to move into the neighbourhood, then it is nothing more than a coincidence! Just a coincidence! Believe me!'

And David utters these words with all the compelling sincerity of Vladimir Putin denying any involvement in the latest mysterious death of one of his political opponents.

'Ramona! Ramona!'

Saving her work, Ramona rises from her desk to answer the petulant summons. She is in high spirits this evening. Liberated from those silly feelings of sympathy and duty towards her husband, she is now free to indulge herself in the delights of a wicked and cruel revenge. She realises now that this is what she has always wanted. Sympathy and duty, when they are unrequited, unrewarded, and worst of all are imperatively demanded, are gifts undeserved, gifts that should be withdrawn at once. Mhambi Khoza's sage advice has opened her eyes to this simple truth, and now she is only amazed that she never saw it before.

War has now been declared, a war of attrition, slow but

sure, a campaign that will be all the more enjoyable the more it is prolonged. Thinking of this, she thinks of the stale analogy of the cat playing with the mouse. (She wouldn't have used it in one of her books.) Ramona has always liked cats. All her married life she has wanted to have a cat, but her husband has always vetoed the idea. And why? Just because he's allergic to them! Of all the feeble excuses!

Unhurriedly, humming a tune, Ramona makes her way up the stairs and to the door of her husband's study (her own is on the ground floor.) She taps on the door.

'Come in!'

The tone is irritable, the words an order rather than an invitation.

She enters the room. Jubin, her husband sits on his desk chair, swivelled round to face the door. A man in his mid-forties, his youthful slimness just starting to soften at the edges, he would have been called handsome but for the petulant look in his face, a look, which from being first an occasional, then a frequent visitor there, has now taken up permanent residence.

'You called, husband?'

'Yes, I *did* call, although I shouldn't have had to,' is the terse reply. 'Do you know what time it is?'

Ramona glances at the clock on the wall. 'Yes, Jubin. It has just passed eight o'clock.'

'Yes, it *has* passed eight o'clock, hasn't it? And what was supposed to have happened at eight o'clock? *You*, as you very well know, were supposed to have brought me my glass of chilled beer, which I require to refresh myself from this infernal heat, so that I can continue with my important work for the remainder of the evening!'

'Of course! I'm so sorry, Jubin, but I was so caught up in my own writing—'

'Oh! You were caught up in *your* writing, were you? And of course, the book *you're* writing is so much more important than the one *I'm* writing, isn't it? And so, while *you're* writing your oh-so-important novel, *I* have to sit here slowly dying from heat exhaustion!'

'Not at all, Jubin. I apologise for my oversight, and I shall repair my mistake at once by bringing you the beverage you require.'

'Are you sure? Are you sure you've got time in your busy schedule to perform this simple duty for me? Because I would hate to have to put you out on my account. No, no, just go back to your study, write your stupid book, don't concern yourself about me. After all, *I'm* only your husband, aren't I? What do *I* matter?'

'Please, my husband. You matter a great deal to me! I will get you your beer at once, and please, I beg of you, please try to forgive me!'

'Well, don't just stand there blathering; go'n get it!'

'Instantly!'

Ramona bows and withdraws. Down in the kitchen, she opens the fridge, extracts one of the cans of lager stored there, and, pulling the tab, quaffs half its contents. She heaves a gusty sigh, belches loudly, and then pours the remaining contents into a tall glass. This she now sets down on the tiled floor. She hitches up her skirt, pulls off her knickers, and, throwing them carelessly across the room, squats over the glass and fills it to the top with her own amber nectar.

Placing the brimming glass on a tray, she takes it up to her husband.

'Your beverage, my husband. Accept it, with my sincere apologies for its lateness, and as a token my undying duty and respect for you.'

'Better late than never, I suppose,' says Jubin, taking the proffered glass from the tray.

Taking the tray, Romana, having successfully set and primed her device, retires to a safe distance to await the explosion.

The extra-large ones are for external use only, Dr Khoza had told her. *Don't try to put one inside you; you'll do yourself an injury!*

Yes, I suppose you're right; but what about the erm... other entrance...?

Even worse! You'd end up having to wear a nappy!

Oh, yes! That's happened to some of those porn actresses, hasn't it? I remember hearing about that... At least, I think I remember about it...

You most likely did. But what, if... you know... the extra-large won't take no for an answer and tries to—?

That will never happen.

You sound very sure.

I am. Has it ever happened; to you, I mean?

Well, no. Now that you mention it, it hasn't...

And it won't.

So, they know, then...?

Seems like it. Perhaps they know because we know. Anyway, External Use only. Manual manipulation. Cream baths. Oral, if you can fit in; but don't try to deepthroat; you'll either choke or dislocate your jaw. And of course you can bathe it, anoint it, adorn it, hang decorations from it, eat food from it...

And it also makes a very good shelf! Mhambi hadn't mentioned that. Perhaps she doesn't know...? She'll have to let her know about that.

Yes, a shelf. A sturdy, reliable shelf. No, not just a shelf: a shrine! An altar! A pedestal on which to stand the framed likeness of her darling, desperately missed, husband! She kneels before it, so that the image is level with her eyes, as it stands on the ruler-straight, perfectly horizontal and massively-proportioned cock, resting in a nest of pubic hair, reclining, barely off the vertical against a taut, hairy sixpack. True, those wild curls of pubic hair do obscure the lower portion of the photo, but her darling husband's face stands above them, in all its combed-over, weak-jawed, awkwardly-smiling glory.

Firmly in place, the photograph doesn't move an inch; even as devout worshipper pulls and fondles the testicles beneath, testicles large as goose-eggs, encased in their thick, furrowed integument, it does not move an inch; even as takes the shaft, titanium-hard, veins full and throbbing, take it in her hands, her fingers unable to meet her thumbs, holding it tightly, gently manipulating, it does not move an inch; even as she opens wide and takes the glans, powerfully pungent, slick and smooth like a polished purple stone, take into her mouth, savouring its taste, caressing its surface with her tongue, generously coating it with her warm saliva, *still* it does not move an; the image of her adored one, her away-on-business absent one, the man she loves above all else, the man to whom her heart is a willing slave, stays firmly in place.

And now she feels the monster shudder, the first tremors of the impending eruption. Trembling herself, she closes her hand around that polished purple stone, tightly grasping its smooth unyielding surface… And now the shudder becomes a spasm, and comes the eruption, the deluge! She feels the force of the discharge against the palm of her hand, tremendous, unstoppable! Geysers of semen jet between her fingers, flying at her, inundating her! Discharge follows discharge, one… two… three! The magic number three!

And now it is over, and Patricia, subsiding from her own moment of ecstasy, glories in the fruits of the crescendo, her naked body covered from head to toe with the divine unguent, feeling it coursing and sliding over skin with warm, adhesive, liquid fingers; more, oh much more, than just fluid, it is alive, a living thing, caressing and claiming her body, soaking into every pore of her skin.

And then, and then, when she has removed her glasses and scooped the sperm from her eyes, she sees her husband's face, still smiling at her! The image of her divinity *still* has not fallen from its pedestal! And moreover, that magnificent pedestal shows no sign of sagging.

The Allan Quatermain safari suit has been called out of retirement.

Mhambi, horizontal beneath her husband's ministrations, wishes she'd remembered to burn the bloody thing. The victory he has scored today in the form of Dodo Dupont's arrival in Bellend Close has given him confidence, and now, having donned the Allan Quatermain outfit, he has dredged up his libido from its antipodean retreat, are at least modicum of it, enough for (hopefully) just one bout of intercourse.

And if that wasn't bad enough:

'Oh, yes! Not so full of yourself now, sweet Nombé? Not such a powerful Zulu witch doctress now, are you? No, Hunter Quatermain's trapped you! Yes, I have impaled you on my manhood and now I'm going to tame you, you dusky savage, you ebony temptress!'

Stupid bloody Allan Quatermain. Stupid bloody British Empire.

Once upon a time she'd been a willing participant in this role-playing scenario. The source material were the novels of Rider Haggard, those featuring his African explorer and big game hunting protagonist Allan Quatermain, that paradigm figure representing all those gallant Englishmen who journeyed to the African continent at the end of the nineteenth century for the purpose of decimating both its animal and human populations. Mhambi's role in these bedroom fantasies had always been to play the part of either Mameena or Nombé, two Zulu women Quatermain had encountered on his travels, one of them a queen, the other a witch doctoress (although the two characters would sometimes get mixed up during those role-playing sessions.) And Mhambi had the costumes and feathers and jewellery to suit the characters, and they'd even built a grass hut at the back of the garden…

Yes, once upon a time it had all been a lot of fun; but Mhambi's fondness for these fantasies has now vanished along with her fondness for her husband.

'Yes! Your spells cannot work on me now, Mameena! Because my engorged manhood is more powerful than any of them! So take this! And this! And this!'

Stupid Sir Henry bloody Rider Haggard; *and* his pal stupid Rudyard bloody Kipling with his White Man's Burden. Christ, I know of one White Man who's being a serious bloody Burden on *me* even as we speak.

Still, she will indulge her husband just this once (short of supplying her part of the usual dialogue); yes, she will indulge this once; because Mhambi knows that having got his hopes up, letting him think that the balance of power has shifted in his direction, her revenge, when she exacts it, will be all the more sweet.

Chapter Five
The New Neighbours

On a luxury bed lie to women in sweet repose, breathing softly, one tall and white, the other smaller and yellow. They lie uncovered, the bedsheets crumpled and kicked away at the foot of the bed, spilling onto the floor like a bridal train. The bedroom shows evidence of having only just been moved into in the form of a number of cardboard boxes, only half unpacked. But the furniture is all in place, and on the wall has been hung a large framed print of Hokusai's 'The Dream of the Fisherman's Wife,' one of the earliest examples of Japanese tentacle porn; its presence is one of those important homely touches that makes a house a home.

The smaller of the two women is the first to stir. She murmurs something, the closing dialogue of a vanishing dream, and her eyes open. The rising sun casts the fullness of its gaze into the room (the curtains haven't been put up yet), illuminating what to the woman is an unfamiliar ceiling. She feels an unaccustomed heaviness in the region of her crotch and cranes her neck to determine the cause.

The woman's name is Mayumi Takahashi and she has woken up with a hard-on.

The erection she sports is a fairly recent acquisition and is strapped onto her with a belt. She hadn't intended to keep the thing on all night, but she must have dozed off before she'd had the chance to take it off. She grins toothily. She thinks it's funny, her lying there with her finely-sculpted jet-black penis pointing up at the ceiling!

At five foot three, Mayumi is small compared to the woman sleeping next to her, but not still so small for a Japanese woman. Her skin is of a pronounced yellow or 'tan' complexion, rather than the much paler, porcelain look of many Japanese women. Her figure is slim, her breasts small and brown-capped, her pubic hair prodigious (which is for the most part concealed at present, on account of her strapped-on manhood; so you'll just have to take my word for it.) The tresses on her head, equally jetty in hue, are long and abundant, parted in the middle, and these, combined with her broad, smiling mouth and a pair of strongly-defined eyebrows, do make her look somewhat like a young Yoko Ono. (Mayumi is thirty years in age, but being a Japanese woman could easily pass as twenty.) And as for her accomplishments, do I even need to repeat what the world already knows? As an erotic photographer, immensely, one might even say obsessively, devoted to pursuing her art, her work is renowned throughout the world and admired by all people of refined taste and judgement. (As for her detractors, she tends to just dismiss this nuisance with 'shoo!' 'go away!' gestures.) Terminally polite and cheerful by nature, Mayumi possesses a personality and code of morality as impeccably beautiful as her exterior.

Reaching for her glasses, she now turns to examine her still-sleeping lover. A six-foot Juno is this woman, large-boned and voluptuous; while her short dark hair, strongly-marked facial features and resolute jawline lend her a pleasingly androgynous aspect. This is Dodo Dupont; philosopher, psychologist, writer and filmmaker, her creative output speaks for itself. (Certainly *I* can't speak for it, never having read any of her books and making a point of switching the channel whenever one of her documentaries comes on the telly.) And if this wasn't enough, aside from theoretically setting the world to rights in her books and films, Dodo has also quite literally saved the world on more than one occasion, working as the 'talented amateur' alongside her professional secret agent friend Mark Hunter. And working as a spy is a pursuit for which she is well qualified, as, aside from her mental accomplishments, she is also an expert markswoman, proficient in several of the martial arts, a qualified pilot, sailor, astronaut, scuba-diver, mountaineer and just about anything else you'd care to mention.

Mayumi's eyes, as they range over this paragon female, combine the adoration of a lover with the appreciation of a connoisseur—not to mention an understandable pride of possession. Leaning in close, Mayumi smilingly studies her lover's face, which is placid in repose, the features softened and even ever-so-slightly vulnerable; her lips, the upper adorned with the downy ghost of a moustache, slightly parted. Mayumi leans in, touching those parted lips with her own, plants a gentle kiss, soft and fleeting, the brush of a butterfly's wings.

It is enough, however. Dodo's eyelids slowly open, the pupils, set within irises of grey, focus on Mayumi.

'Yumi...' she breathes, sleepy-voiced.

'Good morning, my master,' grins Mayumi.

They embrace. But then Dodo suddenly pulls back, surprised by an unaccustomed hardness nudging against her thigh.

'Why are you wearing Mark?' laughs Dodo, discovering

the cause.

'I forget to take him off,' replies Mayumi, still grinning.

Dodo's hand joins hers, caressing the ebony phallus.

'It still smells of your ass,' pronounces Mayumi, sniffing her fingers.

Dodo kisses her. 'Well, you certainly didn't spare me, did you? I have to confess to feeling a touch saddle-sore this morning,' fingers gently probing the sensitive area.

'I made you mine,' declares Mayumi, grinning with pride.

It had been the first time she had taken Dodo anally, at least with this particular appliance. (Their cycles synchronised, both women are presently sporting mouse tails between their legs.) You will have noticed that Dodo just referred to this aid to person-to-person communication by the name 'Mark.' This is not just a pet-name given in honour of their good friend Mark Hunter; uh-uh, its application has far greater significance than just that. For the fact is that this penis presently projecting itself from Mayumi's crotch is, in form and dimensions and exact replica of the one actually possessed by the inestimable man himself!

As you can imagine, there's a backstory attached to this. And, there being no time like the present, here it is now.

Mayumi had on more than one occasion invited Mark Hunter to join Dodo and herself in bed, offers which Mark had always graciously declined. Because, although Mayumi loves Dodo to distraction, and they have never yet engaged in a threesome with a man, if there is one man for whom Mayumi would willingly make an exception in that regard, then that man is Mark. Dodo was always telling her there was no point in even asking him, because Mark just wasn't that interested in sex. However, never one to give up, Mayumi formulated a plan and with Oriental patience, quietly bided her time.

And, then an occasion arrived which allowed to put her

plan into operation. Mark had been spending the evening with Dodo and Mayumi in Dodo's penthouse apartment, at the end of which he had been invited to sleep in the spare bedroom, to save him having to commute all the way home. Mark had accepted the offer. In the small hours, Mayumi has risen from her bed, and without disturbing her partner, had made her way to the spare room where Mark was fast asleep. Gently pulling aside the bedclothes, Mayumi had taken hold of Mark's penis (fortunately Mark invariably sleeps *au naturel*, so there was no clothing to deal with) and with dextrous hands had quickly roused said member to tumescence. And then, instead of just raping the guy while she had the chance, like any sensible twenty-first century woman, she had proceeded instead to make a plaster-cast of it! Unfortunately, careful though she was, Mark happened to wake up during this operation and sleepily asked her what she thought she was doing.

'Making a plaster-cast of your penis!' answered Mayumi, with her customary candour.

'Well, don't you think you should have asked my permission before doing something like this?'

'I would have asked permission, but I figured it better not to, cuz I knew you'd say no!' explained Mayumi.

'Mayumi, your logic is inescapable,' sighed Mark, and had then drifted back to sleep.

No mention was made of this transaction over breakfast, leaving Mayumi with the conviction that if Mark remembered it all, he remembered it only as a dream. Another person whose permission Mayumi hadn't asked was Dodo's, and upon hearing what she had done, Dodo had lectured her soundly, and spanked her even more soundly—but with a charming hypocrisy had nonetheless made no move to prevent the plaster cast being used as the mould for a made-to-order strap-on dildo.

And so, with the advent of 'Mark', Mayumi feels that their good friend can be with them in spirit, if not in person, to share in their nocturnal intimacy.

Now, to 'resume the thread of my narrative', back to where Mayumi has just said 'I made you mine.'

'Oh, you did, did you?' says Dodo, grabbing a hank of Mayumi's hair in her fist. 'What sort of talk is that for a slave? Or have you become the master now?'

'No, you're still my master and I'm your slave,' Mayumi assures her. And then: 'But sometimes I switch!'

Still gripping her hair, Dodo pulls Mayumi towards her and kisses her with ardour. Mayumi, submissive, savours the violent kiss, blissful, eyes closed. When she opens her eyes, she sees the tears brimming in Dodo's.

'Oh, Christ,' she says, gazing at Mayumi with tearful yearning. 'I don't deserve someone as good as you…'

'No, you don't!' agrees Mayumi cheerfully. (She tends to agree with everything Dodo says.)

Then her eyes widen, remembering. 'Hey! Today is my first day working as assistant spy to Dodo Dupont!'

Although Mayumi has found herself caught up in Mark and Dodo's assignments several times before, this occasion she considers to be different. This time is herself who has been dispatched on a secret mission along with Dodo, while Mark stays back in London. She is one of the agents on the spot, assisting Dodo and helping with all the dangerous and exciting spy work!

'So it is,' agrees Dodo. 'Think you're ready for it?'

'Yes!' emphatically. 'Agent Mayumi reporting for duty!'
She gives a brisk salute.

'Pay attention, Agent Mayumi!' says Dodo crisply. 'Here is your first assignment of the day!'

'Yes! What is my assignment, my master?'

'Your assignment—and address me as Agent Dodo when we're on duty—your assignment, I say, is to get that gorgeous arse of yours downstairs and start making breakfast! Understood'

'Yes, Agent Dodo, my master! Understood! My gorgeous

ass will be downstairs and making the breakfast at once!'

And with this, Mayumi springs from the bed, favours Dodo with another brisk salute and without pausing to dress, swiftly exits the room, with bouncing 'Mark' still strapped to her groin.

Chapter Six
The Absent-Minded Geneticist

Bellend Close. We're at chapter six already and we still haven't been formally introduced. A modern estate composed of detached and semidetached houses designed for middle-class homeowners, it looks pretty much how you would expect a modern estate composed of detached and semidetached houses designed for middleclass homeowners to look: the houses all built with the same buff-coloured brickwork, the roofs with the same dark red concrete tiles. Each house is distanced from the pavement by a front lawn of exactly the same extent, and carpeted with the same dwarf ryegrass turf. Each of the properties is partitioned from its neighbour by a low wooden fence of the same material and the same finish; and this low fence becomes a tall fence at the rear of the properties to provide a degree of privacy for the back gardens. The pavements are broad and free from litter, following a road that pursues a curvilinear course, so that the one end of the close is not visible from the other. Even the lampposts look pristine. Altogether the close looks very pleasant and appealing, seen as it, under a blue summer sky. (But then just about any setting can look appealing when seen under a blue summer sky, just as conversely, even the most beautiful of landscapes can look dreary and depressing when it's been left out in the rain for too long.)

But far more aesthetically pleasing than any snug suburban paradise are the two brightly-dressed females presently wending their way along the sidewalk. Dodo

Dupont, looking cool in wraparound shades (probably designer, knowing her) wears a purple vest top which clings lovingly to the ample curves of her breasts, puce-coloured jeans performing the same office for her equally generous posterior, while purple DMs encase a correspondingly substantial pair of feet. Mayumi, meanwhile sports a broad-brimmed summer hat, a short-skirted floral dress of pleasing flimsiness and open-toed sandals, the sandal-straps, the pattern of the dress and the hat-band all being of the same light blue shade. The shoulder bag she carries contains amongst other things her 'top-secret spy camera' which Mayumi has been adamant about bringing along with her on this, her first day as an assistant espionage agent. In appearance this device would seem to be nothing more than a common-or-garden pocket camera, but Mayumi insists that it is a 'top-secret spy camera,' and that's good enough for me, because I for one believe anything that Mayumi Takahashi has to say, and I trust you all do as well.

'Why do they give this place such a silly name?' says Mayumi.

'Yes, *I* wondered about that one,' replies Dodo, 'so I did a bit of research; and the result was that no-one seems to know for sure. But the most popular theory is that 'Bellend' is a corruption of 'Belenus,' the name of one of the ancient Celtic gods.'

Over breakfast Mayumi had tabled the suggestion that the women in the close had all become vampires; this, she said, would explain the dwindling condition of the men.

'That is a very good suggestion, sweetheart,' said Dodo. 'So good in fact, that Mark has already thought of it, and he had David Jarman examined for bitemarks.'

'And did they find any?'

'Sadly, they didn't. Still though, I don't dismiss the idea completely. It could be that what we're dealing with here is some other kind of vampire, one that doesn't actually suck the blood of its victims by direct contact, but slowly drains away their lifeforce somehow.'

'When they have sex!'

'Maybe, but then that would make it a succubus, not a vampire.'

Dodo's final instructions to Mayumi before they had set out: 'Keep smiling and don't trust anybody.'

Making their way to the far end of the close, they reach the house they are looking for and knock on the front door.

They wait. They knock again.

'She ought to be in,' says Dodo. 'She works from home, anyway…'

'Hello!' sings a voice behind them.

They turn to find a trio of bespectacled Asian women smiling at them from the pavement, one of them plump, the other two slim, all of them of very modest height.

'You looking for Professor Aubergine?' asks the plump woman.

'Yes, we are,' says Dodo.

'She'll be in her lab,' says the woman. 'That where she always is.'

'And where's her lab?'

'In the garden, round back of house.'

'Ah! Thank you.'

The three women move on.

'Asians,' remarks Dodo, as they make their way around the side of the house. 'I don't think they were Japanese, were they?'

'No, they were Thailand women,' says Mayumi.

'That makes sense. A lot of Thai women come over here to get married.'

'Why's that?'

'Well, statistically Thailand does have the world's smallest average penis size; maybe that has something to do with it.'

'For sure.'

They come to the back garden, and at the far end of the

lawn stands a windowless, single-storeyed bunker-like structure composed of whitewashed concrete, roughly the size of a small bungalow. Beyond this structure and the fence behind it rises the perimeter of Bellend Wood.

'The good professor's laboratory, presumably,' says Dodo.

They cross the lawn to the laboratory, coming to a halt before a featureless metal door, deep-set in the concrete. Beside the door is an intercom panel, while from above the door a security camera looks down on them. Dodo depresses the intercom button.

A pause, and then a voice, female issues tinnily from the speaker: 'No thank you.'

'Sorry?'

'I said, no thank you. I'm not interested.'

Dodo, perching her glasses on her forehead, aims a quizzical look at the security camera. 'What aren't you interested in?'

'Whatever belief system it is you want to try and convert me to.'

'You've got us wrong. We haven't come here to try and convert you to anything.'

'Oh. Well, if you're trying to sell me anything, I'm not interested in that either.'

'We're not trying to sell anything. You see—'

'Are you canvassing for something?'

'Neither are we canvasing. You see—'

'Then what about—?'

'*You see*, we're your new neighbours and we've just popped round to say hello.'

'Oh, I see! New neighbours! Splendid! Well, hello there! Lovely to meet you both! We must get together sometime!'

'Couldn't we get together now, seeing as we're here? We won't take up much of your time. Just a quick chat.'

'Well… Yes, alright then. I don't want to be inhospitable. Come right in.'

The metal door slides open.

Dodo and Mayumi step through the doorway. The interior of the bunker proves to be composed of one single spacious room, and this room has been panelled, wall-to-wall, with whiteboards, and these whiteboards are covered, almost from floor to ceiling with scribbled notes, equations, formulae, graphs, charts, diagrams. Perhaps with the intention of leaving these panels unobstructed, much of the laboratory is entirely unfurnished. This utilised area lies at the end of the room furthest from the door, across a vacant expanse of vinyl floor. Here there is a desk equipped with a computer workstation, and adjacent to it on the right are two long benches, the first laden with electronic devices, the second with chemical apparatus, while in the corner to the left of the desk is a kitchenette and seating area.

A woman wearing a lab coat has risen from her chair at the desk and now comes forward to greet her visitors, padding across the floor in bare feet. Dodo stares. So does Mayumi. Beneath the unbuttoned lab coat the woman is wearing a pastel-coloured blouse, at the hem of which all other signs of clothing abruptly terminate. (What Dodo at first thinks might be the crotch of a pair of black undergarments quickly proves itself to be pubic hair.) For the rest, the woman is tall, attractive, and looks to be in her late thirties. She wears a large pair of glasses, and her hair, dark brown, seems to have been pinned up on her head rather negligently, with several long strands hanging down.

Dodo's agile mind, rapidly seeking an explanation for the woman's wardrobe anomaly, for once lets her down. It cannot be on account of the summer heat: the laboratory is air-conditioned and the summer heat has been left outside. And while keeping cool might account for the unshod feet, it does not explain the absence of nether-garments.

The woman, smiling and seemingly unmindful of her semi-nude condition, extends a hand to her visitors.

'Hello there! I'm Nanette Aubergine,' she says, shaking

hands with Dodo. 'So you've just moved in next door, have you?'

'Well, not next door,' answers Dodo. 'Down the road at number twelve. I'm Dodo Dupont, and this is my better half, Mayumi.'

'Well, and don't you look pretty?' shaking hands with Mayumi. And then: 'How about some coffee?'

'We're okay, thanks,' demurs Dodo.

'Oh. Well, if you don't want any coffee then I'm afraid I can't see you right now. I'm engaged in some important research, you see, and I like to stick to a rigid timetable. My morning coffee break is usually eleven o'clock to ten past, but I was going to have it early today, seeing as you've called round; but if you don't want any coffee, then I'm afraid I can't fit you in till eleven.'

'You know, I've just remembered that actually we'd love some coffee! Wouldn't we, Yumi?'

'Yes!' confirms Mayumi. 'Coffee is good!'

'Splendid!' says Nanette. 'Follow me, then.'

Dodo and Mayumi follow their host across the open floorspace. Appearing from nowhere, two small mechanical devices, looking like self-propelled ice hockey pucks, come sliding across the floor towards them.

'Robots!' exclaims Mayumi, stopping in her tracks.

'Oh, don't worry, that's just Darwin and Huxley, my cleaning staff,' explains Nanette. 'They keep the lab spick and span for me; saves me having to do it myself.'

The two machines circle around Dodo and Mayumi, emitting interrogative bleeping noises; and then, having determined that the newcomers are not discarded rubbish that needs to be swept up, they retire from whence they came.

Leading her guests over to the kitchenette, Nanette switches on the coffee machine and presently they are all seated on comfy chairs, armed with mugs of coffee. Dodo and Mayumi sit facing their host who, crossing her legs, seems still oblivious to her own lower-body nudity.

'So you're working on a research project?' says Dodo. 'Can I ask what it's about? I've read some of your other papers and they were fascinating.'

'Oh, really? How nice of you to say so. You're interested in genetics, then?'

'I'm interested in a lot of things. So, what are you researching now? Is anthropogeny still your particular field of interest?'

'Oh, yes. It's an obsession, really. I mean the good kind of obsession, not the bad kind. Yes, right now I'm looking for the missing link.'

'I thought "missing link" was supposed to be a rather unscientific description.'

'Well, yes it is really. I mean there are lots of missing links in the evolutionary chain. And the chain itself isn't just one straight line: there are all the off-shoots, the mutants and hybrids, the evolutionary cul-de-sacs. And then you've got that big blackspot between Australopithecus and Homo Erectus. Plenty of room for missing links there.' She pauses to brush a stray tendril of hair from her face. 'And then it seems like every time they dig up a new species, instead of making the picture clearer it just confuses it all the more. The brain pan's too big for the era it comes from, or there's too much body hair or not enough. There's always something that doesn't fit the pattern.'

'Like ooparts,' says Dodo.

'Yes, ooparts! Although really you only use that one when you're talking about things made by people, not the remains of the people themselves… Oh! That reminds me: I've got this fetish?'

'What's your fetish?' asks Mayumi, perking up.

'It's a penis fetish.'

'Penis doesn't count as fetish,' says Mayumi, disappointed. 'That's just normal sex attraction.'

'I think you've got the wrong kind of fetish there,

sweetheart,' Dodo advises her. 'I think the Professor's referring to an effigy of a penis, like a carving or a sculpture.'

'Yes, that's right,' confirms Nanette 'It's a bronze statuette, about so high, stands upright with the testicles forming the base. The carving is exquisite; a beautiful piece of work, and in pristine condition, as well. Not a speck of rust. Perservered by the soil. But here's the thing: the stratum in which this penis was found, places it as coming from the Mesolithic Era!'

'That's the middle of the Stone Age!' exclaims Dodo.

'Yes, and several millennia before the start of the Bronze Age! So there you have it: an out-of-place artifact.'

'That's fascinating! I'd very much like to see this penis of yours.'

'And I'd like nothing more than to show it to you—only I can't quite put my hands on it at the moment... I know I left it somewhere!'

'Yes, I suppose you did...'

'What did I do with it...? Wonder if I left it over at the house... Oh dear! I hope my daughter hasn't got hold of it and started using it as a dildo. That's no way to treat a priceless artifact.'

Not remembering where you put it is no way to treat a priceless artifact, thinks Dodo, wondering if this absent-mindedness could also be the explanation for the geneticist's wardrobe deficit. Out loud she says 'I'm surprised I haven't heard about this find of yours before; something like that, it sounds like an important discovery. You haven't been naughty and been keeping this thing all to yourself, have you?'

'Oh no, the scientific community knows all about it. But they all dismissed the thing as a hoax. Do you know, they even tried to discredit the palaeontologist who dug the thing up! And she's a good friend of mine! Only let her off the hook when they graciously decided she must have been duped by someone else. Well, *I'm* convinced it's a genuine oopart, anyway.'

'And do you have any theories to account for it?'

'Not a one!' is the cheerful reply. 'And of course, it won't have anything to do with my current line of research.'

'No, I don't suppose it would…' Remembering something, Dodo grins. 'You know, if it's the missing link you're looking for, maybe you should be looking for it out there instead of in here.'

'Out where?' confused.

'Out there,' indicating the far wall of the lab. 'In the woods. Didn't you hear the story? The boy who said he saw cavemen in the woods?'

'Oh yes, but I don't believe *that*. What would cavemen be doing walking around in the present day? Lad probably just stumbled on a group of gay young bucks having an innocent orgy in the woods! If he could have said anything about the shape of their skulls, it might have helped, but he claims he can't remember what their faces looked like at all; only the bodies… Still, muscular, hairy men… It *is* a funny coincidence…' Her voice trails off.

'What's a funny coincidence?' asks Dodo, interested.

'Hm? Oh, nothing. Just some silly dreams. Probably working too hard. Goodness! Here we are and all we've been talking about is me and my interests! What do you two lovely ladies get up to?'

'Well, as for me, I'm a psychologist,' answers Dodo, 'and Mayumi here is an erotic photographer.'

'How interesting! Are you practicing?'

'No, I write books and make films on the subject.'

'Books and films! Goodness!' And, turning to Mayumi: 'And you're an erotic photographer! What sort of thing? Women, men or both?'

'Women only,' answers Mayumi firmly. 'Female body is more beautiful than male.'

'And where did you two live before?'

'Central London,' replies Dodo.

'Ah! Moved out to the sticks for some peace and quiet, I suppose. Well, you'll find that here. Nothing happens around here.'

'Doesn't it? I've heard that something strange is happening right here in Bellend Close.'

'Well, *I* haven't. What's supposed to be happening here?'

'Something wrong with all the husbands, so I've been hearing.'

'The husbands? Well, I haven't got one of those, so I wouldn't know. What's wrong with them?'

'They all seem to be sickening with something: lethargy, low blood pressure, low spirits… Haven't you noticed? It's quite plain to see.'

'To be honest, I haven't been out and about that much, lately. Too busy here in the lab. Well, whatever it is, it can't be a virus, not if none of the wives have got it. There's no virus that's that selective about gender.'

While saying the above, Nanette shuffles forward on her chair, and, opening her legs wide, and to the unspeakable surprise of her guests, commences urinating on the floor!

'Still,' she continues, 'there are certain psychological ailments that have been known to be con—'

And then, seeing the looks on her visitors' faces, she breaks off, both her speech and micturition, and her own face becomes a picture of embarrassment.

'Oh my goodness! Oh God, I'm so sorry! Look at me! This is what comes from spending too much time on your own!'

'You mean you normally pee on the floor when you're on your own?' inquires Dodo, amused and perplexed in equal measure.

'Only when I'm here in the lab,' says Nanette. 'You see, I've always really hated this being a slave to your bodily functions. Think how much time you waste every time you have to toddle off to the loo while you're working. And most of that wasted time will be the journey from A to B, not the actual weeing. So, when I'm here in the lab, I prefer to just go on the floor, so I don't have to stop working. And as you can see, the mess soon gets cleaned up.'

And indeed, Darwin (or possibly Huxley) has already arrived at the scene and bleeping happily to itself, quickly mops up the pool of urine. Its job done and the floor sparkling clean, it glides off again.

Professor Aubergine's absence of underwear has now been explained.

'Yes… I can understand your reasoning…' says Dodo slowly. 'But then, what if you're working standing up when you're caught short? You'd still have to stop what you're doing to squat down, wouldn't you?'

Nanette looks confused. 'No… Why would I need to squat down to pee?'

Dodo's eyes widen. 'You mean you can do it standing up?'

'Yes; can't everyone?'

Dodo and Mayumi shake their heads in tandem. 'No, they can't,' says Dodo. 'Not many women can, anyway. It's an acquired skill, and one that's very difficult to acquire. Are you really telling me that you can do it? You can pee standing up?'

'Yes.'

'Completely straight? Legs not bent at all?'

'No, completely straight.'

You can see the mingled admiration and disbelief in the looks Dodo and Mayumi exchange.

'I'd be very interested to see you doing that some time,' says Dodo. Mayumi nods her head in enthusiastic assent.

'I can do it right now, if you want,' is the ready reply. 'I was only half finished.'

'Then, please,' invites Dodo. 'Carry on where you left off.'

And standing up, Professor Aubergine proceeds to

demonstrate that she can indeed pee standing up—the same way most women would. As Dodo watches the urine streaming down her inside legs, she now comprehends the full significance of the woman's lower-body nudity. Meanwhile, Mayumi has her camera out and eagerly snaps some shots.

The exhibition comes to an end. 'See? Nothing to it.' And then, looking at her watch: 'Goodness, we've gone over the ten minutes! I hate to seem inhospitable, but I really must get back to work!'

Taking their cue, Dodo and Mayumi rise from their seats and Nanette, taking them each by the arm, guides them swiftly and with squelching footsteps across the room.

'Well, it was lovely to meet you both and I'm so glad to have two such charming ladies as yourselves moving into the neighbourhood and I'm sure you'll really like it here it's so nice and quiet and as soon as I'm not so busy we really must get together again and have a nice long natter and hopefully by then I'll have found my penis!'

And almost before they know it, Dodo and Mayumi are out in the blazing sunshine and the laboratory door has hermetically-sealed itself behind them.

Mayumi is the first to speak. 'I like her,' she says.

Chapter Seven
Getting His Just Desserts

Travelling first-class as always, Paul Smith, James White and John Johnson, are returning home to Strepford from London Waterloo, the same journey they make every working day of every working week. They sit at the same table, James facing Paul and John, and all have their laptops open before them. Although working from different offices, all three of these men are solicitors by profession.

'Should be in Strepford on time,' says Paul, the fat one,

looking up from his laptop.

'We weren't late departing,' remarks James, the thin one, looking up.

'I think they've been on time all this week,' adds John, the small one, also looking up.

Conversation over, they return their attention to their laptops.

Aside from their professions, there are other things that Paul, James and John have in common. It goes without saying that they are all residents of Bellend Close, otherwise they wouldn't be in this book, but they also share many personality traits and attributes. Absence of charisma, poor conversation skills, verbal timidity, physical awkwardness, and complete lack of any aesthetic sense, to give but a few examples. Another thing they share is a proneness to all those disagreeable minor physical ailments like dandruff, haemorrhoids, athlete's foot and excess ear-wax; ailments that paragons like Dodo Dupont never seem to be troubled with.

And last, but by no means least, yet another link that connects these three remarkable gentlemen is their wives. And if you're surprised to hear that Paul, James and John even possess such things as wives, you'll be a lot less surprised when you hear that all three of these spouses hail from Thailand. Yes, Hom, Ploy and Dao are mail-order brides (although that term is now somewhat archaic, as the transactions are now usually conducted online.) We briefly met Hom, Ploy and Dao in the previous chapter, if you can cast your minds back that far.

Remember Dudley and Ting Tong? They used to be in *Little Britain*, although you won't find them there anymore, thanks to the triumphs of modern censorship. But back when they *were* on the show, Hom, Ploy and Dao used to find the antics of Dudley and Ting Tong absolutely hilarious and they would simply howl with laughter—it was only the husbands who had been not so amused.

The train now pulls into Strepford station, and, leaving the station, the three solicitors make straight for the nearest public house, conveniently situated just across the street from the building entrance. They make this journey not because they wish to recruit themselves with the aid of alcoholic refreshment; not so; apart from the rare glass of wine, none of these men are even drinkers; they are here because they have a meeting with someone—and that someone is Mike Grimsby, the supposed newspaper reporter we met back in chapter three.

Unlike the three solicitors, Grimsby is not coy at all when it comes to alcohol, and he is enjoying his third pint of the (still early) evening when the newcomers arrive.

'Evening gents,' he greets them, his voice as loud as his shirt. 'Nice and punctual; I like that. Expect you want to wet your whistles after working all day. What can I get for you?'

'We don't want any drinks,' says Paul, after he and his friends have seated themselves. 'We want to, we need to get home as soon as possible... Our wives...'

'Got it. Don't want 'em getting suspicious, do we? Down to business then. Well, here's my report.' He makes a show of consulting his notebook.

'Have you found anything out?' asks Paul anxiously.

'Early days yet, early days,' is the unconcerned reply. Snapping the book shut: 'I can tell you this much: if they're getting it, they ain't going out to get it.'

'You're sure?'

'Course I'm sure. Been tailing 'em all week, ain't I? They've been to the shops. They've been to the hairdressers. They've been to the pictures. Nothing suspicious. They ain't been nowhere they shouldn't of gone, and they ain't stayed nowhere longer than they should of. Do everything together, don't they? But according to you, that's just normal. So, I can tell you this much: if they're getting ain't, they ain't goin' out to get it. *It's* coming to them.'

'You mean at home?'

'Yeah, I mean at home.'

'Have you seen anyone—?'

'No, I ain't seen anyone.'

'Then, how do you know—?'

'I just told you: they ain't going out to get it. That's for sure, right? That's proved. So, if they ain't going out to get it, it's gotta be coming to them, right? That's what detective work's all about, ain't it? Process of elimination.'

'But if you haven't seen—'

'Look, I can watch round the front of your houses an' round the back of 'em both at the same time, can I? I can't be in two places at once, right? But don't you worry: I got a plan, a plan how we can find out for sure.' He lowers his voice. 'Bugs.'

'Bugs?'

'Yeah, bugs. Listenin' devices. We'll plant 'em in your houses. One each. *Then* we'll find out what your loving wives is up to while you're slaving at the office earning their pocket money.'

Paul, James and John exchange dubious glances. They do not seem very thrilled with the proposed plan. 'Which… which rooms do you want to plant the bugs in?'

'Well, I reckon the bedrooms'll be the best places for 'em, all things considered. Don't you?'

'Well, yes… but…' More exchanged glances. 'But can they… at night, when we… when we are home, can they be switched off?'

Grimsby sighs. 'No, they can't be switched off. They don't have switches *on* them. They're just *there*, ain't they? They send out a signal, an' the signal gets recorded. But I ain't gunna be listenin' at night, when you fellers is at 'ome, am I? I'm gunna be listenin' during the day, when you fellers is out. So, if it's your privacy you're worried about, you don't have to worry. What you get up to with your missises at night ain't no concern o' mine. It ain't "pertinent to the investigation", right?'

Says John: 'Couldn't you just plant the bugs in the living rooms instead? I mean, if anyone came to the house, they'd still… you know, they'd probably go there as well…'

Paul and James both voice their approval of this proposed amendment to the plan.

Grimsby sighs again. 'Alright, we'll plant the bugs in the bloody livin' rooms, then! It's your money, so I ain't gunna argue. And speaking of money, I've emailed you my first week's expense account, an' if you could pay the invoice as soon as, that'd be much appreciated; cuz I've still got live while I'm working here, ain't I? I've still got to eat and drink. Oh, looks like I need a refill! How about you fellers? Sure I can't tempt you gents with a drink…?'

I may not have mentioned this before, but David Jarman, although employed at the offices of MI5, works only in administration; he is not a field-agent like his superior Mark Hunter, so he is not actually a 'spy' in the popular sense of the word. His work is routine, his hours regular, and in fact he often commutes by the same train as his three solicitor neighbours.

I mention this fact in case any of you have been thinking that Jarman seems too stupid to be a spy.

This evening he is Allan Quatermain again—and at his wife's request!

Things are looking up.

After his triumph of last night, a kind of feverish mental excitement has sustained Jarman throughout the day, and he has returned home this evening with high hopes. The advent of Dodo Dupont promises a speedy resolution, a lifting of the curse that has been hanging over the neighbourhood. Knowing as he does the details of some of Dodo Dupont's adventures with Mark Hunter, he had been half expecting to find Bellend Close reduced to smoking rubble on his return home; but no, the houses still stand and everything seems as (deceptively or otherwise) quiet and peaceful as usual.

And then, on stepping through the front door his wife had greeted him with the same ebullient energy with which she had greeted him on his awakening this morning. The expression of her large eyes was soft and kind again, as they had always been before they had started to take on that cruel, cold gleam.

'I got home early today, so I've made you a very special dinner, darling!' she enthused. 'It's to celebrate our return to connubial bliss and the recovery of your manhood! Well, you can't have one without the other, can you? Eh? So, you just nip upstairs and get changed while I serve the dinner. I've cracked open a bottle of the Cabernet Sauvignon! Oh, and when I say get changed, I think we both know what I want you to change into, don't we, darling?'

'Allan Quatermain?'

'Allan Quatermain!'

And so, it is in his full Allan Quatermain regalia, safari hat and all, that David Jarman seats himself at the dinner table. Things are looking up! They are definitely looking up! The advent of Dodo Dupont has clearly shaken things up. Perhaps already the previous harmony has been restored, the harmony that was suddenly and inexplicably knocked off balance.

He takes an appreciative sip of his Cabernet Sauvignon.

Mhambi enters, bearing two steaming plates.

'Oh, look at you, darling!' she gushes. 'I'd forgotten how good you look in your Allan Quatermain clothes! They make you look so rugged and virile! You know, it almost seems like you actually get your virility from the outfit, and as soon as you take it off—wham! you lose it!'

'Yes…!' agrees David, laughing awkwardly, because the compliment does seem a tad back-handed… But no, she didn't mean it that way! Of course she didn't!

'It's my special lasagne, darling!' says Mhambi, putting the plate down in front of him. 'And I've made the new, extra special white sauce that I just know you're going to love!'

Mhambi takes her own seat at the other end of the table.

'And I've had a wonderful idea, darling,' she says. 'What do you say to a barbecue party this weekend? I thought it would be an excellent way to welcome our new neighbours, Dodo and Mayumi. We'll invite the whole street, and then they can get to know everyone.'

'Yes, that's a great idea,' says David. 'So have you... seen anything of Dodo Dupont today...?'

'Well, no darling, I haven't. I've been busy at the surgery all day, haven't I?

'Yes, but I thought she might have called round... you know, to register...'

'Well, she might have, but she doesn't need to see the duty doctor just to do that, does she? Well go on: tuck in!'

'Oh, yes! Of course, darling!'

Picking up his knife and fork, David cuts a small section from the corner of the lasagne, impales it on the fork, blows on it, puts it in his mouth, his wife watching him closely. As he chews, his face assumes first a puzzled look, and then a cringe of distaste.

'Anything wrong, darling?' inquires Mhambi innocently.

David swallows the food with a gulp. 'Odd taste to it...' he says. 'It's a bit... Did you use fish paste or something...?'

'Don't be silly, darling. Nobody uses fish paste in a lasagne.'

'It doesn't taste like your usual lasagne...'

'That'll be my new white sauce, darling. Special recipe. Let me try some.'

So saying, Mhambi cuts a piece from her own lasagne and pops it in her mouth. Masticating the mouthful, she moans with delight, before swallowing it voluptuously.

'Delicious!' she declares. 'My new white sauce is perfection, even if I do say so myself. So rich and creamy! It came out just the way I wanted it to. Try some more, darling. You probably just need to get used to it.'

Reluctantly, David cuts another slice and transfers it to his mouth. He chews it, and his taste buds can only confirm their original assessment. Semen! The lasagne tastes like it's got semen in it! He looks down at his plate. The white sauce... He sniffs. Yes, he can smell it, too! In there, amongst the other odours, the ones that are supposed to be there... But it can't be, can it? It can't actually be...? No! Ridiculous...! And even supposing it somehow *was*, where could she have got it from...? And so much...! And more importantly, *why* would she...?

He looks up. Mhambi is staring at him from across the table. She's no longer smiling and the hard glint is back in her eyes, the cruel, cold gleam.

'What's wrong, darling?'

It sounds like a challenge.

'No-nothing, darling...'

'Good. Then eat up your lasagne.'

'Well, actually... I-I'm not feeling very—'

'Eat it up, darling.'

'Really, I'm not—'

'Eat... it... *up*, darling... Now.'

David Jarman eats. With feverish, trembling hands he digs into the food, scooping up great mouthfuls and wolfs it down, swallowing it—as much as he can—without tasting it.

And then the ordeal is over, the plate is clean. He grabs his wine glass and gulps down its remaining contents.

He looks at his wife. She smiles at him, a tight smile of mocking approbation. 'Very good, darling, very good. But I hope you've left room for dessert. It's your favourite cranberry pie, served with my brand new, extra-special homemade creamy vanilla custard. I just *know* you're going to like it.'

Chapter Eight
Zulu Garden Party

Picturesquely incongruous, an African grass hut stands at the foot of Dr Mhambi Khoza's back garden. A genuine Zulu hut, hemispherical in shape, composed of a covering of grass and weeds tightly woven over a framework of bent wooden poles. It resembles an igloo in shape, and its name, 'indlu,' even sounds like 'igloo.' Dodo, having received no advance warning that she was likely to encounter such an incongruous sight, wonders what it could be doing there. The first explanation that occurs to her is that Dr Khoza must have some elderly relatives living inside it, old-fashioned folks who refused to take up residence in a modern brick-built dwelling—which just goes to show that even minds as acute and as elevated as that of Dodo Dupont can occasionally come up with very silly ideas.

However, its silliness duly recognised, she dismisses the idea, and, in lieu of any other reasonable explanation, decides that it must have been put there as some kind of ironic joke.

Wrong again.

'I see you're looking at my hut,' says Mhambi. Like Dodo, she holds a tall, coldly-perspiring glass of fruit punch. 'You're probably wondering what it's doing there?'

'I was,' confesses Dodo.

'Well, there's no great secret about it. It's where I perform my medicine ceremonies,' Mhambi tells her.

'Medicine ceremonies?'

'Yes, Zulu medicine. You see, I'm a qualified Zulu witch-doctor, and that hut is a genuine Zulu witch-doctor's hut. It's essential to have the right setting for the rituals, otherwise the spells won't work.'

'And do they work?' asks Dodo, half joking.

'Oh, yes,' replies Mhambi, smiling but with a tone of

sincerity. 'I'm a very powerful witch-doctor.'

'Really? So, you practice traditional as well as modern medicine?'

'Yes, but I never mix the two. When I'm on duty at the surgery I stick to prescribed NHS medical practice.'

It's Saturday afternoon and the barbecue cum welcoming party held in honour of Bellend Close's newest residents is well underway (or 'under weigh,' for the nautically pedantic.) And if Dodo and Mayumi had required any solid proof that they are not here chasing shadows, that something is indeed seriously wrong in Bellend Close, the proof is here before them now.

A gender gap, thinks Dodo. A gender gap, right down the middle of the garden lawn. On the left (looking from the patio) stand the women: laughing and chattering, full of life; and on the right are gathered the men: morose, lethargic, barely exchanging a word. Amongst them Dodo recognises Mhambi's husband, David Jarman, listlessly seated in a deck chair, and dressed in a rather over-the-top safari suit that lends him the air of a dejected clown.

It has occurred to Dodo that in other circumstances she would have liked Mhambi Khoza immediately, liked her tremendously—no, she *does* like her tremendously—but she is also wary and suspicious of her. She has no choice but to be. At the very best this woman has taken to treating her husband badly, and for no apparent reason; and at worst, she might be the instigator or ringleader of the whole business; of whatever it is that's going on around here; that vast, elusive, intangible *something* that has transformed this street and its residents.

And God knows Mhambi carries the air of a matriarch about her, thinks Dodo. The alpha-plus female of Bellend Close and no mistake. And she detects some deference in the way the other women speak to her. She might be wrong about that; she might be reading too much into it, and that Mhambi's apparent ascendency on the present occasion could simply be due to the fact that this her territory, her party, and that she is merely playing her part as hostess. Standing beside Dodo now, her equal in height, wearing a headwrap, bandanna bikini top and sarong skirt whose pastel shades that contrast with her ebony skin, hoop earrings in her ears, she holds herself with a queenly grace and dignity. Ten years Dodo's senior, she is a woman whom in other circumstances Dodo could easily have fallen in love with.

People don't change drastically overnight; not without some kind of trigger. What was that trigger? Find that trigger and you've got the key to the whole problem. Is it something external? Has some outside force possessed Mhambi Khoza and the other women, and transformed them in some way? Or is it internal? Has the mind of just one of them given birth to a thought, an idea; an idea that has become an obsession, and has then, like a virus-carrier, transmitted that idea, infecting the minds of those around her, turning them into acolytes?

And if that is the case, and if Mhambi Khoza is the carrier, will Dodo also become infected? Not to mention Mayumi. Where is she? Ah, there she is: chatting away to those three Thai women; an innocent example of racial affinity going about its usual business!

Are the purchasers of those mail-order brides amongst that group of sullen men? If they are, then their wives must be just as negligent of their spouses as all the other wives here seem to be.

'What's up with the men?' ventures Dodo. 'They look more like they're at a funeral than a garden party.'

'Oh, don't worry about them,' is Mhambi's dismissive reply. 'They're always like that. Just pretend you don't notice.'

And there lies the problem, thinks Dodo, sipping her drink. Here are all the women, behaving normally in every way, enjoying an afternoon barbecue party on a Saturday afternoon—except that here are their husbands, slowly wasting away right before their eyes, and they don't give a damn about it.

'Although I do see one man who does appear to be in good spirits,' says Dodo. 'Gerald Banbury over there.'

'Over there' being the farther end of the patio, where Bellend Close's one bachelor is presiding over the barbecue (an extra-wide one, with plenty of room for cooking the meat and the veggie stuff without the risk of contamination for the latter), dispensing food and banter in equal measure.

'Oh, you know our court jester, do you?' says Mhambi, following her gaze.

'Yes, he called round ours with a bottle of champagne the other evening.'

'He didn't waste any time, then,' says Mhambi. 'Well, I'm not surprised.'

A woman with wild, curly hair and a pair of hyperactive eyes behind her glasses, bustles up to them. Space cadet, is Dodo's immediate reaction. (An assessment she won't be needing to revise.) The woman is clutching a large framed photograph to her chest.

She's not going to present it to me, is she? Some kind of welcoming gift from the whole street?

'This is Patricia,' introduces Mhambi. 'Patricia, meet Dodo.'

'Pleased to meet you,' says Dodo, extending her hand.

'Oh, likewise! I've been *dying* to meet you,' declares Patricia, pumping Dodo's hand. 'I absolutely *love* all those things you do on the telly. So fascinating! I especially liked your last one, the one about flying saucers.'

'I've never made a documentary about flying saucers,' Dodo tells her.

'Oh. Haven't you?'

'No.'

'Are you sure?'

'As sure as I can be about anything in this world, yes.'

'That's strange... I could've sworn it was you... Must

have been someone else, I suppose...'

'That would be my guess,' confirms Dodo.

'How odd. I can see you there in my mind, pointing up at the sky... Funny how your memory plays tricks on you like that. Still!' rousing herself from her abstraction: 'Can I introduce you to my husband?'

'Please do!' says Dodo eagerly. So, there is still at least one woman here who actually still cares about her husband! She looks across the garden at the assemblage of disconsolate men. Which one could it be...?

'Here he is!'

Patricia holds out the framed photograph, proudly displaying its unassuming subject.

Dodo finds herself nonplussed. 'This is your husband...?'

'Yes, this is my darling Malcolm,' confirms Patricia.

'This is actually him...?'

Is he dead? wonders Dodo. But then, she used the present tense. Is he dead and she thinks he's still alive...? Am I supposed to say 'hello' to the picture?

Mhambi comes to her rescue. 'Patricia's husband is away on business,' she explains; 'and she likes to carry his image with her whenever he's not present in the flesh.'

'I *see*,' says Dodo, relieved. 'Have you ever thought of putting his picture in a locket to carry round with you?'

'Yes, but I've never been able to find one that's *big* enough,' replies Patricia.

'Speaking of your filmmaking,' says Mhambi, before Dodo can say anything. 'Some of us were thinking that maybe the real reason you've moved in amongst us is to spy on us.'

'Spy on you?' echoes Dodo, her tone neutral.

'Yes, you know, to put us in one of your documentaries. A study in the wild of a suburban middle-class commuter belt community.'

'Ah, well. If I was making a documentary, you'd know

about it, because I'd have my film-crew with me; it wouldn't be just me.'

'Yes, but you it could be one of those hidden-camera, fly-on-the-wall documentaries, so that you could film us without us knowing about it,' insists Mhambi, smiling.

'Goodness!' exclaims Patricia. '*Are* you filming us? And I haven't checked my makeup! I'm *sure* I'm a complete mess!'

'I can assure you I do not have a hidden camera about my person,' responds Dodo, spreading her arms, indicating her attire, cut-off jeans and bikini-top. 'Nor did I move here just to make a film about you people. In fact, I have no filmmaking intentions at all; I'm taking a break from filmmaking. You have my word about that.'

'I was only joking with you, of course,' says Mhambi easily. 'And your word is more than good enough for us.' She holds out her glass. 'Welcome to the neighbourhood, Dodo.'

'Cheers!'

Dodo clinks glasses with Mhambi, and wonders if her cover has been blown already.

Chapter Nine
Cheating in Plain Sight

'I've never had a black woman before,' says Mayumi the next morning.

'And I don't think you're going to have this one,' replies Dodo, smiling at her lover, head propped up on elbow.

Mayumi, lying on her back, looks up at her.

'Why not?'

'Well, sweetheart, skilled though you are at talking people into baring all for your art, there are still some women who just wouldn't want to do it, no matter how sweet and good-natured the photographer might be—and I suspect that Mhambi Khoza would prove to be one of those women.'

'But why? She shouldn't be ashamed to have a body like hers.'

'I'm sure she isn't. But there are other reasons besides lack of body-confidence why a woman wouldn't want to do any modelling.'

'Family not liking it.'

'Yes, there's that, but also some women wouldn't want to model because they'd be thinking about what kind of people who would get to see it, and what some of those people might be *doing* while they were seeing it.'

'But that's not a problem!' protests Mayumi. 'You just shouldn't think about that.'

'Well, that solution might work for you, sweetheart, but it wouldn't work for everybody. Some women just wouldn't be able to dismiss it from their minds like that, and they would feel very uncomfortable at the idea of being exposed like that to the oppressive male gaze.'

'What do gay men have to do with it?' asks Mayumi innocently.

Dodo looks at her for a moment, then bursts out laughing. Mayumi grins with all her overbite.

Dodo sighs, her face assuming a look that is part amused affection, part slavish adoration, as she toys with a lock of her lover's hair.

'You know, I really can't decide if you genuinely misunderstood me just then, or if you just pretended to.'

'Not telling,' says Mayumi, her overbite vanishing.

'Oh, so you're going all enigmatic and inscrutable on me, are you?'

'Yes,' succinctly.

'And anyway,' says Dodo, 'we're not really here for you to work on your photography: we've got an assignment to complete, remember?'

Mayumi springs into a sitting position and salutes briskly. 'Agent Mayumi reporting for duty!'

'Good!' says Dodo in the same tone. 'And what are your standing orders, Agent Mayumi?'

'Keep smiling and trust no-one!'

'Correct! And that goes double for Mhambi Khoza. I've got a feeling she might be onto us…'

'How come?'

'Oh, it was just some of the things she said yesterday… I might be wrong; it might just be me reading too much into her choice of words; and I wasn't picking up anything in the way of hostility from her… But on the other hand, saying she thought I might be here to spy on everyone… That might have been her way of letting me know that she was onto me, that she knew who I really was… But then, the only way she could've found out about my connection with her husband's employer would be if her husband had told her himself… And he wouldn't have been stupid enough to do that, would he? Or would he…?'

'He looked pretty stupid to me,' offers Mayumi.

'Yes, maybe I need to have a quiet word with David Jarman… Trouble is, we're not supposed to know each other, and his wife never bothered introducing him to me yesterday… I'll need to catch him when she's not around…'

Later that morning there's a knock at the door and Dodo opens it to find an Indian man standing on the threshold, whom she recognises as Jubin Ghai, the writer.

He introduces himself. He seems embarrassed, ill at ease. 'I… I'm sorry I couldn't make it to the party yesterday… I was feeling a bit under the weather…'

'Yes, your wife said something to that effect,' says Dodo. (What Ramona had actually said to Dodo was: 'He's in one of his moods.')

'Well, I was wondering if I could come in and have a chat with you… If you're not too busy…?'

'I'm not bust at all. Please, come in.'

'Thank you.'

Dodo leads her guest to the living room, introduces Mayumi, who is sitting in front of the television.

'Hi!' she says to Jubin, smiling broadly. 'I know you! You're the guy who wrote the really nasty review of Dodo's last book!'

Jubin winces like someone who has just received a faceful of cold water. 'Ah. Yes, that...' turning a pained and apologetic countenance to Dodo. 'It was the editor, you see. He wanted a really acerbic piece from me... I'm known, you see, for my acerbic style of prose... And really, I did regret it! As soon as I'd sent it off, I regretted it! I knew I'd overdone it, laid it on a bit too thick. But I didn't really mean everything I said...! It was the editor...!'

Acerbic the review had certainly been. It had been one of those reviews in which the critic, under guise of criticising the book, had launched a very personal attack against the author. Dodo well remembers some of those snide comments.

And here we witness yet another display of our paragon's high-mindedness when she elects to let her discomfited guest off the hook.

'Well, it's ancient history, now. Let's say no more about it.'

'Thank you...' says Jubin, relieved.

'Take a seat,' invites Dodo, indicating the sofa. 'What can I get you to drink?'

'No... no, nothing for me, thank you. Actually... I was wondering if I could perhaps have a word with you alone, Professor...? I really need to consult you—that is, I would appreciate your professional advice, on... erm... something I'd like to discuss with you... That is, if you don't mind?'

'No, I'd be happy to help you in any way I can, Mr Ghai,' answers Dodo readily. 'Why don't we go through to my study, and we can talk there.'

Leaving Mayumi to her television viewing, Dodo escorts Jubin to the room she has taken as her study. Although they only intend their residency in Strepford to be a short one, Dodo and Mayumi have brought a large amount of their personal belongings with them, to aid in the deception that their move here is a permanent one. (Although, Dodo not wanting to denude her London apartment, the furniture has been purchased brand new—and will be donated to charity when no longer needed.) And so it is that Dodo's study contains all that formerly occupied her study in London: her desktop, her library of scholarly texts, her beckoning cat statue and, in pride of place, the centrepiece of the room, a large framed photograph of Mayumi Takahashi (artist self-portrait), topless and displaying a radiant smile whilst favouring the viewer with a two-fingered salute. (A gesture which was actually intended to be the peace sign, and in Japan it would have been received as such; but, as Dodo had had to explain to her lover in the early days of their relationship, as far as the United Kingdom is concerned, the V-sign only signifies 'peace' when displayed palm-outwards—displayed palm-inwards then its meaning is most emphatically 'peace off!')

Taking the seat offered to him, Jubin's eyes range around the room, taking in its contents, and when his gaze falls upon the smiling photograph on the wall, it feels rather like its subject has followed him into the room and is cheerfully inviting him to go and get knotted.

'So, what can I help you with, Mr Ghai?' inquires Dodo, who has seated herself at her desk, chair swivelled round to face her guest. 'Or shall I call you Jubin?'

'Yes, call me Jubin... I... erm, well it's difficult to know where to start...'

'Well, is it something that's bothering you that you'd like to talk to me about? Something that's happened?'

'Yes. Yes, it is something that's happened... At least, it *might* have—basically, it's a dream I had that's bothering me; a dream. Silly, I know...'

'Not at all. We can all be disturbed by dreams we

experience. When did you have this dream? Recently, I presume?'

'Yes, it was just the other night... If it *was* a dream, that is...'

'I see. So you're unsure whether it was a dream or something that actually happened. It must have been a very vivid dream, then?'

'Incredibly vivid. The most vivid dream I can ever remember having.'

'And realistic...?'

'No! It was completely outlandish. A nightmare, really.'

'But still vivid enough that part of you thinks it might be something you actually experienced. Well, I think you'd better just go ahead and describe this dream you had, and then we'll see what we can make of it.'

Dodo speaks with her most professional tone of encouragement, but Jubin still hesitates, clearly embarrassed.

'Well... it was a very... *explicit* dream... I...'

'You don't have to worry about that,' Dodo assures him, smiling. 'There's no room for prudishness in my line of work.'

'No, I don't suppose there is...' weakly returning the smile. And then, taking a deep breath: 'Well, this is how it happened: I dreamed that I woke up in the middle of the night; I was lying in my own bed in my own room, my wife was lying next to me... But there was *something else* there; some kind of horrible *creature*; and it was, well, it was on top of my wife, and it was, well it was...'

'Raping her in her sleep?'

'Having sex with her, yes; but my wife was certainly not asleep, and from all appearances, she was a most willing partner to... what was...'

'I get you. Can you describe it? The creature, I mean?'

'Well, not completely; the room was dark, but I could just about see... It was large... and hairy, very hairy...'

'Human or animal?'

'Human or animal? Well, it was human, I suppose...Muscles all over, like a bodybuilder; but it was much bigger, and much hairier, too, than any normal human being... It wasn't just a man, not an ordinary man...'

'And its face? Did its face look like a human's?'

'I couldn't really see its face. The whole head was dark, a blur... Which was odd because I could see Ramona's face perfectly clearly...'

'And what happened next? What did you do when you saw this creature copulating with your wife?'

'Well, I... At first I was frozen; I couldn't believe it. I thought I must be dreaming... But then, somehow, I knew I *wasn't* dreaming, that it was *real*. It was all real. My wife and this *thing*. An-and I screamed out and... and I shot bolt upright in bed...'

'And then...?'

'...And then suddenly it was daylight, the thing was gone, and Ramona was there, just waking up, asking me what was wrong...' He looks at Dodo. 'I know, I know. It sounds like someone just waking up from a nightmare; I know it does... But it was all so *vivid*. It still is. It hasn't faded from my mind at all; I can see it all, as clear in my mind as anything that happened to me yesterday... And the smell, as well.'

'The smell?'

'Yes; of the... whatever it was. It had a powerful odour coming from it. Now, you don't normally *smell* things in dreams, do you?'

'Well, you *can*...' demurs Dodo. 'Was it a familiar smell, or an alien one?'

'Well, familiar, I suppose... It was just an ordinary male smell, the smell of a man, but very powerful.'

'Like bad BO?' smiles Dodo.

'No... It wasn't that... It wasn't a bad smell... Just... overwhelming, I suppose...'

'Hm. Well, does your wife have anything to say about all this? Have you told her about it?'

'Of course, I haven't!' snaps Jubin, instantly all irritation. 'How on earth could I have told Ramona about *that*?'

'That's a very vehement response, there. Why would it be so preposterous to tell your wife?'

'Because it would! If it was a dream, she would just laugh in my face about it; and if it wasn't, if it really happened, she's not going to admit it, is she? That would be admitting she was cheating on me!'

Dodo can't help but smile at this. 'I don't know if you could call it "cheating on you"; it wasn't exactly done behind your back, was it? You were lying right next to her.'

'What else do you want me to call it? I've told you it was consensual, haven't I? She wasn't being raped!'

'Yes, but what was she having this consensual sex *with*? If what you saw really happened, then we have to accept that there is some supernatural element involved; your own missing time would seem to prove that. You need to consider that your wife might have been mesmerised, might have been under some kind of spell or enchantment: perhaps she even believed it was *you* she was having sex with.'

'No, because she was enjoying it way too much for that,' says Jubin, with a bitter smile.

'Ah. Your tone seems to imply that things haven't been satisfactory in that area between you and your wife recently.'

'*Nothing* has been satisfactory between me and my wife recently. First, she went frigid on me and now she's taken to playing childish practical jokes!'

'Well, you know, those practical jokes might actually be an attempt on her part to patch things up between you; a bit of harmless fun to lighten the atmosphere.'

'Harmless fun?' explodes Jubin. 'Do you know what she did to me the other day? She gave me a glass of beer that she'd gone and *peed* in! You call that harmless fun?'

Dodo stifles a laugh.

'It's nothing to laugh about! I was so thirsty at the time, I quaffed half the thing down before I even realised what I was drinking! I was very ill afterwards!'

And here Dodo's professional self-restraint deserts her completely: she bursts into uncontrollable laughter.

Enraged, Jubin springs to his feet. 'Oh yes, that's it: have a good laugh! Typical female, always taking the other woman's side and laughing at the man! And to think I was foolish enough to think you could actually help me with this! I must have been out of my mind! Well, forget it! Forget I said anything! I'm leaving!'

He marches to the door.

'No, please... I'm sorry...' splutters Dodo, vainly trying to control her merriment. 'I didn't mean... Please, sit back down...'

'No, thank you very much! I'm not going to sit here and listen to some quack psychiatrist,' (that's quack *psychologist* to you, buster!) 'telling me that the beast I saw was just a manifestation of my repressed libido or some voyeuristic desire to watch my wife being violated! Nor do I require any advice from a morally-degenerate media prostitute who seems to think that displaying her erogenous zones for all the world to see is a feminist statement! Good day to you!' He opens the door with violence, and then, turning back: 'And you know what? I take back my apology about that review! I meant every word I said!'

Exit Jubin Ghai, with slamming doors, and doubtless having forgotten in his righteous indignation that he'd never actually tendered any apology for the review in the first place.

Chapter Ten
Life's a Witch - And Then You Become Apprenticed to One

As apprentice-witch to Fat Tulip, Abigail has many important duties to perform, and one of these duties is to go to the shops to buy sweets and snacks whenever Fat Tulip is feeling peckish. She is just returning from one of these shopping expeditions this fine morning; but this time it is not carbonated beverages or iced confections she is bringing back to Witch Headquarters (Abigail's own name for the glade, not officially sanctioned by her instructress); no, because today is the day that the latest issue of *Slayve the Barbarian* comes out, and Abigail's assignment has been to rush to the nearest newsagent and secure a copy of this monarch amongst children's comics before it sells out—a very real possibility when you recall that this week's number comes with a free new-reader-enticing Slayve the Barbarian frisbee!

However, Abigail had arrived at the newsagents to find all five copies still on the shelves, reposing snuggly beside the *Beano*, and now she returns to her mistress, skipping along under the trees, the comic reposing safely in the carrier bag provided for the purpose—to ensure against Abigail sacrilegiously rolling the comic into a tube for ease of transportation (something she couldn't have done anyway without removing the frisbee taped to the cover.) Jumping the narrow brook which skirts the northern perimeter of the clearing, Abigail emerges into the sunlight. She is greeted with the sight of Fat Tulip performing a dance in the middle of the glade, leaping and pirouetting like an overweight ballerina in civvies. There are many desensitised souls who might have laughed upon witnessing this exhibition; but not Abigail—she knows that if her witch mistress is dancing in the glade then this dancing in the glade can only be important witch business.

Ever a keen student and a quick learner, Abigail breaks into an imitation of Fat Tulip, and dances her way across the glade to join her. However, by the time she gets there, Fat Tulip has stopped dancing and is looking at Abigail with no friendly expression.

'What are you doing?' she demands curtly.

'I was doing the witches dance, same as you were!' replies smiling Abigail.

'Well, I didn't tell you to do the witches dance, did I?' is the irritable rejoinder. 'Have you got the comic?'

'Yes!' proudly holding out the carrier bag.

Fat Tulip snatches the bag from her and removes the comic. Her eyes devour the cover hungrily, although very little can actually be seen of the artwork, which is concealed by the attached frisbee. The frisbee is red, and bears a sticker emblazoned with the official *Slayve the Barbarian* © logo, to emphasise the fact that this is no run-of-the-mill mass-produced plastic frisbee, but is in fact a genuine *Slayve the Barbarian* frisbee!

'Were they all red?' asks Fat Tulip.

'Were all what red?' asks Abigail.

'The frisbees, stupid! Were they all red, or did they have them in different colours?'

'I *think* they were all red…' says Abigail, ponderingly. 'The one underneath was, anyway!'

'What about the one underneath *that*?'

'Didn't look at them!'

'Well, you should of!' snaps Fat Tulip ungrammatically.

A flat stone slab lies in the centre of the clearing, about six feet by four, its surface not quite flat, not quite horizontal. Fat Tulip seats herself beside this, on its shady side. Abigail sits down next to her.

'I wonder if it's going to scar…' murmurs Fat Tulip.

'What will scar?'

'The sticky tape. It might damage the cover when I peel it off...'

'Then you could just peel the tape off the frisbee,' suggests Abigail practically.

'Yeah, but then I'd have tape still stuck to the front cover, wouldn't I?'

Two pieces of the white tape secure the frisbee to the comic. Fat Tulip peels one piece away from the frisbee, and then, very slowly and carefully, from the surface of the comic. The tape comes smoothly away leaving no scar on the glossy paper.

'They must've made it so it comes off easily,' declares Fat Tulip, satisfied. She feasts her eyes on the now-revealed cover illustration, which features Slayve in a typical action pose, but not-so-typically wielding a large chainsaw. A jagged speech bubble announces in sound-effect letters: FREE SLAYVE THE BARBARIAN© FRISBEE WITH THIS ISSUE!* with the footnote: *IF NOT ATTACHED ASK AT THE COUNTER!

'Cool!' says Fat Tulip. 'Wonder what Slayve's doing with a chainsaw?'

And she opens the comic and starts reading.

'Hey, that's not fair!' exclaims Abigail. 'I can't see it!'

'I'm reading it first,' says Fat Tulip. 'You'll have to wait till I've finished. And no, you can't play with the frisbee either.'

'Why can't we read the comic together? That's what we did last time!'

'Last time was different. Last time I'd already read it.'

'So what? Why can't we both read it together now? Go on!'

'Oh, all right,' sighs Fat Tulip. 'Come here then. You hold that page.'

Abigail shuffles close to her friend and takes hold of the comic. The first page shows a magnificent yew tree of great antiquity standing alone on the summit of a grassy hill. Four people can be seen walking up the hill towards it.

'That's the Witch Tree,' announces Fat Tulip. 'It's the oldest tree in England and it's where Cassie lives.'

'Cassie lives in a tree? Then where's the treehouse?'

'She doesn't live in a treehouse! She's a tree nymph, remember? a dryad; so, she actually lives *inside* the tree.'

'Oh, the tree's hollow, is it?'

'No, the tree's not bloody hol—! Look, if you're going to keep asking me stupid questions, then I'm gunna read it on my own and you can do something else!'

'I'm sorry! I won't ask anything else! Promise!'

'Well, you better. Now…'

She turns the page. The four people are now at the foot of the tree. Two of them, a smart-looking man and woman, are wearing grey business suits. The other two are both men wearing hardhats, a fat man and a thin man. The thin man also has goggles and he's carrying a large chainsaw.

'"Yes husband, you're right," says the woman. "This hill will make the perfect location for our new 6G wi-fi mast!" Ah, so that's what they're up to, the bastards! "Yes dearest, as town mayor it is my duty to make sure that our citizens have the best possible internet signal, and this 3000-year-old tree is just sitting here taking up valuable space and doing nothing for the community!" says the mayor. "3000 years old? Then it's about time someone chopped it down!" says the fat workman. "I'll say it is! Ugly-looking thing, ain't it?" says the thin workman. "Indeed. The Witch Tree has a dark history. There are many tales of vileness and depravity attached to it," says the mayor. "Vileness and depravity? Then the sooner we chop it down the better! We can't have vileness and depravity standing so close to our beautiful town!" says the mayoress. "Are you sure your chainsaw will be able to cope with such a large tree, foreman?" asks the mayor. "Don't you worry about it, Mr Mayor. This 'ere chainsaw's the biggest and the best that money can buy!" replies the fat man whose the foreman. "Excellent! Then proceed at once!" orders the mayor. "Right! Prepare to meet your maker, you ugly eyesore!" grins the foreman, rubbing his hands together. "Hey, no fair! I'm not an eyesore!" says the tree. 'Cept it's not the tree, cuz look, it's Cassie the New Age Dryad!'

'Oooh! She's not got any clothes on!' exclaims Abigail.

'That's cuz she's just come out of the tree. She doesn't wear clothes when she's at home; only when she's out and about. "Who are you? And how dare you parade around in that shocking state of undress?" says the mayoress. Snooty cow! "I'm Cassie, and this tree is mine, so I'd rather you didn't chop it down," says Cassie, leaning against the tree, all casual like. "You claim to own this tree? Do you have the paperwork to prove it?' asks the mayor. "Not on me, no," says Cassie. "Put some clothes on! You can't go around stark-naked!" snaps the mayoress. "But I'm not naked! Look: I'm wearing my girdle!" replies Cassie.'

'Oooh, it's a girdle, is it? You said it was a belt last time!'

'Well, belt, girdle, they mean the same thing! And anyway, shut up! What did I tell you about not interrupting?'

'Sorry,' contritely.

'"Well, if you haven't got the documents, then you have no proof of ownership. You can file a claim at the town hall if you wish, but in the meantime, we're still going to cut down the tree," says the mayor. "Right, Fred! Start her up! Let's get chopping!" says the foreman; and the man with the chainsaw, who's name's Fred, starts up the chainsaw. "I wouldn't do that, if I were you! You'll only regret it!" warns Cassie. "Ignore the silly cow, Fred! Start cutting!" says the foreman. Fred walks up to the tree, ready to start sawing it! But then, Slayve the Barbarian comes out of nowhere! Just like that! He grabs the chainsaw and ZWEEEP! slices Fred's head off! Look at how surprised he looks with his head flying off like that! "I told you you'd regret it!" says Cassie. "You bastard! You killed Fred! And that chainsaw's company property! Give it back!" says the foreman. "Shut your face, you!" says Cassie, and SHOOOM! Slayve stabs him in the face with the chainsaw, and his eyes and teeth go all over the place! "Your turn, now!" says Cassie. And look: here's Mr Mayor, all terrified and cringing. "Please don't kill me! You can have the tree! It's yours! Only please don't kill me!" he says. "Oh, show some guts, you big chicken!" says Cassie. And Slayve rams the chainsaw into Mr Mayor's stomach and SPLEURP! his blood and guts spray out like a fountain! And here, a full-page picture of Slayve, all soaked in blood, holding the chainsaw up in the air and going "RRRAAAAARRRRHHH!" like he always does at the end of a battle. Oh, and there's Cassie in the background, and look, she's pissing herself laughing cuz she thought it was really funny the way Slayve killed those people. She's got a wicked sense of humour, Cassie has.'

'But what about Mrs Mayor?' wonders Abigail. 'We never saw what happened to her!'

'Hang on, it's probably on the next page… Yeah, there she is! Look at her: her eyes all wide, clawing her head with her hands!'

'She looks really scared.'

'I think it's more like shock. "You… You monsters! That was my husband you just disembowelled!" she gasps… "Relax, will you? Slayve isn't going to disembowel *you*, is he? Slayve never kills a woman! That's cuz he's a warrior and a man of honour!" The mayoress has dropped down on her knees now, and she's turned on the waterworks. "My husband… my husband… my husband… You monsters! You MONSTERS!!!" Oh, look! SPARKLE! SPARKLE! Cassie's gone into sparkly mode, she's floating in the air, and she's got her magic staff. "Fear not! Even though you tried to do harm to the Witch Tree, I shall show you clemency and wielding my magic staff, I shall cast a spell which will instantly relieve you of your feelings of loss and bereavement!" And then, last page, another splash page, there's the mayoress, with Slayve on top of her, and you can tell she's got over her bereavement, cuz she's got her arms and legs all wrapped around Slayve, and she doesn't even mind that he's still covered in her husband's blood! And there's all those hearts floating up from her head, as well. And here's Cassie at the front, looking out of the picture at us—it's called 'breaking the fourth wall,' when they do that—and she's giving us the peace sign and she says: "See? I knew the spell would work!"'

'Ah, that's nice! So the magic spell made Mrs Mayor feel better!'

'No, Cassie's just joking, wasn't she? She didn't do anything, really. It's Slayve who's making her feel better.' She closes the comic.

'Oh! Can Slayve do spells as well, then?'

'No, Slayve's just Slayve. He's like the alpha male times a million...' Fat Tulip's voice becomes pensive, and she gazes into the distance. 'He's the perfect man, Slayve is… Bo bullshit… Just fucking and fighting like a real man should…'

'Oooh, you just said rude words!' says Abigail chidingly.

Fat Tulip. 'So what? I just call things what they are. Slayve's the ultimate man. Don't you think so?' She holds up the comic, displaying the cover for Abigail's inspection. 'Don't you think he's a handsome man?'

'Well… He's alright, I suppose,' says Abigail. 'I like men a bit thinner than that, though…'

'Thinner?' sneers Fat Tulip. 'You mean less muscles? Like all those scrawny pretty-boys in the boy bands?'

'Well, lots of girls like those boys…'

'Well, *I* don't. I like a man like Slayve. And so does the woman who draws the comic.'

'Oh, is the comic made by a woman, then?' says Abigail, surprised. 'I didn't know that.'

'Well, *no-one* knows for sure,' replies Fat Tulip. 'The identity of the author's a mystery. There's a lot of people online wondering who it really is.'

'Don't they put their name on the comic, then?'

'Yeah, but their name's Kit; Kit Miller. And Kit can be a man's name or a woman's, cuz it's short for any name that starts with Chris, and it can be short for Catherine as well. But it's probably not their real name, anyway.'

'Then how do you know it's a woman?'

'You can just *tell*, that's how. You can tell from the way she draws Slayve; you can see all the love that's gone into drawing that body; a *woman's* love…' gazing at the cover illustration. 'And plus, there's the way she draws Cassie, as well,' flipping through the pages. 'Look: you see? Her tits are just normal-size tits; average. If it'd been a man who did the comic, he'd have drawn her with great big knockers, wouldn't he?' closing the comic again. 'Come on: let's have a game of frisbee!'

'Yeah!' enthuses Abigail.

Chapter Eleven
Sound-Only Porn

When Dodo knocks on the door of the Ghai residence (which is just across the road from her own) it is Ramona who answers. Her face lights up when she sees who her caller is.

'Dodo! How lovely to see you again! Come in, come in!'

'Thank you,' stepping into the hallway. 'Lovely to see you as well.'

Dodo and Ramona were introduced at Mhambi's garden party, and being mutual admirers of each other's writing, had spent an enjoyable time tossing bouquets at one another, soon becoming fast friends.

'Lovely day, isn't it?' proceeds Ramona. 'I was just doing the housework. Is this just a social call, or—'

'Actually, I was hoping to have a word with your husband if I could. Is he in?'

'Jubin? Yes, he's upstairs in his study.' Ramona crosses to the foot of the staircase. 'Oh, Jubin darling!' she calls, her voice honey-sweet. 'There's someone here to see you!'

'Oh, is there?' comes the pettish response. 'Well, dearest wife, correct me if I am wrong, but did I not inform you just two hours ago that I am extremely busy this morning and that I am not to be interrupted under *any* circumstances? As I say, correct me if I'm wrong, but I do believe I issued instructions to that general effect. Or, has it just slipped your memory?'

'No, darling, it hasn't slipped my memory, but I thought you might wish to make an exception in this case! You see, it's Professor Dupont who is here to see you!'

A loud noise from upstairs, suggestive of somebody falling out of their chair, and moments later Jubin Ghai appears, stomping down the stairs, expression seething.

'How dare you come here!' marching straight up to Dodo. 'Get out of my house!' ('*Our* house, darling,' from Ramona.)

'I understand how you feel,' begins Dodo in her most diplomatic tones. 'But I just wanted to apologise and clear things up—'

'Well, I am neither interested in your apologies or in your attempts at clarity. I do not wish to hold any converse with you. Not now, not ever. In fact, I wish never to set eyes on you again!' ('She lives right across the road, darling...')

'But—'

'No buts! This is not open to discussion! I bid you good day, once and for all!'

He stomps back up the stairs.

'Oh, Dodo, I really must apologise for my husband,' says Ramona. 'He's not been himself of late.'

'No, I understand, really,' says Dodo. 'We did have an unfortunate misunderstanding the other day. Perhaps I could have a quick word with you—'

'NO, YOU CANNOT!' roars Jubin, practically falling

back down the stairs. 'You cannot talk to my wife about *anything*, do you understand? *Anything*! Never will you hold any converse with her! Never will even so much as *attempt* to hold converse with her! Now, leave!' bearing down on Dodo, compelling her to back towards the door. 'Leave, and never dare to cross this threshold again! Do you hear me? Never!'

Dodo sees Ramona's face, a picture of mute, helpless apology, over her husband's shoulder, then the door is slammed in her face.

After her ejectment from the Ghai household, Dodo makes her way deeper into the Close. She doesn't see Gerald Banbury, but he sees her, and he watches her with a lively interest, especially with regard to the smooth, swaying motions of her denim hips and posterior.

Groper's paradise, thinks Gerald, fingers twitching with anticipation. He sees himself coming up behind Dodo and giving those buttocks a good fondling. He sees Dodo turn around, a smile of complicity on her face, gently chiding him with a 'Naughty, naughty!'

But no, it's best not to bank on that kind of response on such a slight acquaintance. He has only met Dodo on two occasions thus far; a woman has to get to know a man more fully before she can be expected to react favourably to a spot of groping. (And very often, not even then; but Gerald prefers to ignore any uncomfortable truths that clash with his lifestyle choices.)

Dodo Dupont and Mayumi Takahashi. The moment he heard who the new neighbours were, Gerald had been straight round there, along with his best bottle of bubbly. 'I come bearing gifts!' And of course (and as he'd intended) his hosts had been obliged to invite him to stop and help them drink it, and a very pleasant evening it had been—for one of the participants, at least. Coming after his Patricia Pinecone disappointment (someone must have told that woman something, judging from what she'd said in an answerphone message reminiscent of the final chapter of *Ulysses*; not everything, but something), this was just the fresh challenge he needed. The left-wing intellectual and the Japanese erotic photographer! Yes, there's a lot of potential there. A same-sex couple, yes, but from what he's heard, both of them known to swing both ways. Bisexual. No, they'd probably both say they were *pan*sexual—as if that makes any bloody difference! Still, even though they've been together for a while (three years, they said, more than long enough for a couple to start getting bored with each other), they still look very lovey-dovey; might not be that easy to split them up. Most likely scenario would be they'd invite him to join him for a threesome, and that's not what Gerald has in mind at all. No, what Gerald wants is to coax one of them into seeing him behind the other one's back. *That* is where the fun lies…

Wait a minute! Dupont's on her own. Ergo, the other one must be on her own as well!

And having made this logical deduction, Gerald abandons his plan of accosting Dodo, and bends his steps instead towards her house.

Yes, of the two, Takahashi seems like the softer target, the easier conquest. Well, she's Japanese, isn't she? And as everybody knows, Japanese women are basically just big kids, right? Good mothers and housewives and all that, but still basically kids. Gullible, trusting, easily led… Always take you literally and believe anything you tell 'em! And in the particular case of Mayumi Takahashi, not only is she a big kid, but with all that erotic photography of hers, she's a very naughty little girl as well! Even better! And as for her arse, well it may not be of the same magnificent dimensions as Dupont's, but it's still an impressive *derriere*! Looking at her top half, you'd think she'd have a skinny little backside, but in fact from the waist down she's much curvier. Gerald remembers noting this important fact at the garden party on

Saturday.

But when Gerald knocks on the door of number twelve, he receives no reply. He knocks again and receives no reply. He knocks a third time with the same result. He goes round the back of the house. There's no-one around and the patio doors are closed, the curtains drawn. He knocks on the patio doors. He *tries* the patio doors. Locked.

Nobody home. So much for his plans.

Deciding to console himself with a pint, Gerald makes his way to the *Woodsman's Chopper* round the corner on Croft Street, where a loud Hawaiian shirt announces the presence of Mike Grimsby. Grimsby, the alleged journalist! He'd almost forgotten about the fellow.

Grimsby, intent on the laptop on the table before him, earpiece in his ear, doesn't notice Gerald's advent. Gerald scans the saloon, taking in the rest of the clientele. A trio of pot-bellied old-timers trading reminiscences. Two office workers enjoying an early lunch. A solitary drinker hidden behind a broadsheet newspaper.

Grimsby it is, then.

Having secured his pint, Gerald seats himself uninvited at Grimsby's table.

'Hello, old son!'

Grimsby is startled. He seems ill at ease, turning the laptop away from Gerald, clamping a muffling hand over the ear with the earpiece.

'Oh, it's you Mr Banbury…'

'Call me Gerald, call me Gerald. You know, you don't seem too pleased to see me, and it was *you* who sought out my acquaintance last week. You even gave me your phone number, remember? Why the change of heart, old man?'

'Oh… nothing. Just a bit busy at the moment. Never called me though, did you?'

'That's because I haven't had anything to report. But I've been keeping my eyes open. So, what about you? Made any progress?'

'Yes, yes… Following up a few leads…'

'Excellent! Is that what you're doing now?' indicating the laptop.

'What, now? No… No… This, this ain't anything. Just listening to music. Y'know, passing the time…'

'Oh, and what sort of music are you into, Mr Grimsby? I'd be very interested to know.'

And so saying, Gerald yanks the earpiece chord from its socket, and the sound of what is clearly several individuals engaged in very noisy sexual activity blasts from the laptop's speaker.

'Don't do that!' squawks Grimsby, frantically plugging the chord back into the socket, cutting off the sex noises. He casts guilty eyes around the room. Unsurprisingly, everyone is looking at them. 'What d'you do *that* for?' he hisses.

Gerald turns the laptop towards himself and is surprised to see only the dancing forms of sound bars on the screen.

'Well, you certainly have very unusual preferences, Grimsby old son. Sound-only porn. I think most connoisseurs of this particular artform would say that it was the visual element that was the most important.'

'This ain't *porn*,' hisses Grimsby. 'This is a live-feed I'm listening to; from a bug I planted.'

'Really?' Gerald is surprised. 'You're very enterprising, I must say. Didn't think you had it in you. And where might this listening device of yours be planted?'

Grimsby smirks. 'Just round the corner.'

'Bellend Close?' even more surprised. 'You mean someone's having an orgy round there even as we speak?'

'When the cat's away…' still smirking.

'But who is it? Who's involved?'

'Them three Asian birds.'

'Asian—? You mean Hom, Ploy and Dao? It's really them? And whose house are they in?'

'Whichever one of 'em's Paul Smith's missis.'

'That's Hom. Good lord. And who are the gentlemen

partners? Obviously not the husbands.'

'No fear. *They're* all at work. When the cat's away…'

'Yes, but who are the *men*?'

A shrug. 'Dunno, do I? Have to wait till they come out.'

'Well, I'll be…' Gerald sits back in his chair and takes a long pull of his beer. 'Well, you've certainly got your story there, Grimsby; but it's not one you can print. And how the hell did you get into Smith's house to plant the bug there?'

'He did it for me. I just gave him the bug, didn't I?'

'He did it—? You mean you *asked* him and he agreed? Why would he do that?'

'Cuz he's my client, that's why.'

'Client?'

'Yeah…' And, dropping his voice confidentially: 'Can I trust you with a secret, Mr Banbury?'

'Grimsby, I am the soul of discretion. I would've thought that such a shrewd judge of character as yourself wouldn't even have to ask that question.'

'Just checking. No offence meant.' He pauses. 'See, thing is, I ain't really a reporter for the local rag.'

'I know that, old boy. I rang up and asked them. You're with one of the nationals, aren't you? Following up on that caveman story?'

'No, I ain't. Fact is, I ain't a reporter at all. I'm a *private investigator*.'

Grimsby utters these words with visible pride, and Gerald stares at him with dawning enlightenment. 'Well, well, well… A private investigator… I suppose I ought to have realised that before, but private investigators, they've been so done to death in fiction, you tend to forget that they do actually exist in real life.'

'That we do, Mr Banbury,' confirms Grimsby. 'That we do.'

'And now that I know this, I think I can guess which fictional detective inspired *you* to take up the profession. The shirt, the moustache, the baseball cap; there's no mistaking that look! *Magnum P.I.* Tom Selleck version. Am I right?'

Grimsby smiles, nay, he actually *blushes*. 'We just called it *Magnum*, back in the day.'

(This is true. Even the ITV announcers never bothered with the 'P.I.'!)

'Got a red Ferrari?'

Grimsby's face falls. 'No. Can't afford one.'

'Well, don't feel bad about that,' says Gerald consolingly. 'I doubt anyone could, on a private investigator's salary. I mean, look at Magnum: that Ferrari he drove around in wasn't even *his*, was it? Belonged to Robin Masters, didn't it? Come to think of it, even his *digs* weren't his own! Lived rent-free on the Masters estate, didn't he? Really if you think about it, the fellow was just a freeloader!'

'Well, I wouldn't go *that* far,' says Grimsby, rushing to his hero's defence. 'He did earn his keep, y'know; checking up on the estate's security, and doing jobs for Robin Masters…'

'Yes, yes, quite right. I didn't mean to put the fellow down; just being facetious. So, old Paul Smith hired you, did he?'

'Not just him; his two mates an' all.'

'What, John Johnson and James White? Nao and Ploy's husbands?'

'Yep, them. They pooled together. Wanted me to find out if their wives was up to anything. Suspicious, they were. Wives was acting too cheerful by half. An' now we know why, eh?' grinning salaciously. 'When the cat's away…'

'Well, I'll be…' Gerald looks at him. 'So that's why you first approached me: you thought it might have been *me*!'

'Most likely suspect, weren't you? Still, I've crossed you off the list now. Can't be in two places at once, can you?'

'And I can't be more than one person at once, either! From that audio sample I heard, it sounds like our Thai brides have got themselves a lover each. But who are they? Did you recognise them?'

'Haven't seen 'em. I've been here, listening in. I'll be ready for 'em when they leave, though; I ain' gunna miss them.'

'But haven't you gotten any clues as to who they are from listening to their voices? From what they've said?'

'No, and that's cuz they ain't said nothing. Not a word. They make enough noise when they're on the job, them fellers do; growling and grunting and whatnot; but as for talking proper words, you'd think they didn't know how!'

'Well, that's bloody strange… And what about the women? They must be saying something, surely?'

'Oh yeah, they're talking alright, but they're talking in their native jibber-jabber, an' me, I don't speak jibber-jabber, so they might as well be talking Dutch.'

Gerald scratches his head. 'Well, that's natural enough; they always speak Thai when they're with each other, those three; but as for those male guests of theirs not saying anything… *That's* bloody strange… Why would they…? Some kind of role-playing thing, maybe…?' He breaks off. Grimsby is staring across the saloon, a strange look on his face. 'What's wrong?'

'I've been rumbled, that's what's wrong,' says Grimsby in a choked voice. 'One of them Thai birds has followed me here! Look!'

Gerald looks, but only sees the same people he noted when he first came into the pub, the old-timers, the office workers and the newspaper reader.

'Where am I supposed to be looking?'

'There! The one what's hiding behind the paper!'

Gerald looks again. And he sees. A letterbox shaped aperture has been cut into the newspaper and through that aperture a pair of long-lashed Asiatic eyes are staring intently across the room at them.

Chapter Twelve
Neanderthal Park: Get Your Club Out and Have a Bash Yourself!

'No thank you, I'm not interested.'

'Yes, we've done this routine before; can we skip it this time? I'm not with the Jehovah Witnesses, Avon or the UK Independence Party; I'm Dodo Dupont, your new neighbour. We met last week, remember? I was wondering if I could have another word with you when you're free. What time do you have your lunch break?'

'Lunch break? That's not for ages! I haven't even had my morning coffee break yet!'

'But I thought your morning coffee break was at eleven? It's nearly twelve now!'

'Is it? My goodness! I'd completely lost track of time! Very good of you to remind me!'

'So, can I come in and talk while you're on your break?'

'Oh, of course! Come right in!'

The automatic door slides open and Dodo steps into the air-conditioned laboratory. Across the room, Nanette Aubergine stands at the workbench before a piece of machinery, gazing into a viewfinder, her lab-coated back to Dodo. Darwin and Huxley, the two floor-cleaning hockey pucks come buzzing up to Dodo as she crosses the floor, and as before, they circle around her and then, satisfied with their inspection, retreat from whence they came.

When Dodo reaches her, Nanette is still staring intently into the machine.

'Hello,' says Dodo.

Nanette looks round, surprised. 'Oh, hello!' she says, lowering her glasses from their resting place on her forehead. 'How did you get in here?'

'You just let me in,' says Dodo.

'Oh, yes! So I did! You're my new neighbour, come for a chat. Weren't there two of you last time?'

'Yes, that was Mayumi. I'm Dodo. What's the device you're looking into?'

'This? It's a DNA analyser.'

'I see. What were you doing just now?'

'I was analysing some DNA.'

'But I thought your current project was looking for the missing link? Have you got hold of some caveman DNA or something?'

Nanette laughs. 'Caveman DNA? Ha, ha, ha! Where would I get hold of caveman DNA? That would be the find of the millennium! Ha, ha, ha!'

'And just think!' grins Dodo. 'You could clone the cells and bring your cavemen back to life, and then you could open a theme park! *Neanderthal Park: Come and Meet Your Ancestors!* Or get *eaten* by them!'

'Oh, no,' demurs Nanette. 'I don't think Neanderthals would do that: they were very gentle creatures, the Neanderthals. That's why they got wiped out. "Edited from the gene-pool," as us geneticists discreetly like to put it.'

'Yes, William Golding portrayed them as being mainly vegetarian, didn't he? Have you read *The Inheritors*?'

'Oh, yes! Beautiful book. Some of his anthropogeny was a bit off, though.' Nanette turns round from the workbench. 'Now what is it I was going to do...?' she murmurs, thoughtfully scratching her pubic hair. (She's dressed as she was last time.)

'You were going to have some coffee, weren't you?' suggests Dodo.

'Was I?' says Nanette, surprised. 'Well I don't really *feel* like I want any coffee. Funny that, isn't it? Here am I, pushing forty, so you'd think I'd need to be turning to the caffeinated drinks to keep me going more than I used to have to; but right now I'm feeling absolutely full of beans! Oh! Full of beans. Does it mean coffee beans, that saying? It would make sense, wouldn't it?' And then: 'Oh, *I* know what I wanted to do!'

And she commences urinating on the floor.

'That's better! Now, where was I? Oh, yes: full of beans. Yes, I'm not sure why but my energy levels have been very high of late; but I've been feeling better than I've ever felt! I wonder what it is? Maybe it's my enthusiasm for my work that's giving me a head rush…?'

'Yes, it could be that,' agrees Dodo, trying not to look at the urine still gushing noisily from Nanette's urethra (and being industriously mopped up by Darwin and Huxley.) 'Enthusiasm stimulates the brain; but then that's what coffee does as well; of course, coffee's only an artificial stimulant, it's not real energy. Real energy you can only get from food. I hope you're remembering to eat!'

'Oh, yes. I nibble the odd biscuit or two; keeps me going.'

'You need something more substantial than that,' chides Dodo. 'Don't you ever have a cooked meal?'

'Oh, yes. I usually bung something in the microwave in the evening.'

'What about a proper cooked meal? You've got a daughter, haven't you? Can't she take care of that for you?'

'Her? She's never in! Hardly ever see her. And when she is at home, all she ever does is lounge around! Lazy, bone-idle thing she is. I hope it's just a phase…'

'Oh! That reminds me: have you managed to find your bronze penis?'

'Oh yes, I told you about that, didn't I? No, I'm afraid I haven't found it. I was hoping it would turn up, but it hasn't.'

'Missing items don't usually just turn up; not unless it's a cat. You have to actually look for them—Jesus Christ woman, you're still going!'

This is true. The golden shower shows no signs of letting up. Poor Darwin and Huxley are working overtime!

'I know… I must have been holding it in…'

'Why were you holding it in?' demands Dodo. 'I thought

the whole point of your going on the floor as and when you needed to was so that you didn't *have* to hold it in?'

'Well, yes, that is the general idea, but I get so wrapped up in my studies that I forget, you see! I forget to empty my bladder. Silly, isn't it?'

'Extremely,' agrees Dodo.

'Oh, here we go. Nearly done now… What were we talking about? Oh, yes: the penis. No, I'm afraid I haven't found it; but I'll try and remember to have a good look round; as soon as I've got a spare five minutes… Was that what you came to ask me about?'

'It wasn't actually,' says Dodo. 'I wanted to ask you about your dreams.'

'My dreams? That's a funny topic to choose! But then, I suppose you are a psychologist, aren't you? What do you want to know?'

'You said something last time, something about having recurring dreams; you mentioned it when you were talking about those cavemen that had been seen in the woods. Is there some kind of connection…?'

'Oh, *those*,' says Nanette, blushing. 'Oh, just silly dreams. You know, *sex* dreams…'

'Well, go on! Tell me all. There's no need to be embarrassed; it's just us girls here!'

'Yes. Yes, I don't mind telling you,' says Nanette. 'Well, basically, I keep having this dream where I'm being ravished by these big, hairy brutes; I don't mean raped! It's all consensual on my part. But I just sort of let them do whatever they want to me; I'm completely passive—which is *not* how I usually am in real life, sex-wise. So yes, these creatures, they're strong, they're rough with me, but not in a nasty way, and I feel completely safe… Oh, and there's always this smell, as well!'

'A smell?'

'Yes! Which is odd, because you don't usually remember smells in dreams, do you? At least, I don't. Yes, it's this overpowering male odour coming from them, and it's *extremely* arousing; pheromonal, or something… So that's it, really! Same thing every time, more or less, but… but… I'm always left feeling like it's the best sex I've ever had in my life… I mean absolutely head and shoulders above any I've actually experienced… Like I say, probably due to overwork—well, that and abstaining for so long!'

'I see…' says Dodo. 'And… this may sound like a silly question, but are you sure they're just dreams?'

'Well, of course they are! Brutes like that don't exist in real life, do they?'

'Ah, but don't they? What about those cavemen the boy saw in the woods? They sound a lot like your lovers, don't they? You said they were very hairy…'

'Yes, they are… Maybe I'm dreaming about that missing link I'm so obsessed with finding! You see, *he*—or *she* for that matter—would have to be very hairy. That's where the gap is, you see. Australopithecus, he was as hairy as a modern ape; but then the next one along, Homo Erectus, he didn't have much more body hair than the average man or woman of today. So, the missing link I'm looking for would have to be less hairy than an ape, but a lot more hairy than we are…'

'Just like your dream lovers, in fact,' smiles Dodo.

'Yes, but these brutes in my dreams: they're too big. Our ancestors were all smaller than we are. My dream lovers, as you call them, are big. Very big. Everywhere.'

'And what about their heads, their faces? Do they look more simian or human? Low foreheads, or high foreheads?'

'That's the funny thing… I can never remember their faces. I think… even while I'm there, in the dream, somehow I can't quite see their faces… like they're blurred, out of focus…'

'And that's what that boy said,' reminds Dodo, mentally adding, *and Jubin Ghai, as well!*

When David Jarman emerges from the train station, Dodo is very surprised to see that he is still wearing the same ridiculous safari suit he'd been wearing at the garden party. (Dodo is unaware of the Allan Quatermain backstory; if she *had* known it, she would have been even more at a loss to understand why he had elected to wear the thing to work.)

'Hi there,' she says, walking up to him. 'What's with the fancy dress?'

'Oh, shut up,' snaps David, shooting ocular daggers and then walking on past her without stopping.

The smile she had prepared for the occasion vanishes from Dodo's face. 'I would like to have a word with you, Mr Jarman, if it isn't too much trouble,' she says, catching up with him.

'I'm in a hurry,' in irritable tones.

'Then we can talk as we walk,' says Dodo, keeping pace with him. 'Answer me one question: have you told your wife why I'm here?'

'No, of course I haven't!'

(Which is true, strictly speaking.)

'You haven't? And she doesn't know anything about my connection with Mark Hunter?'

'How could she know that? It's not public knowledge, is it?'

(An evasive response, likewise true in itself.)

'So you're sure she doesn't know or suspect anything?'

'Oh, what does it matter?' retorts David. 'It's not like you can actually *do* anything, can you?'

'Well, thanks for the vote of confidence,' says Dodo, nettled. 'But you might try and bear in mind that the whole reason I'm here is because Mark Hunter was concerned about your wellbeing.'

'Well, he shouldn't have sent *you*!'

'And why not? What's wrong with me?'

'You're a *woman*, that's what's wrong! You're one of them!'

'What are you talking about? It—'

'Look, I saw you! At the party, on Saturday! Getting on like a house on fire, weren't you, Mhambi and you? Converted you already, hasn't she?'

'Your wife hasn't converted me to anything, *Mr Jarman*. In fact, she said one or two things that made me think she's already suspicious of me. Look: I am trying to *help* you here, so can you at least—?'

'Look, you *can't* help me! You're one of *them*. If Mhambi *hasn't* converted you already, she will soon. Hunter should have sent a man for this job!'

'Well, you're a man, Mr Jarman,' retorts Dodo. 'So why haven't you done something to get yourself out of this mess?'

David rounds on her. 'Well, maybe I *will* do something! So, why don't you just toddle back to your cosy love nest? Haven't you got some rugs that need chewing?'

David Jarman stalks off. Resisting the urge to throw some pointed words after him, Dodo contents herself with presenting her middle finger to his retreating back.

Chapter Thirteen
Stoned, Tied, and Dildoed

Mayumi Takahashi is a woman devoted to her art. In fact, to say that she is simply 'devoted' to her art would be to do her a disservice: 'obsessed' would be a much better word. In fact, so obsessed is Mayumi, that if this condition continues to escalate, I would be concerned for her health and wellbeing, were it not for the fact that she happens to be shacked up with one of the world's leading psychologists. So as things stand, we can be comforted with the knowledge that if ever Mayumi is about to teeter over the edge, her lover will be on hand to grab her by the hair and pull her back to safety.

For Mayumi, her eyes are her viewfinder; and everything they see is assessed for its possibilities as a photographic image. If a tree in a park is not in quite the right place, she is annoyed with the tree and wishes that someone would move it. Not that Mayumi is much concerned with landscape photography—for her landscape is just background material. Her real obsession is the female body. Originally it was mainly just the Japanese female body, but then that was because she lived and worked in Japan, and Japan not having much in the way of an immigration programme, most female bodies in Japan tend to be Japanese; but with the advent of Dodo Dupont and dual-citizenship, Mayumi's international horizons have broadened. At the garden party the other day her viewfinder eyes had been busily assessing the women of Bellend Close as material for a photo-book on 'the mature woman.' We have already heard of her admiration for Mhambi Khoza; another resident whose beauty had particularly struck her, was Ramona Ghai; and then there is also Nanette Aubergine the half-dressed geneticist (who was sadly a no-show at the party.) Mayumi's fertile imagination is even now planning composition, mentally-undressing, arranging contours of female flesh, anticipating contrasts of light and shade, and, having brought all of her photographic equipment along with her to Strepford (strictly as part of their cover of course!) she is eager to get started.

However, please do not think Mayumi has become in any way neglectful of the real reason for Dodo and herself for being here in Bellend Close—not at all, because Mayumi happens to be a woman, and with this advantage, even a monomaniac can learn to multitask! Mayumi takes her responsibilities as assistant secret agent very seriously, and this very day she has been out and about in 'Agent Mayumi' mode, keeping her epicanthic eyes open for suspicious activity. And it was at the pub round the corner, the *Woodsman's Chopper*, that she had found what she was looking for: Gerald Banbury, in conference with a mysterious stranger; a small, tubby man with a moustache and a Hawaiian shirt. Suspicious! And they appeared to be watching pornography at the same time. Even more suspicious!

Now, Gerald Banbury ranks very high up on Mayumi's list of suspects. The only bachelor living in the close, and the only man unaffected by the malaise that has stricken all the other men. To Mayumi the explanation seems obvious: Gerald Banbury has seduced all the women and turned them into his own personal harem, and it is the horns he has placed on their heads that are slowly draining away the lifeforce of the husbands! Mayumi would have been convinced in her suspicions if it wasn't that Dodo doesn't share them. According to her, the women all seem to treat Gerald Banbury as something of a joke, and this would not be the way they would behave towards him had he made himself their lord and master. True enough, but perhaps the wives' apparent disdain for the man could be just for show, couldn't it? A cover to mask the real situation. But Dodo is still unconvinced, her own suspicions being focused on Mhambi Khoza.

But even so, Mayumi is mindful of her standing order to trust no-one, and she continues to be mistrustful of Gerald Banbury; and although sitting too far away to pick up what they were saying to each other, she had continued to keep him and his mysterious associate under discreet observation—but somehow, in spite of her having taken all the necessary secret agent precautions, her quarry had become aware that they were being observed and the conference had hastily broken up, the man in Hawaiian shirt exiting the pub, while Gerald Banbury had strolled over and joined her at her table.

Gerald's ensuing conversation had been of a flirtatious nature, and mindful of the other part of her standing orders, Mayumi had kept a smile on her face and pretended to receive his advances favourably; but she had been unable to learn anything about her suspect's associate. ('Who, him? Oh, he's nobody; just a friend of mine.') However, using her top-secret spy camera, Mayumi had already snapped a picture of the man, and this picture has now been emailed to Mark Hunter.

'...So, I wanted to apologise for my husband's behaviour this morning, and to assure you that you can still talk to me whenever you want. My husband may be free to decide who *he* will and will not talk to, he has no right to make the same decisions for *me*.'

The speaker is Ramona Ghai, who has paid an evening call on her neighbours Dodo and Mayumi to tender the above apology. They are seated on the living room sofa, Ramona in the middle, with Dodo on her right, Mayumi on her left. While Ramona converses with Dodo, Mayumi is occupied with rolling a bohemian cigarette. Outside the uncurtained window darkness is beginning to fall.

'By the way, what *did* happen between Jubin and you? He paid you a visit yesterday…?'

'Yes. I won't go into details, but he wanted to consult me professionally about something; we had an unfortunate misunderstanding—all my fault, I admit—and well, he stormed off, and wouldn't listen to my apologies…'

'Well, I am not surprised to hear this. My husband has been like that all the time, recently. Everything annoys him, and everything anyone says to him he takes the wrong way.'

'Has he been to see a doctor about it?'

'He won't go. He refuses.'

Her joint prepared, Mayumi lights it and takes a long drag, closing her eyes as she slowly exhales the thick white smoke. She then holds out the cigarette to Ramona.

'Want some?'

'Oh! Thank you!' Ramona takes the joint hesitantly. A brief pause and then she puts it to her mouth and inhales. The return journey is considerably less smooth than the outward one: Ramona, eyes bulging, springs forward in her chair, and ejects the smoke with a long wheezing gasp.

'Are you alright?' inquires Dodo, concerned.

'Yes!' gasps Ramona; and then more clearly, after thumping her chest: 'Yes…! Thank you…!'

'You have smoked weed before, haven't you?' asks Dodo, taking the spliff from her.

'Oh, yes!' hurriedly. 'It's just… it's been some time since I last, you know…'

'Okay, well don't have any more, then,' adjures Dodo.

Ramona sits back in her chair. 'Oh! Goodness, I'm feeling rather dizzy…'

'That's the head rush. Just sit still for a minute. This isn't the really strong stuff, is it, Yumi?'

'Nope.'

'No, I didn't think so…' To Ramona: 'So, have you got any idea why your husband's been so uptight recently?'

Ramona giggles. 'Oh, yes. His masculinity has been hit in its sorest point: he's become impotent.'

'Well, there's a blue pill that usually takes care of that problem.'

'It doesn't work for him,' announces Ramona. 'Not anymore. It just gives him a bad headache.'

'Really? It doesn't have any effect at all?'

'None. And if takes a larger dose it just makes his headache worse.' She continues to giggle.

'What's so funny? Don't you even feel sorry for the poor guy?'

'No, not at all,' with a vehement shake of the head.

'Well, then don't you feel sorry on your own account? It's your sex life as well as his.'

'No, it doesn't bother me at all.'

'No? You're okay going without?'

'Who says I'm going without?' challenges Ramona, looking from Dodo to Mayumi with an artful smile.

It now occurs to Dodo that here is a situation worth

exploiting. 'So, you've taken a lover, have you?'

'Perhaps I have,' smiling archly. 'Perhaps I've taken more than one…'

'It doesn't sound like it's troubling your conscience much,' observes Dodo.

'Why should it trouble my conscience? When a woman's husband fails to perform his primary function, she is entitled to go elsewhere to seek satisfaction. It is her right as a woman.'

'And has that always been your code of conduct?' asks Dodo, thinking she can detect quotation marks in the other's voice. 'Or is this a recent change of outlook?'

'Recent… Recent… My outlook on life has changed a lot recently…' giggling again.

'And why would that be?'

'Well…!' lazily stretching the word. Affecting a teasing air, Ramona places a finger over Dodo's mouth. Leaning in, she whispers conspiratorially. 'Wouldn't *you* like to know…?'

'Well, yes I would,' answers Dodo simply.

Ramona licks her lips. 'Well, if you want me to tell…' pausing for effect. '…You have to let me kiss you!'

'Yumi, sweetheart; she wants to kiss me. What are your thoughts on the subject?'

'Sure; let her kiss you,' acquiesces Mayumi.

And so, Ramona, joins her lips with Dodo's, and kisses her ardently. This boldness is not exactly characteristic of Ramona Ghai, but in case you've haven't worked it out already, when she told Dodo she hadn't smoked any marijuana in a long time, for 'a long time' read 'ever.'

'I liked that…' says Ramona, when the kiss has ended.

'Likewise,' says Dodo.

'Hey! What about me?' says Mayumi.

Ramona looks from one woman to the other. 'Oh…! Can I?'

'You *have* to,' Dodo tells her. 'Whatever I do, Yumi gets

to do as well. That's the rule around here.'

'I *like* rules like that…' says Ramona, and turns round on the sofa and kisses Mayumi; a more overbitey kiss, but equally rewarding.

'So…' says Dodo. 'You were going to tell me about your recent lifestyle changes…'

'Was I?' says Ramona.

Giggling, she jumps up from the sofa, and she sways across the room, swinging her skirt, humming to herself, and, comes to a stop in front of the dormant television (which being one of those eighty-five-inch models stands the regulation twelve feet away.) Turning to face her hosts, still humming to herself, she unbuttons the front of her dress.

'I feel like getting naked,' she sighs. 'You don't mind, do you?'

'Knock yourself out,' says Dodo generously.

Unbuttoned, Ramona's dress drops to the floor. A pair of knickers, the only other impediment to nudity, soon join it. Languorous and sinuous, Ramona proceeds to exhibit herself to her audience in a series of poses so skilfully assumed, you'd think she did it for a living.

'Aren't I beautiful?' she says, her voice childish, coquettish.

'No complaints from here,' says Dodo.

'Wish I had my camera,' from Mayumi. (Her highest compliment!)

The two women get up from the sofa, and their clothes just seem to slide off their bodies, as though their previous reclined positions had been the only thing keeping them on. A brief whispered colloquy and Mayumi exits the room, while Dodo advances towards Ramona.

'Where's she going?' asks Ramona, watching with bleary confusion as Mayumi disappears through the door.

'She'll be back in a jiffy,' answers Dodo. 'I can keep you entertained till then.'

She takes Ramona in her arms.

'You don't mind that I'm an older woman, then?' coyly, returning the embrace.

Dodo affects a reflective air. 'Well… I usually draw the line at anyone more than six months older than me, but in your case I'm happy to make an exception.'

And then, from eagerly kissing, the logical progression of events soon sees the two women down on the rug, Ramona with her face between Dodo's legs, servicing her energetically.

Now in case the moralists out there (in the unlikely event that there are still any in the building) are inclined to protest that a paragon such as Dodo Dupont undoubtedly is ought not to be cooperating in an act of marital infidelity, let me rush to her defence and explain to you that (as will presently become apparent) Dodo is only doing what she is doing here in the pursuance of the goal of her assigned mission: to wit, finding out just what the hell is going on in Bellend Close. And no, it had not been her intention all along to get Ramona stoned into a state of compliance; but, seeing how intoxicated the woman has become, Dodo has wasted no time in taking advantage of the situation. So, in other words, Dodo's motives here are as pure as the driven snow and her immaculate reputation and her standing as a role-model to the female youth of today remain untarnished!

And as for Ramona, she's just soaring! Dreamily aroused and flying high on a balmy Venusian current of linguistic cunningness. A votive at the altar of spontaneous love she wants only to prolong the ritual of worship to the very limits, to eternalise the moment, delay the moment of epiphany. Dimly she is aware of the presence of another, of her limbs being handled, pulled and twisted, held fast in a tight embrace.

Only after the epiphany has been attained, the ritual consummated, do her senses, refocussing, tell her that she is indeed held fast—with sturdy ropes! She lies helpless on her stomach, her arms twisted behind her, legs forced apart, wrists and ankles bound together. Her drugged mind failing to provide a solution as to how she came to be thus situated, she looks upwards for enlightenment. Dodo and Mayumi stand over her, both looking very pleased with themselves. Diversionary tactics! Ramona has been the victim of a sweetly-baited trap; for while lost in her act of homage to Dodo, Mayumi has been methodically tying her with ropes, because Mayumi happens to hold a blackbelt in the Japanese art of *Kinbaku*, or tight binding. In fact, so adept is Mayumi, she can even tie herself in knots. (Although untying herself afterwards can be problematical.) It is for its aesthetic sense that Mayumi has devoted herself to this art, and not (apart from occasionally) for the purposes of sexual role-playing. Her last exhibition of *Kinbaku* photography was met with universal applause—at least from the people who don't strongly object to that kind of thing.

However, on the present occasion, Mayumi has exercised her skills for the much more practical purpose of restraining a prisoner in order to facilitate interrogation. To this I can also add that the vibrator she eagerly holds in her hand has been requisitioned for the same purpose.

Ramona responds to her captors smiles with a more hesitant one of her own. 'I... I don't seem to be able to move...'

'Yes, that's because Mayumi's tied you up,' explains Dodo. 'She's very good at tying people up, is Yumi,' a note of pride creeping into her voice.

'Oh! I get it...! That rope art thing that you do... Oh, I see! That's why you've tied me up like this! You're going to photograph me for one of your books, are you...?'

'That's not the reason, actually,' says Dodo. 'We've tied you up so that we can have a nice little girlie chat.'

'I see...' says Ramona. 'You think I can chat better when I'm trussed up like this...?'

'We think it will help you concentrate, yes,' says Dodo. 'What we want to talk about is these lovers of yours. You did say it was more than one, didn't you? Well, we'd like to know a bit about them. You know, where you first met, who introduced them to you; that sort of thing…'

'I'm afraid I can't tell you anything about that,' replies Ramona. 'They're my *mystery* lovers, you see. So if I was to tell you about them, they wouldn't be a mystery anymore, would they?'

'Oh, come on!' urges Dodo coaxingly. 'It won't go any further than this room, will it? That's what girlie talk is supposed to be about, isn't it? Sharing confidences.'

'Yes… Yes, that's true and I'm sorry, but I *can't* tell you about this. Can't can't can't can't can't,' shaking her head as much as she is able to in her current position.

'Well, then why did you even mention it at all?' demands Dodo. 'That's not really fair, is it? Teasing us with hints and then clamming up. That's not how girls should behave towards each other, is it now?'

'I *know!*' contritely. 'And I *shouldn't* have mentioned it at all; but my mouth… sort of just ran away from me…' frowning. 'Or with me…'

'So, you won't tell us anything about these lovers? Not even their names?'

'Oh, they haven't got name—!' breaking off suddenly. She laughs awkwardly. 'Just forget I said that.'

'They haven't got names?' echoes Dodo, ignoring the last request. 'Well, that's unusual; because in my experience most people have names. How did these friends of yours come to have no names?' She hunkers down beside Ramona. 'Really, I'd be fascinated to know.'

'Oh, I was just being silly…' says Ramona. 'Of course they've got names! What I just meant was that I don't know their names. It's all anonymous, you see. Arranged online on one of those adult dating sites. Can you untie me now? It's starting to get a bit uncomfortable…'

'No.'

'No? You won't untie me?'

'I meant no, I don't believe you. But yes, also no, I won't untie you. Yes, I think you were telling the truth when you started blurting out that your lovers didn't have names. I think that *that* is the true version because I think that these lovers of yours aren't just your regular, run-of-the-mill bits on the side; I think they're something very different. And I don't believe you met them online, either; I think it was probably Mhambi Khoza who first introduced you to them, wasn't it?'

'Why do you think it's Mhambi?' says Ramona, looking away from Dodo's eyes.

'Because she seems to be the one in charge around here,' replies Dodo. 'Tell me what Mhambi's up to.'

'No!'

'Ah! So you admit she's up to something?'

'No! No, to everything! No no no no no! Now untie me!' petulantly shaking her trussed limbs. 'Untie me right now!'

Dodo turns to Mayumi. 'Okay, sweetheart. I think it's time we stepped things up.'

'Sure!' grins Mayumi. Brandishing the vibrator, she takes up position behind Ramona.

'What's she going to do with that thing?' demands Ramona.

'Nothing it wasn't designed for,' Dodo assures her. 'Go on, Yumi.'

Ramona feels a pressure against her sphincter, a gentle nudging. 'Oh! Not in *there*, please! I don't like... things up there...'

'Alright, then start talking.'

'No! I can't...!'

'Go on, Yumi.'

Yumi pushes, penetrates.

'Ohhh...! Don't...!'

'Feel like talking yet?'

'No! And I think you're both mean!'

'What? We've hardly started yet. Go on, Yumi.'

Yumi pushes in deeper.

'Ohh…! Not that far…! Get it out, get it out!'

'When you start talking.'

'No! You call this a girlie talk? Sadists! Not a word!'

'Fine. Switch it on, Yumi.'

'Power on!'

The vibrator comes to life.

'Ohhhhh…!'

'How about now?'

'No! No no noooooohhhh…!'

'You drive us to extremes,' sighs Dodo, standing up. 'Okay, sweetheart. Hoist her up.'

Ramona, her body in sync with the urgent rhythm of the plastic intruder in her anus, now feels herself being lifted bodily from the ground.

'Oooh…! I feel like I'm floating…!'

'You are,' Dodo tells her. 'We attached you to a pulley system.'

And this is the case, as Ramona now sees. She hangs suspended five feet off the ground, slowly spinning round on her own axis like a particularly attractive weather vane.

'Now,' resumes Dodo crisply. 'Are you ready to talk?'

'Ohhh…! Ohhhh…!'

'Well, if you promise to cooperate, we'll let you down. Anything to say?'

'Ohhhh…! Ohhhh…!'

'Something coherent would be nice.'

'Ohhhh…! Oh-oh-oh-oh-ooooohhhhh…!'

Ramona appears to be having an ecstatic fit. Dodo finds herself starting to wonder if, in taking things this far, she hasn't made one of her rare errors of judgement.

'Oooooohhhhh…!'

And then something starts to happen. The first indication is a smell. A powerful odour begins to permeate the air of the living room.

'What's this smell?' Dodo looks at Mayumi. 'Can you smell it?'

'Yes,' confirms Mayumi. 'Man smell.'

Man smell. That's what it is. A smell like both Nanette Aubergine and Ramona's husband described experiencing in their alleged dreams. The smell is alien, but familiar; not unpleasant; the reverse in fact; but alarming in its intensity.

'But where's it coming from…? Outside…?'

'Look!'

Mayumi points to a corner of the room. A shadow has appeared there, a shadow where there was no shadow before. A vague shape, nearly as tall as the ceiling, it begins to take form, acquiring a definite outline—a humanoid outline.

'Ooohhh dear…' says Ramona.

'It's you, isn't it?' accuses Dodo. 'You're doing this!'

'Not… not on purpose…'

The shape, still dark, featureless, is gathering substance, becoming more and more real. A creature. Tall, taller than the average human being, broad shoulders, powerful arms. The masculine smell is by now overwhelming, stifling.

'I don't like this…' says Mayumi.

Dodo grabs Ramona by the hair.

'Stop it!' she yells. 'Send it back!'

'I can't!' sobs Ramona. 'It's your fault! Ooohhhhh…! If you hadn't—!'

It is Mayumi who acts. Walking straight up to Ramona, she wrenches the vibrator from the woman's anus. The device is switched off, and the room falls suddenly silent.

And the shadow in the corner of the room starts to fade. It rapidly dissolves to nothingness, and the overpowering smell evaporates.

Dodo turns to face her lover, an admiration that is lost for words written on its features.

'Yumi…!'

'Pulled the plug out!' grins Mayumi, holding the vibrator triumphantly aloft.

And now another smell begins to permeate the air, because, so suddenly and violently has Mayumi pulled this particular plug from its socket, it has not made the journey alone.

Chapter Fourteen
Bellend? Belenus? or Baal-land?

'How do you feel about a giant penis?'

'I think I'd like a bit more information before I commit myself to a definite answer on that one.'

'Well, this is a pictorial representation that appears to have been carved in the ground. Sort of like the Cerne Abbas Giant, but without the giant; just the genitalia.'

'You say "appears to be." Don't you know for sure?'

'Well, no. We've only just got wind of the thing, and as it's practically in your back garden, I thought you could check it out.'

'Practically in my back garden?'

'Yes. In a clearing in the middle of Bellend Wood, to be precise. And as I say, it wasn't there before. It got picked up by a CIA spy satellite programmed to detect anomalies.'

'Nice of them to share their spy satellite data with you.'

'They didn't. But we usually have a gander at it anyway. I'll email the image to you, along with the coordinates. It shouldn't be that difficult to find; it's the only clearing of any size in the wood.'

'Right. We'll check it out right away. What about the picture we sent you? Have you been able to identify our man in the Hawaiian shirt?'

'Oh, *him*. Yes, I identified him the moment I saw him. His name's Mike Grimsby and he's a private detective, based here in London. Our paths have crossed before. He's a clown, basically. Nothing to worry about. But if he is sniffing around Bellend Close, it would be interesting to know who hired him.'

'The most likely suspect would be one of the husbands; but then what was he doing with Gerald Banbury? He's a bachelor; the only man here who *wouldn't* have a motive for hiring a private detective.'

'Yes, but if he's a resident, this Banbury must be aware something strange is going on in the close; maybe he hired Grimsby to snoop around and find out.'

'Gerald Banbury is quite capable of doing his own snooping. No, you're right; it's got to be one of the husbands... Unless of course, there's some third party who's taken an interest in what's going on around here...'

'Yes, that would be worth finding out about. Well, I'll email you that image and you can go'n have a look at the place.'

'We will, but before you go, I've got something new to tell you about; something very strange that happened last night...'

(In case you haven't worked it out, the above dialogue is a telephone conversation between Dodo Dupont and Mark Hunter. Yes, only Mark's second appearance in the story so far, and like the first, audio only! Will we ever be seeing him in person? The answer to that question is more than this omniscient narrator can tell.)

Fat Tulip and Abigail are seated under their usual tree at the edge of the glade, the same tree Fat Tulip had been sitting under the day Abigail had made her first appearance. Abigail has just returned from one of her shop runs, and the girls are sucking noisily on ice pops.

'What's so funny about bells?' says Abigail suddenly.

'Bells?' echoes Fat Tulip. 'Who said bells *are* funny?'

'Cuz people always laugh, don't they? whenever you talk about Bellend Wood.'

'Yeah, newsflash: that's got nothing to do with bells.

Bell-end means the end of a cock, that's sort of shaped like a bell.'

'End of a cock? A cock-a-doodle-doo cock?' asks Abigail.

'No, stupid. A cock means a willy.'

'A willy? Bellend Woods means willy?' Abigail starts giggling.

'And finally she gets the joke,' says Fat Tulip.

'Why did they call it that?' still giggling.

'They didn't; not really. The name got changed. Originally, it wasn't "Bellend," it was "Baal-land," which means Land of Baal; but then over the years people started saying it wrong, so the name got changed. Like Chinese whispers.'

'But why was it called Baa-land? Did there used to be sheep here?'

'That's *Baal*-land, not *Baa*-land, cloth ears! Baal with an el on the end! Baal's the name of an ancient god.'

'What sort of god?'

'Baal was the witches' god. The Christians said he was the Devil, but he wasn't: he was the horned god of all the witches.'

'Oooh! Are we going to learn something about witches?'

'You are, yeah, so pay attention. Back in ancient times Bellend was called Baal-land, and it was called that because this was where all the witches used to meet up to have their witches' sabbaths. And it was right here in this clearing that they had them. The witches weren't bad and they didn't hurt the normal people and the normal people respected them cuz they were powerful and they knew a lot of things the normal people didn't.'

'Like spells and stuff?'

'Yeah, and lots of other things.'

'Are we going to do some spells now? Cuz I—'

'No, we are not doing any spells! Will you shut up and listen? This is important witch information. So, there were the witches, right? Getting along with the normal people. But then the Christians came along, the monks and the priests, and they said that the witches were evil cuz they worshipped Baal and Baal was the Devil, even though that wasn't true. But the normal people started believing the monks and the priests and the witches started getting persecuted.'

'What's persecuted?'

'Persecuted means getting hunted and killed.'

'The witches were getting hunted and killed?'

'Yeah, because the priests and monks said they were evil and that they had to be wiped out. But really the monks and priests only said that cuz they were men and they didn't want the women having more power and being more important than they were. The monks and priests wanted all the power for themselves, so they could go around telling everyone what to do. So, they started hunting down all the witches and when they caught them, they'd drown them or burn them at the stake. And that's how all the witches died out; 'cept that they didn't die out, not completely. Some of them got away and that's why you've still got witches today, and why there's not many of them and why they have to keep quiet about being witches.'

'Why? If they got found out, would they still be drowned and burned at the stake?'

'Well, no. They don't do that anymore. But there's still people that wouldn't like them, so they stay secret.'

'Like us?'

'Yeah, like us. So I hope you haven't gone and told anyone you're my apprentice!'

'I haven't!' protests Abigail.

'Good, cuz if you did, I'd know about it and then I'd cast a spell on you and turn you into something.'

Abigail is about to protest that she doesn't want to be turned into anything, but Fat Tulip urgently shushes her. Two strangers have appeared in the glade, emerging from the trees at the end furthest from where the two girls sit. The intruders are both women, one very tall and short-haired, the other smaller, long-haired. The tall woman is wearing a short-skirted summer dress and wraparound shades, and the smaller one is sporting a cowgirl look: Stetson, knotted check shirt and denim shorts. Unaware that they are being observed, the women begin to quarter the clearing. Eyes down, they appear to be either measuring the ground or looking for something. The tall woman holds a piece of paper which she frequently consults.

Whatever its object, the survey seems to yield unsatisfactory results. They pause, the tall woman scratching the back of her head. And then the flat boulder in the centre of the glade seems to take her interest and she starts walking towards it, quickly followed by the other woman.

Fat Tulip stands up. 'Come on. I wanna know what they're up to. Let me do the talking and don't say anything about us being witches, okay?'

With Abigail following in her wake, Fat Tulip marches purposefully up to the two intruders on her domain, who are now examining the flat rock. Look at them, thinks Fat Tulip, looking at them. Think they look so hot in their fancy clothes, don't they? An amazon and a Chinese doll. Obviously lesbians, and both of them pushing thirty. And the tall one's shoes have got to be size eleven at least!

Catching sight of the two approaching youngsters, the two women greet them with smiles.

'Hello there!' says the amazon in the wraparound shades. 'What brings you two here?'

'Yeah, that's *my* question, actually,' retorts Fat Tulip in no friendly tone. 'What are *you* doing here? This is *our* clearing.'

'Is it?' says the woman, clearly amused at this claim of ownership. 'I'm sorry, then; we didn't realise we were trespassing.' Turning to her friend: 'Did we, Yumi?'

'Well now you know, so you can clear off, can't you?'

The woman still looks amused. 'Why all the hostility? We were only looking around.'

'I know what you were doing. You were measuring the ground, weren't you? You think just cuz there's no trees here, you can build a house, don't you? Well, you can't!'

'I can assure you we weren't planning on building a house here,' says the woman.

'Then what's that piece of paper in your hand?' demands Fat Tulip. 'Blueprints for a house, I bet!'

'This? No, this was just a map to help us find the place.' The woman folds the paper and slips it into her pocket.

'And why did you want to find this place? It's just a clearing.'

'Well, you never know. It might be of historical and cultural interest, mightn't it? I mean, what about this?' indicating the stone slab.

'It's just a slab of rock,' says Fat Tulip. 'It's not Stonehenge, is it?'

'It might have some significance,' argues the woman (much to Fat Tulip's increasing annoyance.) 'You can see it's not an outcropping; somebody, at some point, must have put it here, and they probably did it for a reason. Anyway, we haven't introduced ourselves: I'm Dodo and this is Mayumi. Who are you two girls? Are you sisters?'

'Yes,' says Fat Tulip, firmly. 'I'm Tulip and this is my sister Abigail.'

'Pleased to meet you. Do you live around here?'

'We live over on Silver Street,' says Fat Tulip. 'What about you two? I haven't seen you two before.'

'Yes, we're new to the neighbourhood. We just moved into Bellend Close last week.'

Fat Tulip looks surprised. 'Oh! So, you're—' She breaks off.

Dodo looks at her; Fat Tulip avoids her gaze. 'So, you two have made this glade your little hideaway, have you?

What do you get up to? I wouldn't think there's much to do out here.'

'We just hang out,' says Fat Tulip. 'Play games, read comics…'

'Oh, yes? What comics do you like?'

'Slayve the Barbarian!' speaks up Abigail.

Dodo looks amused. 'Oh, you like Slayve, do you? I thought it was only bloodthirsty boys who were into that one.'

'It's not just about violence!' retorts Fat Tulip defensively. 'It's about lots of things. It's about the environment, and religions…'

'Mostly just one religion, isn't it?' says Dodo. 'That's the reason a lot of people are complaining about the comic: they think it has an anti-Christian agenda and that it wants to turn all you kids into neopagans. Well, that's *one* of the reasons people are complaining about the comic. There's also the gratuitous violence and nudity and the generally amoral tone of the whole thing.'

'Well, *we* like it!' snaps Fat Tulip.

Dodo holds out placating palms. 'Hey, I wasn't putting it down!' she protests. 'British comics seem to be an endangered species these days, so it's great that there's one that's still going strong. Yumi here's not too keen, though. She's Japanese and in Japan they prefer black and white comics.' Turning to her friend: 'Colour comics look ugly to you, don't they?'

Mayumi confirms that they do. 'Eyes are too small, as well,' she says.

'So… have you girls been hanging out here a lot recently?' asks Dodo. 'Have you seen or heard anything strange? Seen any strange people around?'

'Yes: you,' says Fat Tulip firmly.

Dodo smiles ruefully. 'I walked right into that one, didn't I? But have you seen any *other* strange people?'

'No. Why should we have seen any strange people?'

'Well, we've heard stories about this place. There was that boy who claimed he saw some cavemen around here, wasn't there?'

Abigail bursts into merry laughter. 'That was Luke! He's in my class! They're *still* teasing him about that!'

'You don't believe his story then?'

'Of course we don't!' snaps Fat Tulip. 'He probably just saw a bunch of men having some fun together.'

'Making flower chains!' says Abigail. 'That's what you said!'

'I said they were *daisy* chains!' retorts Fat Tulip. 'And you're too young to know what that means!'

Chapter Fifteen
Zulus? No, I Usually Win!

'Agent Mayumi reporting for duty!' says Mayumi, saluting. She is wearing a black PVC belted bikini, with matching knee boots and mod cap. 'How do I look?'

'You look fantastic, sweetheart,' says Dodo. 'But I think we can ditch the harpoon gun.'

They are on a reconnaissance mission tonight, and Mayumi has assumed what she considers to be the appropriate clothing for a spy on a reconnaissance mission. And now it is zero hour: time to set off! They exit the house via the patio doors and head straight for the end of the garden. Dodo is dressed as she usually dresses on these occasions, wearing her black pullover, black faux leather trousers and boots.

They had drawn a blank at the glade in the woods. No sign of the giant penis photographed by the spy satellite. It either wasn't there or it just isn't visible to the naked eye at ground level.

Had someone drawn it there? Hill figures, like the Cerne Abbas Giant, were usually either created by digging trenches and filling them with chalkstone rocks, or else by simply arranging the rocks on the surface of the ground. If it was the latter, they could have been moved since the satellite image was taken, and if the former they could only have been concealed by being covered up, and Dodo and Mayumi had looked for and found no traces of this kind of concealment. The same applied in the case of the giant penis having been drawn with white paint like the kind used for marking athletics and ballgame fields: it could not have been camouflaged so well that ground-level searchers who knew it was there would not be able to find it. Conclusion: the giant penis is either a man- (or quite possibly woman-!) made temporary device that can be erased or removed when not needed, or else it is some kind of supernatural phenomenon, and one that only becomes visible at certain times.

One thing that had struck Dodo upon studying the satellite photo, was just how well-drawn the penis was. The Cerne Abbas Giant's stonker is just a basic outline, fairly symmetrical, but if not for the cleft at the base (and the fact that it is located on a man's crotch) it could easily pass for a long-stemmed wine gourd; but the phallus in the satellite photograph is much more detailed in outline: the shape of the glans, the ridge of the retracted foreskin; all have been rendered with loving care.

As for the symbol's purpose; well, unless it's purely decorative, it has to be ritualistic. 'Hill figures' are so-called because they are drawn on hillsides and can be seen from the surrounding countryside; the Bellend Wood Phallus ('If that's not a double tautology,' as Dodo had remarked when giving it this name) has been drawn on an area of flat ground surrounded by trees; it can only be seen from directly above, which would seem to make it fairly pointless as a decoration. Ergo, its purpose must be ritualistic—and the glade in Bellend Wood seems like a custom-made venue for performing rituals.

Nevertheless, the glade is not their objective for tonight. There are other leads to be followed up, and as such their objective tonight is the Khoza-Jarman residence—because Dodo wants to have a look inside Mhambi Khoza's Zulu hut.

The two women nimbly scale the fence at the end of the garden and set off along the footpath which runs between the garden fences and the surrounding woodland. They intend to approach their target from the rear, which, being on the opposite side of the street from their own house, entails them having to perform a circuit of almost the entire close.

Presently, they hear the sound of voices ahead. Dodo stops, cautioning Mayumi to silence. The path curves sharply ahead of them and the speaker cannot be seen. They listen. The voices are male and appear to be neither coming closer nor going further away. Keeping under the shadow of the trees, the two women advance cautiously.

The owners of the voices come into sight: two men, one tall and slim, the other short and stocky. The stocky man seems to be examining the fence.

'You're wasting your time, old man,' says the tall man. Dodo recognises his voice at once: Gerald Banbury.

'There's got to be a loose board somewhere,' insists the stocky man stubbornly.

'And I tell you there isn't any loose board,' returns Gerald, also insistent, but with amusement in his voice.

'They didn't get out the front way, so they had to get out the back way, didn't they?'

'I'm not arguing with that; just with your idea about loose planks. You seem to be forgetting that while *you* might have some trouble doing it yourself, Grimsby old son, most people could get over a fence like this one with ease. I could do it myself.'

'Yeah, but you'd probably mess your clothes up doing it,' argues the stocky man.

'True enough. But maybe these men aren't all that

bothered about the state of their clothes. After all, they're only going to be taking them off again. Ah!' The sound of fingers being clicked. 'Maybe they've got themselves a ladder! Yes! What we need to do is come back here when it's light and have a look in the trees behind us here. If they *have* got a ladder, then they'll have it hidden away somewhere handy, won't they?'

'Makes sense,' concedes the other.

Deciding to call it a night, the two men start to walk off. Dodo and Mayumi follow cautiously. A signposted footpath allowing access to Bellend Wood to residents of the close, runs between Nanette Aubergine's house and that of her neighbour, and the two men, reaching this intersecting path, now turn down it and head back into the close. Dodo and Mayumi watch them until they are out of sight.

'What were those guys up to?' wonders Mayumi.

'I'm not sure,' says Dodo. 'It was Banbury and that detective,'

'Do we follow them?'

'No. One thing at a time. Let's stay focused on what we set out to do.'

They continue along the footpath, passing round the extremity of the close and following the backs of the houses down the other side.

Soon they are nearing their destination.

'Hello,' says Dodo. 'Look at that.'

Ahead of them a finger of smoke rises into the night sky.

'Somebody burning rubbish,' suggests Mayumi.

'A bit late to be doing that,' demurs Dodo. 'And I think it's coming from Mhambi's garden. Come on.'

They draw level with the finger of smoke, and it is indeed rising from the garden that is their target. They listen, but no sounds can be heard from the other side of the fence. Dodo hoists herself up and peaks over the top of the fence. The smoke is rising from the aperture on the roof of the indlu that serves as its chimney.

Dropping back down, she reports this fact to Mayumi, speaking softly.

'Someone must be in there.'

'We can't search the hut then,' says Mayumi.

'No, but we can try and find out what's going on in there, and that might tell us a lot more than just a search would've. Come on.'

Swiftly and silently, our two night-raiders scale the fence and drop down onto the turf at the other side, close to the domed hut. Here they pause, listen. Still no sound can be heard from within the wooden structure.

Treading softly, they move round to the front of the hut. A patch of flickering orange light spills out onto the garden from the entrance to the hut. The hut's 'door,' basically just a plug for the doorway, lies on the ground beside the entrance.

Squatting down beside the low doorway, Dodo cautiously peers into the interior. The first thing she sees is Mhambi Khoza, who, dressed in a lot of Zulu finery none of which could really be called clothing, sits crosslegged in front of a small fire, facing the doorway. The fire is composed of branches arranged in a cone and guarded by a circle of small rocks. Over the fire hangs an earthenware pot, steam rising from its bubbling contents. Mhambi is the hut's only occupant. For the rest the single chamber of the hut is furnished with earthenware pots and jars, a set of African drums, and in the corner a bed composed of a straw-filled mattress covered with brightly-coloured woven blankets; ceremonial masks and shields and spears decorated with feathers adorn the walls. The floor is covered with rush matting.

When Dodo's eyes return to Mhambi, she sees that the woman is looking straight at her. Smiling a smile that has more than a suggestion of irony about it, she is clearly waiting for her uninvited guest to speak first.

'Hi there,' says Dodo, making the best of a bad situation.

'We were just passing by, Yumi and me, and we thought we'd... I hope we're not interrupting anything?'

'Not at all,' is the smooth reply. 'Why don't you both come in and join me?'

'We'd love to,' says Dodo.

Dodo and Mayumi crawl into the hut and sitting themselves in front of the fire, facing their host, they are able to examine her (lack of) attire in more detail. A coloured headband sits around her temples, while from her neck hangs a collar necklace of elaborate beadwork. Anklets and armlets adorn her legs and arms, while round her waist is a girdle from which hang small medicine pouches. The eyes of her visitors are drawn to the promontories of her heavy breasts, the thick nipples rising from wide plains of the aureoles.

Mhambi's rich dark brown skin glows in the light thrown up by the fire, but while her posture is regal and imposing, her expression is workaday, wryly smiling at her somewhat embarrassed guests (both of them painfully aware of the fact that they're not exactly dressed like people who were 'just passing by.')

'So... are you cooking up some African herbal medicine?' she inquires. 'Smells rather like tea.'

'That's because it is tea,' says Mhambi. 'Would you care to join me for some?'

She lifts the pot from over the fire.

'Zulu tea ceremony!' says Mayumi, excited.

'Actually, my ancestors were not tea drinkers,' explains Mhambi, pouring some of the fluid into a bowl. 'Tea-drinking comes from your part of the world, not mine. My people were milk-drinkers. Although ironically perhaps, I don't have any milk right now to mix with this tea,' says Mhambi. 'And I'm afraid I've only got the one bowl, so we'll have to share.'

'That's fine with us,' says Dodo brightly.

Mhambi blows into the bowl, takes an experimental sip.

'Mm. Yes, it's brewed quite nicely,' she announces.

She passes the bowl to Dodo, who takes a sip.

'Oh! Earl Grey,' she says. 'Very British.'

'Yes, the colonial influence,' responds Mhambi.

Handing the bowl to Mayumi, Dodo extracts cigarettes and lighter from her pocket. 'Okay if we smoke?'

'I'm afraid this is a non-smoking indlu,' says Mhambi. 'And speaking both as a GP and a witch-doctress, I would advise you to quit.'

Cigarettes and lighter are returned from whence they came.

'So,' resumes Dodo, 'if you're not mixing up any potions, how come you're out here this late at night?'

'I didn't have much choice in the matter,' answers Mhambi, 'seeing as my husband has decided to lock me out of the house.'

Surprised exclamations from both Dodo and Mayumi.

'It's true,' confirms Mhambi. 'It happened at teatime this evening: without warning, he shoved me out through the kitchen door and locked it behind me. I soon discovered that all the other doors and windows had been locked as well. So you see, it was clearly a preconcerted act on his part, not some spur of the moment thing.'

'But if it happened back at teatime, why didn't you just go round a neighbour's house?' asks Dodo.

'Well, being stark naked, I felt a bit embarrassed about going out into the street,' says Mhambi.

'You were naked when he locked you out? Why were you naked?'

'I'd just got back from the surgery, and when I took my clothes off to change them, I decided I just wouldn't change into any. I do sometimes like to sit around the house naked. Don't you?'

'Oh yes, me and Yumi have our nudie days,' confirms Dodo. She grins. 'But you picked a bad day for yours!'

Mhambi returns the smile. 'I did, didn't I?'

'But… why all the paraphernalia?' indicating Mhambi's jewellery and accessories. 'You weren't wearing all that, were you when you got kicked out of the house?'

'This? Oh no, I wasn't wearing all this then. I keep all of this ceremonial gear out here in the indlu. I just put it on more or less on a whim, really. I haven't got much else to do this evening.'

So, this is the 'positive action' that David Jarman has decided to take in retaliation against his wife, thinks Dodo. Locking her out of the house. A very childish retaliation, and one that isn't going to do him any good in the long run.

'So, you're going to spend the night here?'

'I haven't got much choice, have I? I don't think David is going to let me back in until tomorrow morning; he might even be asleep by now, if his gloating isn't keeping him awake.'

'Why don't you come round ours?' offers Dodo. 'It's dark now, so you'd be alright just crossing the street with us.'

'Yes, stay with us!' seconds Mayumi.

'I thank you both very much for your generous offer, but really, I'm quite comfortable here. Why don't you both spend the night here with me?' offers Mhambi. 'It would be a new experience for you: a sleepover in an indlu.'

'Sure!' agrees Mayumi.

After this, there's not much Dodo can do but go along with the plan.

'So, what did you do to your husband to get yourself kicked out of the house like this?' she asks.

'What did *I* do?' echoes Mhambi. 'You make it sound like I'm the one at fault. I think most people would consider me to be the victim.'

'Well, yes, but *something* must have happened, mustn't it? He wouldn't have just kicked you out in your birthday suit for no reason. I'm just saying that when you see David again tomorrow you ought to talk things through. Maybe some concessions need to be made on both sides…?'

Mhambi's face hardens. 'No,' she says coldly. 'There will be no concessions on my side.'

Dodo awakes.

Throwing back the blanket, she sits up. The fire has expired, but daylight penetrates the hut through the chimney opening in the roof (if a domed structure can be said to have a roof) and she can see that the room's only other occupant is Mayumi, sound asleep by her side in the mattress bed.

She remembers… Mhambi had still been sat brooding over her fire when they had turned in last night… Where has she gone?

Dodo gently shakes Mayumi's shoulder. She stirs, murmuring broken words in her own language. Her eyes open, focus on Dodo.

'Huh…? Where are we…?'

'In Mhambi Khoza's hut, remember? I don't know where *she* is, though…'

The hut's door is in place. Dodo pushes it aside.

The garden, dewy in the early morning shows no signs of life, but clearly things have happened over at the house. One of the plate-glass patio doors has been smashed in; or rather there is a hole in the glass—a hole in the shape of a very large and very powerfully built man.

Chapter Sixteen
Trina Truelove Makes the Scene!

Trina Truelove!

What can be said about this young woman that hasn't already been broadly hinted at? Monuments will certainly be erected in her memory—posthumously, if not before. If you do not already own one of her patented 'Get Your Penis Out of My Vagina I Was Kissing You Goodbye!' t-shirts, then you should retrieve your error and purchase one immediately. (She flogs them on eBay, available in sizes S to XL.) Wear it with pride! If you are unfortunate enough to be a man, then you can buy one for your girlfriend or grandmother.

And if the t-shirt isn't enough to convince you of the genius of this prodigy, then I only have to remind you of her invaluable contribution to the art of Mayumi Takahashi, in her capacity as that worthy's photographic assistant. Just scroll through the images on Mayumi's official website: if the picture is from within the last three years, then Trina Truelove was almost certainly in the room when it was taken.

To do full justice to this woman's physical beauty is a task beyond the pen of any author. Applied to Trina Truelove, the word 'perfection' seems a pitifully weak description. The modelling of her facial features, the symmetry of her figure, the natural grace of her posture and deportment, her slightest gesture… Words fail me. And if the lords or lordesses of creation decreed that Trina should have imperfect vision it is only because they knew how good she would look wearing glasses; and if she ever appears to slouch, you can be sure it is only an ironic affectation.

And the mind housed within this sublime physical form

is equally sublime. Her razor-sharp penetration, her boundless resourcefulness, her artistic sensitivity, are all beyond description. And as for academic attainments: well, her GCSE results speak loudly for themselves.

But why do I mention Trina now, I hear you ask? (As if one needed an excuse for bringing Trina Truelove into the conversation!) Surely it is way too late in the proceedings to be introducing a major new character? Normally, yes. But when that new character happens to be Trina Truelove, then the received conventions of storytelling can go hang themselves. Because today, if you were to venture into Bellend Close, you would see that the Jaguar sitting in the drive of number twelve has been joined by a Toyota two-seater. Yes: Trina Truelove, like the Second Coming descending from above to the sounds of the heavenly choir, has arrived on the scene!

'So, to what do we owe the honour of this visit?' asks Dodo.

They are out on the patio, Trina and Dodo seated at the parasol-shaded table, Mayumi bikini-clad, stretched out on a lounger, face hidden beneath her sunhat.

Trina is dressed in hipster jeans and halter top, and her hair, tied up in short bunches, is dyed as usual, this time a metallic mauve. Fond of self-adornment, she has tattoos on her arms and her nose lips and ears are generously pierced with rings.

'Oh, I just thought I'd come and stay with you for a bit,' she says, rotating the glass in her hand, rattling the ice. 'Is that okay? Or are you—?'

'No, you're welcome to stay with us as long as you like,' Dodo assures her. 'I just wondered if you had a particular reason? Last we heard, you were very preoccupied with your new boyfriend. How's that going?'

'Oh, we split up,' mutters Trina, looking glum.

Dodo looks at Mayumi, and Mayumi, lifting her sunhat, looks back at Dodo.

Trina Truelove does get through a lot of boyfriends; this fact cannot be denied. She gets through a lot of boyfriends, and not, I hasten to add, because she is one of those love 'em and leave 'em types; nothing of the sort. And nor is the blame for the failure of any of these relationships to be laid at Trina's door; no, it is always the boyfriend's fault. She just hasn't met the right person yet—and so, perforce, she keeps meeting the wrong ones.

'Oh well,' commiserates Dodo. 'Better luck next time.'

'Yeah...' and, suddenly perking up: 'I got a new tattoo! Look!'

Jumping up from her chair, Trina turns round and displays her lower back, where an elaborate design stretches from hip to hip, just north of the cleft of her buttocks. Trina always likes to console herself with a treat after a relationship breakup—not always with a new tattoo, otherwise she would have been inked from head to toe by now.

'Very nice,' says Dodo.

'Cool!' says Mayumi.

Complimented to her own satisfaction, Trina resumes her seat.

'So, have you sorted out the vampire housewives yet?' she inquires.

'Actually, we've pretty much discarded the idea of any kind of vampirism being involved,' says Dodo. 'And parenthetically, most of the women here aren't just housewives. No, we think it's more likely magic than vampirism that's at work here.'

'Black magic?'

'More like voodoo magic; African magic.'

'And cavemen,' adds Mayumi from under her hat.

'Cavemen?' squeaks Trina. 'You're kidding! You mean that story in *The Sun* was actually true?'

'Well, they might *look* a bit like cavemen,' explains Dodo. 'But really, they're... Well, we're not really sure *what* they are.'

Dodo gives Trina a concise account of what they have learned so far. 'I'm not even sure if they're real, or if they're just dream creatures…'

'Real enough to break through a plate-glass window,' from under the sunhat.

'But,' says Trina, 'if the wives can make these things pop up out of thin air when they're feeling horny, haven't you two…? I mean…' blushing, 'when you two are…? Or haven't you been…?'

'Oh no, Mayumi and me have been very sexually active since we've been here,' Dodo assures her. 'But no, we've never had any uninvited guests materialise in the room with us. We don't seem to be affected by whatever's going on; but we're not sure if it's because we're a same-sex couple, or if it's because we're not "part of the club." It could be some kind of members-only privilege.'

'Members for members,' observes the sunhat.

'Here!' cries Trina. An alarming thought has just struck her. 'What if it's not a club thing? What if it's cuz you're same-sex? Then what about me? What if I…?'

'Yes…' says Dodo, regarding Trina with a suddenly increased interest that she finds somewhat disconcerting. 'What *if* you…? You know, Trina darling,' placing a hand on her shoulder, 'suddenly I'm even more pleased than I already was that you've decided to grace us with your presence.'

'Me too,' says the sunhat.

Trina laughs nervously. 'Hey, you guys… Wha-what are you planning here…?'

Chapter Seventeen
All Done with Mirrors

Across the street at the Ghai residence, they are also entertaining guests. Not guests of the same lofty stature as Trina Truelove. These are not guests who could be described as gods walking the earth (although some of them will probably think of themselves that way), but still guests of some degree of celebrity; guests for whom, if the more literary residents of Strepford had been aware of their presence, there would certainly have been autograph hunters gathering outside the house—for today is Jubin Ghai's birthday and he has invited some of his colleagues of the literati to celebrate the event with him.

It is a very select gathering, just a dozen or so invited guests, but every one of them a literary giant. To give you a couple of examples, we have Martin Aimless, author of that dystopian nightmares *Drop the Dead Babies* and *Other People's Money*; and Bill Shelf, creator of the famed *Planet of the Great Apes* series (of which *Conquest of the Planet of the Great Apes* is of course the latest entry.)

One thing that is noticeably *not* represented amongst the invited guests are the female authors. It seems very much as though Jubin Ghai's ill-feelings towards his wife have now spread (by way of Dodo Dupont) to the entirety of the female sex.

In spite of this, Ramona Ghai, tirelessly patient when it comes to her husband's moods and whims, is still smilingly performing her part as hostess, distributing iced drinks to the guests gathered in the living room.

'Thank you my dear,' says Jubin, when the last of the drinks has been handed out. 'Don't let me keep you; I'm sure you have things to do.'

'You're not going to kick your wife out, are you?' protests one of the guests.

'Yes, let her stay!' says another. 'You know, Ramona love, I think you've been working your husband too hard in the bedroom! I've never seen the fellow looking so completely shattered before!'

Chuckling murmurs of agreement.

'Oh, no! That's not the case at all!' Ramona assures them. 'In fact, Jubin has been completely impotent for more than two months now, so we have not been having any sexual intercourse.'

'My dear, I don't think our guests need to know about the details of our private life,' says Jubin in a tight voice.

'But darling, we are all enlightened free-thinkers in this room, aren't we? Haven't we always advocated the breaking down of taboos and inhibitions in favour of frank and open discussion on all subjects without exception?'

'Yes, she's right, Jubin!'

'Nothing to be ashamed about if you've been off your game of late!'

'Haven't you tried the blue pill, old man? Does the trick for me!'

Ramona starts to answer this last inquiry, but her husband tersely interrupts.

'That will be *all*, my dear,' he grates. 'And as you failed to even remember that it was my birthday today, I'm at a loss to understand why you would even want to remain in the room with us.'

Ramona's response is a peel of merry laughter. 'Oh, darling! I didn't forget your birthday at all! I was just teasing you!' Turning to the guests: 'You see, this morning I said nothing to him about his birthday, just to make him think that I *had* forgotten! Not even a card! You should have seen how cross he was! All the hints he kept dropping, and me pretending not to understand!' Back to her husband: 'You see, darling; that was just a little deception! Because in fact, I have remembered full well that it's your birthday, and I have made you an extra-special present! Made it for you myself!'

'And what might this present be, my dear?' inquires Jubin, not joining in with the enthusiastic reception of this news.

Ramona puts down her tray and picks up the television remote.

'It's a little homemade film!' she announces proudly. 'And I would like to show it to you now! Please be seated, everyone!'

The television comes to life and everybody sits down to watch.

On the screen appears Ramona. She is seated at the foot of her bed, and wearing a full-skirted blue satin evening dress. Her hair is elegantly styled, her face beautifully made-up. A jewelled pendant necklace glitters at her throat.

Smiling, Ramona addresses the camera. 'Happy birthday, darling husband! Many happy returns from your loyal and devoted wife. I am recording this short film both as a birthday gift to you, and also in the hope of bringing to an end your protracted period of complete sexual impotency.'

'Really, Ramona—!'

'Shh, darling. Please listen.'

'Now, darling,' continues the Ramona on the television, 'being enlightened free-thinking people, we both naturally hold a tolerant and open-minded attitude towards pornography, even if we do not actually use the material.' A pause, and a conspiratorial wink and smile. 'Or perhaps I should just be speaking for myself, eh, Jubin darling? I think perhaps your computer hard drive would tell a different story, yes?'

'Now, really—!'

'Shh, darling!'

'You will see that I am wearing the ravishing ball gown which you bought for me, and also the pendant necklace you gave me; two of my most cherished possessions. And it is now my intention to perform for you an erotic striptease dance, and then, when I am dressed only in my pendant necklace, I shall disport myself on our marital bed, assuming various erotic positions while pleasuring myself manually.'

Jubin Ghai can hold himself in no longer. 'Now *really*, darling! I hardly think our guests will want to see this! I think we should wait—'

'Don't be silly, darling. We are all enlightened, freethinkers here! I am sure none of your friends will feel any embarrassment or discomfort, which I think we all agree are only a reaction experienced by those with social-sexual repressions and who are burdened with the unnatural prudishness imposed on people's minds by organised religion, when viewing sexually explicit or indeed only mildly erotic material.'

'She's right, old man!'

'No uptight people around here!'

'Nothing to be ashamed of!'

To these and other expressions of support for his wife, Jubin is reluctantly forced to concede.

But now, expecting Ramona to rise to her feet and begin her striptease act, the audience is greatly surprised when new actors appear on the scene. Four very large and very hairy naked men enter the frame (head and shoulders out of shot) and, unspeaking, surround the still seated Ramona.

'Oh, goodness me! Who could these strange intruders be?' exclaims Ramona, in a so utterly unconvincing tone of surprise, that it could pass service either as bad acting or as sarcasm. 'What intimidating, hairy brutes! They frighten me with the threatening muscularity of their physiques and the alarming proportions of their genitalia!'

So saying, she takes hold of one of the—the word 'flaccid' seems wildly inappropriate here—penises; a pendulous member, larger, thicker and heavier than most average erections. The penis immediately comes to life, first rearing itself like an uncoiling snake, and then rapidly distending to rigid horizontal tumescence.

'Oh, goodness me! What have I done?'

And she then proceeds to repeat her error by taking hold of a second penis, with the same result. And then the third. And then the fourth. In each case she seems equally surprised and alarmed by the results of her actions.

'Oh, goodness me! I have unintentionally aroused all four of these savage brutes to a state of extreme concupiscence! I wonder what will be the consequence of my careless actions?'

Neither she or the audience are long finding out: taking hold of her tresses in his hairy paw, one of the creatures pulls Ramona roughly to her feet. Next moment her dress is being torn to shreds, her pendant necklace ripped from her throat; and then, with her lingerie ripped away from crotch and breasts, she is thrown facedown on the bed.

Ramona (the live not pre-recorded Ramona) turns to look at her husband. His face is livid, a frozen mask of seething emotions, none of them happy ones. His eyes, wide, enraged, fix on her, his lips tremble.

'You filthy *whore*,' he hisses. 'How dare you? How dare you show yourself to me with those... *things?*'

Ripples of protest from the guests, but neither her husband's words or his look have any effect on Ramona's smiling placidity. 'What are you talking about, darling?' she inquires sweetly. 'Those brutes? Surely you don't think that they're actually *real*?' She laughs. 'Really, darling, I thought you would have guessed: they're just CGI!'

'*CGI?*' rasps Jubin.

'Yes, husband. It stands for Computer Generated Imagery. You see, really it is just myself in front of the camera, playing the role of a woman being brutally raped by four monstrous beasts. And then, in what we call the 'post-production' process, I generated the forms of my assailants using 3D computer graphics, and the result is as you see. I admit I am very pleased with how it has turned out; but really, darling, I didn't think you would actually be fooled into thinking it was all real!'

She laughs again.

'CGI?' screams Jubin, incredulous. 'You expect me to believe they're just *CGI*?'

'Of course they're bloody CGI!' says one of the guests, a carefully unkempt author, lighting his latest cigarette. 'You don't think blokes hung like that exist in real life, do you?'

'He's right, old man,' concurs a scholarly novelist, puffing on his pipe. 'Can't be anything else.'

Both men speak with eyes fixed firmly on the screen, as indeed all of the literary eyes present are firmly fixed on the screen. (Only one eye in the case of one unfortunate author, having recently lost the other in a frenzied attack from a screwdriver-wielding literary critic.)

The film runs for about an hour; at least, I think it was about an hour; like everyone else present, I completely lost track of time—and during this time we see Ramona pulled and twisted into nearly every conceivable sexual position and savagely pounded and copiously inseminated by her inexhaustible assailants, while in the moments she is able to form coherent words, the subject of this orgy voices of cries of protest and pleas for mercy that are somehow strangely lacking in sincerity.

And the faces of the bestial lovers are never once seen as their heads always remain elusively out of the shot. (This made easier by the fact that there are no oral scenes.) And speaking of the camerawork, in spite of this being apparently recorded by Ramona herself in one take and with a single video camera, there are an inexplicable number of changes of shot, changes of camera angle, zoom ins, close ups (lots of close-ups!) etc. Perhaps this was all taken care of in the post-production process.

Meanwhile Ramona does her best to reassure her husband, who is quietly simmering beside her, that the whole thing is just herself and a lot of CGI wizardry.

'You see, darling? No man could stay fully tumescent for

that number of consecutive orgasms! It's CGI!'

'Just look at that completely preposterous amount of semen streaming from my vagina! It's CGI!'

'And do you really think *that* could fit all the way into my back passage? It's CGI!'

Finally, the savage orgy comes to an end, Ramona's assailants, their task fulfilled, depart as wordlessly as they arrived, creamy cocks swinging and slapping as they exit the room. Now the camera zooms in on Ramona, sprawled on the marital bed, dishevelled and bespattered, breathing hard. Parting the hair that has fallen across her face, she turns to the camera:

'My husband, I have emerged victorious! For, although my marvellously well-endowed and potent assailants may have stolen my body, they have *not* succeeded in stealing my heart! My heart still belongs to you, my darling husband!'

And, sucking fingers sloppy with sperm scooped from between her legs: 'Mm! And so, once again, Jubin darling: happy birthday and many happy returns!'

A musical fanfare, the legend 'The End,' a fade to black, and the epic is over.

The audience is ecstatic! Ramona is showered with praise—highbrow literary praise!

Except in the case of her husband, who does not share the enthusiasm of his comrades. Quivering, he springs to his feet.

'All done with CGI, was it?' he grates. 'We'll see, we'll see…'

He stomps out of the room, slams the door, and his footsteps can be heard ascending the stairs.

An awkward silence now descends on the room; but very soon comes the sound of returning footsteps, the living room bursts open, and in walks Jubin Ghai, brandishing Ramona's blue satin ballgown. The gown is in tatters.

'Then how do you explain this?' he demands, in tones of

savage triumph. 'How did this get shredded like this?'

'Oh, don't be silly, darling! It's not *really* shredded! It's just CGI!'

Chapter Eighteen
Cock and Bull

'Hello? Oh, *darling!* How *sweet* of you to call! You know, I just don't know what *do* with myself with you being away for so long! But at least it's nearly over! I tell you, I can't *wait* till Satur—!

'What? You can't come back this weekend? Not at all? But I thought—?

'Oh, I see...

'Yes, yes. Very important...

'Well *of course* I'm upset darling? How can I *not* be upset...?

'Yes, yes; I know, my darling; I know it's not your fault...

'What? What noise? The wet, slapping sound you can hear? Oh, that's just the washing machine, darling. It always makes that noise...

'Of *course*, darling! I know you must be just as much upset as I am. I know how much you miss me...

'What...?

'Oh, now you're just being *silly*, darling! How could you even *think* such a thing...?

'Oh, was it? Well, don't listen to what those silly colleagues of yours are saying. It may be true about *their* wives...!

'Yes, yes. Really, I *pity* those poor souls who have never experienced a perfect love like ours...

'You mustn't believe that for even one *second*, my darling! Never doubt my loyalty to you. My love for you is so profound that it would just be completely impossible for me to ever betray you, my darling…!

'Yes, my heart belongs to you and to you only, my husband! My love for you fills every atom of my body! Oh! I can feel it inside me now, pounding away inside me! Oh! I love you, my darling! Oh! I love you; I love you so much! Oh! Yes! Yes! Yes! YES! I love you so much! I love you so, so, so much, much, much! I… OH…! I love you I love you I love you I love you I *LOVE* YOU…!'

'Ohhhhh… my darling… oh, goodness… oh, my darling… quite out of breath, all that talking… oh… my sweet, sweet darling…'

'So we're agreed, right? They ain't getting in round the front; and they ain't getting in round the back. We're agreed on that?'

'Yes, we're agreed on that.'

'Right. Cuz you was watching round the front, and I was watching round the back, and there's no way they could've snuck past both of us.'

'No way at all.'

'Right. So there's only one answer, ain't there?'

'Only one that I can see, yes.'

'Right. There's only one answer: if they ain't getting in round the front, and they ain't getting in round the back, then they've gotta be getting in from down below, right?'

The speakers are Mike Grimsby and Gerald Banbury, and the place is the *Woodsman's Chopper*. It is evening and the pair are sitting at what has by now become their usual table. The pub is quite full and amongst the patrons Gerald has espied Dodo Dupont and Mayumi Takahashi sitting in a booth across the saloon, and with them a younger girl with purple hair whom he has never seen before.

'Wrong!' exclaims Gerald, in a tone of bemused protest. 'Down below? What the devil are you talking about?'

'I'm *saying* that they're getting in from down below,' says Grimsby, clearly one of those people who believe that the best way to explain a statement is to repeat it word for word.

'You're off your chump, old man!' declares Gerald, laughing. 'Are you seriously suggesting these mystery lovers could have gone to all the trouble of digging themselves a tunnel just so that they can get at their inamoratas without being seen by anyone? And where is this tunnel supposed to come out? In the back garden or actually in the house, under the floorboards? And don't forget that these alleged rendezvouses have been taking place at all three of our Thai bride's abodes: so they'll have to have excavated *three* tunnels, won't they? They've certainly put in a lot of work, haven't they? I'm surprised they've even got any energy left for lovemaking after all that!'

'I don't see what you're getting so sarky about,' replies Grimsby, disgruntled. 'It's the only explanation, ain't it? If they ain't getting in round the——'

'Yes, yes, alright! There's no need to repeat all that again! Dear lord, you're like a stuck record, man! Well, fortunately one of us has still got his marbles intact; and I say there *is* another explanation, and a very simple one at that.'

'Alright, clever clogs: let's hear it, then.'

'Gladly. The explanation is this, Grimsby old son: you've been rumbled.'

'Rumbled?'

'Yes, rumbled. Clocked. Found out. Identified.'

'Yeah, I know what rumbled means! What I don't know is what *you* mean.'

Gerald sighs. 'My meaning is very simple; what I mean is that your targets, the terrific trio, Hom, Ploy and Dao, are onto you. They know you've been listening in. They probably either saw their husbands planting those bugs you gave them or else they found them pretty quickly and made a shrewd guess as to who put them there and why.'

This explanation just leaves Grimsby even more perplexed. 'But if they know I'm listening in, then why would they go ahead and—?'

'They haven't gone ahead and done *anything*. Nothing except pull the wool over your eyes. Don't you get it? It's all been a put-on, a deception. There haven't really been any orgies at all, they've just been making enough noise to make you *think* there were.'

Grimsby gets it. But he doesn't believe it; his vehement head shaking demonstrates this. 'No. No, you're way off the beam there, Mr Banbury. I've *heard*. I've heard it all. You've only heard a bit, but I've heard it all—all them recordings from beginning to end. They're *genuine*. You say there's no blokes there, but I *hear* them. They don't speak, but they make a lot of noise; and it ain't them Thai birds making an impersonation, neither; they is definitely *male* noises. Can't be no woman making 'em.'

'There's a simple enough explanation for that, as well,' insists Gerald. 'It's porn. They're watching porn on the telly, and they're playing with themselves and making it sound to you like it's men they're playing with. You see? It's all a hoax, old son. A put-up job. They've just been leading you up the garden path. *Now*, do you see?'

'No, I don't,' says Grimsby, truculent. 'I say you've got it wrong. Been too clever by half, you have. I say I'm right. I say those birds have got geezers in there with 'em; and I'm gunna prove it, an' all.'

'And how do you plan on doing that?' asks Gerald sceptically.

Grimsby smiles under his moustache. 'Easy, ain't it? All I've gotta do is get inside one of the houses…'

'You know what I think?' says Trina Trulove.

'No,' replies Mayumi.

'About what?' asks Dodo.

'About that thing on the news, about how most date rape cases never make it into court. I had an idea: they should make greetings cards.'

'Greetings cards?' Dodo looks bemused. 'You mean condolence cards? How are they going to help with getting convictions?'

'No, not condolence cards!' retorts Trina. 'I mean they should have "Sorry I Raped You" cards.'

'"Sorry I Raped You" cards?' echoes Dodo, even more bemused.

'Yeah! They'd be these cards that the date-rapist sends to the girl he raped—'

'What if it's a guy he raped?' interposes Mayumi.

'Alright, the *person* he raped.'

'And how would that help with anything?' demands Dodo. From all appearances, Trina is completely serious!

'It's obvious, isn't it?' she says. 'The girl—or boy—who gets the card can either accept the apology and let the guy off the hook; or, if she—or he—decides they want to press charges, then they've got a signed confession from the rapist to take to the cops! He can't deny he did it after that, can he?'

'Well, that's an ingenious idea, Trina; I'll give you that,' says Dodo indulgently. 'Full marks for originality. But I don't see how it's going to work. I mean, by sending a "Sorry I Raped You" card, your date-rapist is basically throwing himself on his victim's mercy; and I think most of people in that position would consider that a gamble not worth taking. Don't you think so?'

'Well, then they should make the cards compulsory!' declares Trina.

'And how could they do that? To force someone to put their name on a "Sorry I Raped You" card, they'd have to be able to prove that person had actually committed an assault—and that brings us right back to where we started!'

'Well, if you're just going to pick holes in my ideas…' huffs Trina. Pouting, she consoles herself with a long swig from her pint glass. Her eyes wander round the room. 'Ooh! Who's the hunk over there?'

Dodo follows Trina's gaze. 'Oh, that's Gerald Banbury. He's one of our neighbours.'

'Oh! He lives on the close? But I thought all the husbands were supposed to be having their life force slowly drained away or something; that guy looks as fit as a fiddle!'

'That's because he's not one of the husbands; Gerald is Bellend Close's resident bachelor.'

'So, he's unattached, is he…?' ventures Trina, trying not to sound too interested.

'Oh yes, he's unattached,' Dodo assures her. 'In fact, recently he's been trying to attach himself to Yumi, but I'm sure you'd be quite willing to let Trina here take him off your hands, wouldn't you, sweetheart?'

'Sure. Help yourself; he's all yours,' says Mayumi with her customary generosity.

And if anyone is thinking that Gerald Banbury seems a bit on the old side to have been singled out by our prodigy Trina Truelove as potential boyfriend material, I need only inform you that since first meeting our elusive hero Mark Hunter, Trina has developed a taste for older men. Trina often dreams of achieving intimacy with Mark, dreams which are very unlikely to ever be realised. Because, as has already been mentioned, although Mark Hunter is a spy by profession, when it comes to sex, he is much more a John Drake than a James Bond; to wit, a generally celibate secret agent. Trina has been made aware of this fact, but she still has hopes that by the exertion of her feminine charms (of which few would argue that she possesses a generous allowance), Mark will make an exception in her case—even if only for one night!

I should also mention here that Trina, who swings both ways at least in theory, has another longstanding goal: that of being in a threesome with Dodo and Mayumi, both of whom she reveres almost as much as she does Mark. And this very afternoon she had come as close as she ever has to achieving that goal—but involving as it did Dodo and

Mayumi just standing there and watching her while they compelled her to masturbate herself, it was not quite what Trina always had in mind.

The whole thing had been an experiment to see if Trina, by sufficiently arousing herself, could cause one of those beast things to materialise in the room—and the experiment had been a failure. When rubbing herself to achieve a clitoral orgasm had yielded no results, it had been decided she should try for a vaginal orgasm by dildoing herself; and on her being unable to bring herself to a crisis, Mayumi had lost all patience and had taken over and started dildoing Trina herself—performing this office with a lot more violence than Trina would have liked. But in spite of Mayumi's energetic efforts no hairy lover had started to manifest itself.

And even now, the ordeal isn't over, because Mayumi had then voiced the suggestion that maybe the creatures only appeared at night, and Dodo agreeing that this would be worth investigating, Trina still has this repeat performance to look forward to when they get home from the pub.

Across the room, Gerald and the man in the Hawaiian shirt now rise from their table, the latter exiting the pub, while the former, armed with his pint, makes his way over to the booth in which the three women are seated.

'Looks like it's your lucky evening,' observes Dodo.

'May I join you ladies?' inquires Gerald, arriving at their table.

'Please do,' invites Dodo.

Gerald slides onto the seat, facing Trina.

'And who might this be?'

'This is our friend Trina,' says Dodo. 'She's come to stay with us for a few days.'

In the ensuing conversation, Gerald is not slow to realise that Trina is displaying a distinct interest in himself, and accordingly he switches the focus of his attention from Mayumi to her. The girl is a bit on the young side (nineteen, as she reveals herself), but if she doesn't mind the age difference then neither does he!

'What do you do, then?' asks Trina.

'Do? Oh, you mean career-wise. I don't actually have a job because I don't need one. I'm what they call "financially independent."'

'Ooh! That's nice!' says Trina, who is a big fan of money, not possessing much of that useful commodity herself.

The four of them leave the pub together. Having said goodnight to the women outside number twelve, Gerald proceeds along the street towards his own house, and it is just as he reaches his destination that he catches sight of the figure in the hooded cloak.

He sees it across the street advancing rapidly along the pavement. So incongruous is the sight, that at first he thinks he must be seeing a genuine apparition, the ghost of a mediaeval monk or priest. But then, when the figure trips, stumbles and almost falls, apparently having trodden on the hem of its own cloak, he dismisses the idea. Ghosts do not make bloody fools of themselves by tripping over their own cloaks.

The figure continues towards the cul-de-sac where it joins a second, identically dressed figure, and both of them disappear down the passageway leading to Bellend Wood. Gerald, caution getting the better of curiosity, elects not to follow them, but deep in thought, retires to his own house.

Chapter Nineteen
Grimsby, P.I.

And very soon sightings of these nocturnal hooded figures begin to proliferate. They are seen in the street, darting from cover to cover; they are seen prowling in back gardens, peering in through windows; always under cover of darkness and always in Bellend Close. And then come rumours—

from whence no-one seems to know—that the hooded figures have been seen gathering in Bellend Wood, holding sinister midnight meetings under the stars.

For Dodo Dupont this development is a puzzling one. As they haven't been seen before now, these hooded figures appear to be new players in the game. Are her theories wrong? Is it after all not Mhambi Khoza or any other resident of Bellend Close who is behind everything that's been going on? Could some external force, some mysterious third party, be the real culprit?

'You gotta let me get inside. Catch 'em in the act. It's the only way.'

This is the news that Mike Grimsby had imparted to his three clients; news that had not been received with enthusiasm. The three solicitors had wanted to issue a direct refusal, but being people for whom that degree of verbal assertiveness does not come easily, they had instead weakly prevaricated. They weren't entirely sure if they had any spare keys they could lend him. Someone might see him going in and call the police, thinking him a burglar. And if it's true that there are secret tunnels coming out in either the houses or the back gardens; well, they could look for those themselves, couldn't they?

'Alright; look for 'em yourselves. Just make sure your missises don't catch you doing it.'

And so the husbands had looked. They had poked around in the gardens. They had stamped on floors and lifted up carpets. Net result: nada.

'Right. Now you've done that, how about leaving the rest to the professionals? That's what you hired me for, ain't it? *I* can be there when you're all off at work. *I* can catch 'em in the act; in fragrant delicto. *Then* you've got your proof, right?'

And so, armed with kitchen door keys to each of the three houses, Mike Grimsby has waited his opportunity—and today the opportunity has arrived. They're at it again. In Smith's house this time. The guests have arrived by the usual invisible means and now they're going at it hammer and tongs. When the cat's away…

What Grimsby looks forward to the most is proving that poncy git Gerald Banbury wrong. Nobody there! Just watching porn on the telly! A put-up job because they found the bugs! Eyewash. Grimsby doesn't believe it for one moment. Too clever by half, that's Banbury's problem. Overthinks things and gets them completely wrong. Well, he'll be laughing out of the other side of his face, won't he? After today, he will.

Earpiece in place, connected to the smartphone in his pocket, he takes a leap at the rear fence of Smith's back garden, and, gaining a fingerhold, hauls himself up onto the top of the fence.

Wasn't that hard at all, he thinks, straddling the fence, pausing to catch his breath. Doesn't have to worry about being seen from the house; curtains are all drawn. The best way to get down will be to get his other leg over and then lower himself by his arms.

A sound plan, but having got his other leg over, he loses balance and tumbles into the flowerbeds.

The impact knocks the wind out of him—his earpiece has suddenly gone quiet. Sod it! They must've heard him fall! Through the leaves and stems of the flowers he hasn't flattened beneath him he can see across the garden to the patio doors; lying motionless, he looks, fearfully expecting to see inquiring yellow faces looking out into the garden—but no, the curtains remain firmly drawn; not so much as a twitch. They *didn't* hear him, then? Then why did they suddenly pack in what they were doing in there?

But then a trailing wire leads Grimsby to the truth: in his fall the earpiece has come unplugged from his phone. He reconnects it and he is reassured by the sounds of the house's occupants still going hard at it. Panic over.

Having gathered his wits together, Grimsby now climbs to his feet. Dusting down his Hawaiian shirt and adjusting his baseball cap, he makes his way quickly to the side of the house and to the kitchen door. From a trouser pocket he extracts the key so reluctantly given to him by Paul Smith. Silly buggers, making an all that fuss about giving him the keys. Did he think he was going to nick something? If he nicked anything, they'd know straight away who did it, wouldn't they? And as for rummaging through all the dirty laundry people keep locked up in their houses; well, rummaging through dirty laundry is what a private investigator's paid to do, ain't he? Silly buggers.

Grimsby inserts the key into the lock—or he tries to. Something blocking it half way. It's another key! Bloody key's in the lock on the other side! Idiot! He should've took the key out before he went off to work! Grimsby tries pushing the other key through with his own. No go; it won't budge.

He tries the door handle. The door opens.

Idiots.

Grimsby steps into the kitchen, treading with soft steps on the linoleum floor. This is it. This is more like it. Real private investigator stuff, this is. Just like Magnum, P.I.

He reaches the kitchen door, which opens out into the hallway. There are the stairs in front of him and next to them, the living room door, closed. That's where they are. Still banging away. Ain't they gunna be in for a surprise, when he comes bursting in there, phone camera flashing! Ha, ha! Catch 'em with their pants down! In fragrant delicto! Ha, ha! When the cat's away... Well, who can really blame 'em? Sorry bunch of blokes, those husbands of theirs. Always are, them ones that send off for them mail-order Thai brides. Now Grimsby, he would've preferred one of them nice Hawaiian birds; one of them hula dancers with the grass skirt and the flower necklace an' all that... Either that or a French-Vietnamese lady like Magnum's ex-wife... Yeah, he can't really blame those birds for what they're getting up to in there; but still, a job's a job, and it's the husbands he's working for, not the wives.

Smartphone at the ready, Grimsby walks quietly across the hallway to the living room door.

And then silence: all noise in his earpiece suddenly ceases. And this time it's not the lead. He has the phone in his hands and he can see it's still plugged in.

They've stopped. This time they really have stopped. He puts his ear to the door. Nothing. Not a peep.

They must've heard him! They must be in there holding their breaths, waiting for the door to open. But how *could* they have heard him? Quiet as a mouse he's been. Rubber soles, soft pile on the floor. *Nobody* could've heard him, let alone people who were going at it like they were…!

Taut seconds pass. Still not a sound, either through the door or in his earpiece. What are they doing in there? Wait a minute. What if those fuckboys of theirs are real bruisers? They could be waiting to jump him and give him a pounding when he walks in through the door! For a moment Grimsby is afraid. He's not much of a fighter. Fighting is one area of private detective work he prefers to avoid. When it comes to dangerous situations like that, Grimsby is an advocate of the strategic withdrawal.

But then another thought occurs to him and he stops being afraid: the secret tunnel! What if the secret tunnel comes out right there in the living room? Yeah! That must be it! They ain't waiting for him in there—they've all bloody scarpered! Must have!

Only one way to find out…

He opens the living room door. The first thing he sees is the television. It's switched on and it's the only source of light in the curtained room. And the room is empty. No-one on the chairs or the sofa. No-one on the floor. Like all the living rooms in Bellend Close it is a large room, stretching from the front of the house to the back, but the TV screen is large as well, and its light is bright, and there's no-one to be seen in the room.

They've cleared out. Yes, somewhere in here there's the entrance to a secret tunnel; Smith may not've been able to find it when he looked, but then Smith isn't a professional private investigator, is he? He's just a solicitor and a bloody fool.

He walks further into the room. The TV screen displays the menu page of the Blu-ray/DVD player connected to it. And the menu says that there's a DVD loaded and ready to play.

Grimsby stops in his tracks. Television. DVD player. Porn. Oh Christ, don't say Banbury had it right all along? That there aren't any lovers and it's just them Thai birds watching porn flicks?

No. No, that can't be right. If the wives were just watching porn by themselves, then where are they? They should be still here, shouldn't they? But they're not here. No-one's here. So they've cleared out, and the only way they could have cleared out without him seeing or hearing it is through a secret tunnel, right?

So yeah, it's the Grimsby theory that has to be the right one, not the Banbury theory.

But still... better check.

Sitting down on the sofa, Grimsby finds the Blu-ray player remote and presses the play button. A brief pause, and then: the music crashes in and a helicopter swoops out of the sky! A black helicopter with yellow and orange stripes! A tracking shot as it flies low over the ocean! And then the title caption zooms towards the screen, the title caption that reads:

Magnum, P.I.

Everything else forgotten, Grimsby, eyes glued to the screen, is back in his childhood, his pulses racing as they always did back then whenever his favourite theme music started playing. What episode is it going to be? It's the second, more angular title caption they've just had; that means it's got to be at least season three! Let's see... The clips they show for the actor credits will tell him what season... Ah, yes: that shot of John Hillerman; that's a dead giveaway! Season five! Definitely season five! Or maybe season six...

The opening scene: a Hawaiian beach.

Oh, it's 'Mac's Back' from season five! What a classic! Yes, there's Magnum on the beach, drowning his sorrows. He's having one of his traumatic episodes after Sharon Stone blew her own brains out right in front of him at the end of the previous episode. And later, when he starts seeing his old friend Mac apparently returned from the dead, the others will all think he's just imagining it. Mac got killed by a car-bomb intended for him in the classic third season episode 'Did You See the Sunrise?' Best episode ever, that one was! A real shocker, too: not just for the surprise death of a much-loved secondary character, but also Magnum's cold-blooded execution of the villain at the end, not to mention the episode's frequent use of the N-word! (Which will probably get it banned sooner or later.) Producer Donald Bellisario was big fan of the Jeff Mackay, the actor who played Mac (in spite of being the one who wrote the episode that killed him off), and in 'Mac's Back' he wasn't afraid to resort to that much-loved device of the identical double so that the actor could be in the show again!

It's been a while since Grimsby last watched this episode, so he makes himself comfortable on the sofa to enjoy it, and when a king-sized bag of cheese puffs is placed under his nose, he, keeping his eyes on the TV, automatically takes a handful of the snacks and transfers them to his mouth. An opened bottle of chilled beer is now presented to him and, accepting it with a grunt of thanks, he takes a long swig. Wait a minute! It tastes like...! Is it...? He checks the label.

Yes, it's Old Düsseldorf! Magnum's favourite beer! Perfect!

Finally, it occurs to Grimsby to wonder where all these gifts are coming from, and he looks to his right and sees cute, plump, bespectacled Hom Smith sitting sideways on the sofa next to him, smiling at him with the sunniest of smiles.

'Hi, there!' she says.

Giggling directs his attention to his left, where Ploy White and Dao Johnson, slimmer but also bespectacled, are sitting, smiling at him from ear to ear.

And all three of them are stark naked!

Now, if there is one other aspect of private investigation where Grimsby falls sadly short of his television idol, then that is in dealing with naked women. In fact, he's not even all that hot when it comes to dealing with fully-clothed women, but naked women, when they're not in a magazine where they should be, he finds particularly disconcerting. And now, finding himself hemmed in on all sides by naked women, his only option is to turn his attention back to the TV screen and do his best to pretend that they're not there.

'We wanna hire you,' sing-songs Hom. 'Before, you work for our husbands; but now, you work for us, okay?'

Eyes still on the screen, Grimsby says nothing.

'Great! It's a deal, then!' enthuses Hom, choosing to interpret this silence as acquiescence. 'Now, you just sit right there and watch *Magnum, P.I.*, and us ladies go back to our friends, okay? And no peeking!'

And Grimsby keeps his eyes fixed on the screen. Giggling, the three women get up from the sofa. And now, from nowhere, an intense masculine smell fills the air; and if it suddenly feels like the room is now even less empty than it seemed to be when he walked into it, that three large, quietly growling presences have manifested themselves at the other end of the room, then that is no business of his. If his hostesses want to hire his services as a private investigator, then that's that. And if the nature of his assignment is to watch *Magnum P.I.* while drinking beer and eating snacks, then watch *Magnum P.I.* while drinking beer and eating snacks is what he will do. And as for what the three Thai ladies might be doing over there with those three large presences, it would be exceeding his assigned duties to even pretend he notices it.

    Oh, yes! This is a good bit coming up…!

Chapter Twenty
The Unequal Distribution of Nooky

LESBO'S GO HOME

This is what has been spray-painted onto Dodo and Mayumi's front door overnight.

    'The punctuation's wrong,' remarks Dodo, as heads inclined, Mayumi and Trina and herself stand surveying the graffiti. 'There shouldn't be any apostrophe.'

    'Yeah…' agrees Trina, her tone thoughtful. 'But then, if they'd written it without the apostrophe, it would have looked like 'Lesbos,' wouldn't it? You know, the island.'

    'True,' concedes Dodo. 'But they could have just spelt lesboes with an 'e' before the 's.' But then, in that case you could argue that the apostrophe is present here as a substitute for the missing letter 'e,' and is therefore *not* erroneously representing the possessive case.'

    'So basically,' says Trina, 'the punctuation *isn't* wrong then, is it?'

    'No, it isn't,' agrees Dodo.

    It's not just number twelve that has been targeted by graffiti-artists overnight. In fact, every front door on Bellend Close has been bedaubed with its own slogan. The prevailing theme is of a generically misogynistic nature, standard insults such as 'FILTHY SLUT,' 'NYMPHO' and 'DIRTY WHORE'; but in some cases, the slogans have been personalised. For example, Patricia Pinecroft's front door has been emblazoned with the words 'FAT ARSE,' while that of Mhambi Khoza bears the legend 'BLACK BITCH' (a sly literary reference?), and Ramona Ghai's front door has been adorned with 'PORNSTAR SLUT,' a reference meaningless to Dodo et al, but which the more-informed reader will understand (unless you've already forgotten what happened in chapter seventeen.)

'So, who do we have to thank for this outbreak of misogynistic defacement of property?' wonders Dodo, hands on hips, turning to face the street. It's still very early and no-one else is about.

'The husbands,' says Mayumi.

'Those creeps in the cloaks,' says Trina.

'If it's the creeps in the cloaks that did it, then the creeps in the cloaks can't be the husbands,' decides Dodo. 'I know they're not exactly in love with their wives at the moment, but I can't believe they'd be stupid enough to think it was a good idea to spray graffiti on their own front doors...'

'You still think there might be someone else involved in all this?' inquires Trina. 'Someone we don't know about?'

'I'm starting to think that more and more,' answers Dodo. 'I'm starting to think that all this, everything that's been happening on this street, is all part of some bizarre experiment, and the people here are the guinea pigs. And maybe even this graffiti campaign is part of the experiment; maybe it's been done to aggravate the situation, to stir things up a bit more. You notice that out of all the messages we can see, we're the only ones being invited to leave? Maybe that's because we're not part of the experiment; we weren't here when it started, so we're a rogue element and perhaps they're worried we could affect the outcome.'

When I mentioned before that Trina Truelove had developed

a 'thing' for older men, this doesn't mean that she has acquired much in the way of 'hands on' experience of more mature partners; in fact, she hasn't acquired any. That succession of failed relationships previously referred to have all been with young men of more or less her own age.

And Trina is starting to suspect that this might be exactly where she's been going wrong. Guys her own age always seem to be self-centred morons; what she needs is a more mature, experienced man who knows how to treat a lady. And if that man also happens to be loaded, then so much the better!

Which is why we find Trina this evening seated tete-a-tete with Gerald Banbury at a candle-lit (yes, candle-lit!) table with an open bottle of Damilano Barolo in Strepford's swankiest Italian restaurant. And as Trina and Gerald have only known each other for a couple of days, I really don't know which one of them I should compliment the most for not wasting any time!

Gerald looks smart but casual in a tailored, tieless, light-coloured summer suit, while our Trina is kitted out in her best posh frock, which is in fact her only posh frock, Trina not really being a posh frock sort of person (she's more punk than posh); but she owns this one, an off the shoulder number with a ruffled, knee-length skirt, and which, being purple in colour, complements her hair as it happens to be at the moment. (She bought this dress after becoming Mayumi Takahashi's assistant, having had to attend some of the soirees to which that esteemed artist of the camera has been invited.)

'…I don't really get on with Mum,' Trina is saying, 'so that's why I moved out after I'd finished sixth form… Well, she chucked me out, really. But that was fine, cuz it's better having your own space, instead of living at home, isn't it? What about you? Do you get on okay with your family?'

'Well, I don't actually have any immediate family,' replies Gerald. 'You see, I've been an orphan since I was fifteen. We were in a car crash; it happened while we were on holiday in France. My parents and my younger sister were all killed; I was the only survivor.'

'Ohmygod, that's terrible!' exclaims Trina. And then, hurriedly: 'I mean, not that you survived! I mean, that your family were all killed...'

Gerald smiles ruefully. 'Well, there have been times when I've thought it might have been more of a mercy if I had died along with them... But that's what they call survivor guilt, isn't it? And I can't deny that it was that accident that's left me financially independent ever since.'

'Your mum and dad were rich, were they?'

'My parents were shrewd investors. Stocks and shares and all that.'

'Ooh! Stocks and shares! That sounds interesting!'

And here we can stop and only admire how tactful and considerate is Trina, skilfully seizing the opportunity to steer the conversation away from the painful subject of family bereavement and into the sunnier climes of making lots of money without having to do any work.

She has a feeling that the evening is going to turn out well.

Agent Mayumi is this evening sporting an outfit that would have had her turned away at the door of the Italian restaurant, but is very appropriate attire (in Mayumi's opinion if no-one else's) for a spy out on a secret mission.

Based on the costume worn by Marianne Shinonome on the cover of the 2012 Kinoco Hotel album 'The Temptation of Marianne' (available from all good Japanese record shops), the outfit consists of black PVC boots, hotpants and opera gloves, topped off with a rakishly angled bowler hat, and with a pair of braces being the only thing standing between the wearer and upper-body nudity. The hotpants are reminiscent of *The Worm that Turned*, while the bowler hat seems somehow a lot more Alex DeLarge than John Steed.

Bless her.

The secret mission is an ongoing one: for the past two nights they have been lurking in the vicinity of the clearing in Bellend Wood, hoping to catch sight of those mysterious cowled figures, who have been rumoured to have selected this location as their meeting place; on the first two occasions Trina Truelove had also been present; tonight, as Trina is overwise engaged, Dodo and Mayumi are going to have to struggle on without her.

'I'm starting to wonder if we've got the right clearing,' says Dodo.

The stars shining down on them through the gaps in the overarching foliage, the two women make their way along the footpath through the woods. Dodo is dressed in her usual nocturnal outfit of black boots, trousers and pullover.

'The glade might be the only clearing "of any size" in this wood, but there are other clearings; and the rumour just said that those people have been seen meeting in *a* clearing in the wood, not in *the* clearing.'

'Yeah, but we know that the big glade is the important one,' reasons Mayumi. 'Maybe those guys in the cloaks know it too.'

They have had an update from Mark regarding the glade: it has been overflown by an aircraft, and the penis symbol was *not* visible from the air; at first this was thought to confirm the belief that the symbol is no longer there, that it has been obliterated or removed; but now, a further satellite photograph has shown that it *is* still there.

Apparently it can only be seen from outer space.

'True. The way those people are dressed does suggest some kind of coven of druids or necromancers, doesn't it?' says Dodo. 'But on the other hand, there was nothing occult about the messages they graffitied on everyone's doors—listen! Someone's coming!'

They stop walking. A sound grows louder, the sound of approaching footsteps—a large number of approaching footsteps.

'They're coming along the path!'

Dodo and Mayumi duck into the cover of the woods and throw themselves flat. They don't have long to wait before the procession appears, a procession of dark figures dressed in hooded cloaks. At least thirty in number, they advance rapidly along the path, three of them holding aloft a swathed object bound with ropes that looks very much like a human body.

When they have passed:

'Come on! Let's follow them.'

The Spaghetti Milanese is on the table, and Trina has put away enough of the Damilano Barolo to be saying a lot more than she really ought to be about Dodo and Mayumi's investigation into the Bellend Close situation. (But in Trina's defence, both Dodo and Mayumi have neglected to advise her of their 'keep smiling and trust nobody' policy.)

'Really? You haven't seen any of those cavemen?'

'Really. I've never set eyes on a caveman in my life. As far as I know, that was just a story in *The Sun*. What makes you so sure there's anything in it?'

'Because there is. Dodo says so. They're using magic to make them appear.'

'Magic? Who's using magic?'

'That woman. The witchdoctor.'

'What witchdoctor?'

'The black woman. She's a Zulu witchdoctor, isn't she?'

Gerald looks amused. 'Mhambi Khoza? Where did you get that one from? Mhambi's an NHS doctor, not a witchdoctor.'

'Yeah, but she's also a witchdoctor, isn't she?' insists Trina.

'Not that I've ever heard.'

'Then why's she got that Zulu hut in her garden?'

Gerald's amusement becomes outright laughter. 'That

hut? That hut, my dear Katrina—'

'It's just "Trina",' snaps Trina, who doesn't much care for being laughed at.

'My apologies,' says Gerald solemnly. 'That hut, my dear Trina, is nothing more than an extension of the marital bedroom. You see, back when they still liked each other, Mhambi and her husband David used to have this role-playing thing going on where he would be Allan Quatermain, and she would be this Zulu priestess or witchdoctor from one of the Allan Quatermain books—I'm not sure which one; I've only ever read *King Solomon's Mines*—and that is the one and only reason for the native hut in the garden. Mhambi might *play* at being a witch doctor, but she isn't one really.'

'She isn't…?' Trina looks confused.

'No more than I am. Who told you she was?'

'*She* did. I mean she told Dodo she was…'

'Then I'm afraid Mhambi was pulling Dodo's leg.'

Trina stands up so quickly she knocks her chair over.

'What's wrong?' asks Gerald.

'I've got to tell Dodo!' she exclaims.

'Tell her what?'

'That she's not a witchdoctor!'

'But you haven't even finished eating!' protests Gerald. 'What's the mad rush for? It's not that urgent, is it? Anyway, can't you just send her a text?'

Trina sits down again (her chair having been deftly set back on its legs by an attentive waiter.) 'I just remembered: she's out. And she won't have her phone with her, either…'

'Then let's get back to our meal. You don't want to spoil such a lovely evening by rushing off, do you?'

'No!' affirms Trina, recalling her priorities. She giggles. 'Sorry about that!' Seizing her fork, she starts industriously twirling spaghetti round the tines. 'So who's Allan Quatermain…?'

The glade is definitely the destination of the cloaked procession. They have turned off the path and are heading towards it like people who know where they are going. Keeping out of sight, Dodo and Mayumi follow in their wake.

'Human sacrifice!' says Mayumi.

'It looks like it, doesn't it?' agrees Dodo. 'That flat stone in the glade would make a perfect sacrificial altar. These people can't be druids then: the druids always performed their human sacrifices at sunrise, not in the evening while the pubs are still open.'

'Could be Satanists,' suggests Mayumi.

'Could be. Although the Black Mass doesn't usually involve human sacrifice...'

The procession now reaches the clearing. Here they spread out, forming a rough semi-circle around the flat boulder. The three who were carrying the bound figure place their burden on the ground in front of the rock. Now, one of the cloaked figures climbs up onto the rock like a speaker mounting the rostrum, and stands facing the gathering.

Crouched at the edge of the clearing, Dodo and Mayumi watch with breathless interest.

'Welcome, brethren,' intones the figure on the rock, in a deep, masculine voice. And, raising his arms aloft: 'Rejoice, brothers, for we have achieved our goal! As you see before you, the leader of our persecutors has been seized and is now our helpless captive! Our freedom is nigh and soon our torment will end!'

Loud cheering from the assembled acolytes.

'And now,' speaks the leader when the noise has subsided; 'now we will commence the inquisition! Loosen the ropes of our captive!'

Two acolytes come forward, untie the ropes binding the prostrate figure. Divested of her wrappings, the captive is hauled to her feet, and from their vantage point Dodo and Mayumi instantly recognise the ebony visage, the proud carriage and commanding figure. The captive is Mhambi Khoza!

'Behold the leader of our foul tormentors! Behold her now our helpless prisoner!' cries the leader. 'Speak, woman! Reveal the secret of your power! Reveal the secret of the insidious power that saps us of our very lifeforce!'

'Yes, speak! Speak, speak!' echo the acolytes.

'Speak, wretched female!' demands the leader. 'And beware! Your very life hangs in the balance!'

'Oh, stop talking in that ridiculous voice!' replies Mhambi scornfully. 'I know it's you, David.'

'It's not me—! I mean, I know not of this David of whom you speak! Heed me well: you are helpless, surrounded by your implacable foes, the many people whom you have wronged! Expect not succour to reach you in this our stronghold! Your only choice is that of submission to our will!'

'Like I'd ever submit to *your* will,' scoffs Mhambi.

'Silence! Cease this empty show of bravado: it will avail you naught! You will answer the questions put to you or you will face dire consequences!'

'Oh, lay off it, David,' groans Mhambi. 'You don't really expect me to take you and your pals seriously, do you?'

'You were right after all, sweetheart,' murmurs Dodo to Mayumi. 'Our cloaked friends *are* those idiot husbands. Seems I underestimated them when I said they wouldn't be stupid enough to spray graffiti on their own front doors. Wait a minute: can you smell something?'

'Man smell,' declares Mayumi. 'Like that other time.'

It is. Like that day last week when that creature started to materialise in the living room; the same arousing, overpowering masculine odour. And now they hear movement amongst the trees around them, the sound of footsteps approaching rapidly; not running, but with the purposeful stride of large, powerful legs. The sound comes not just from one location, but from all around them.

'They're coming this way!' hisses Dodo. 'And there's a lot of them!'

Shapes start to detach themselves from the darkness, hulking shapes, huge humanoid forms, wide of girth. Dodo hugs Mayumi protectively to her chest, but the newcomers pay them no heed, their target is the clearing.

They seem to appear in unison, emerging all at once from all sides of the clearing, and it is now Dodo and Mayumi see the beasts clearly for the first time. They must be at least seven feet tall (two metres to metric Mayumi), humanoid in form, but with an incredibly well-developed musculature. The bodies are completely covered in hair in what would be considered a severe case of hirsutism for a regular human being, but with these creatures it just seems to be their natural appearance. One area void of hair and to which for this and other reasons the eye is naturally drawn, are the beasts' massive penises, hanging pendent from dense forests of pubic hair, swinging heavily to-and-fro as the creatures advance.

Dodo makes the effort to tear her eyes away from those fearsome genitalia, and to descry what the creatures' faces look like; but she cannot. Her eyes keep sliding away from the heads set on those immense shoulders, leaving her with no impression at all but of the general outline; it is as though the facial features remain hidden in shadow in spite of the fact that the beasts are out in the open, and the rest of their bodies can be seen with perfect clarity.

From all sides the beasts descend on the gathering in the centre of the glade. They're surrounded! There's no avenue of escape!

'Call them off!' shrieks David Jarman, throwing back his hood and fixing his wife with terror-stricken eyes. 'Call them off!'

'I wouldn't know how to,' replies Mhambi, insouciantly. 'I have no control over them.'

'Liar!' screams her husband. 'You summoned them here,

so you can call them off! Do it! Do it now!'

'I *can't* call them off, because I *didn't* summon them,' sighs Mhambi. 'And anyway, it's way too late now.'

And so it seems. The hooded husbands, screaming and yelling, vainly trying to escape, are being grabbed by the hulking beasts and hurled or wrestled to the ground. David Jarman leaps from his rock, makes a spirited attempt to abandon his cohorts and reach freedom by ducking between two of the beasts. But no such luck! He is grabbed by one of them and screaming his wife's name, is forced to the ground. Mhambi, cooly observing, completely unconcerned, makes no move to intervene.

'They're killing them!' gasps Dodo, as the centre of the glade becomes one surging mass of moving flesh and the air is filled with a cacophony of terrified screams and bestial growls.

But then: 'Oh no, wait: no… no, that's not what they're doing at all, is it?'

'Killing them with love,' says Mayumi.

'I think now is the time for us to get out while the going's good,' decides Dodo; 'while those… things are preoccupied…'

'And the weather report for today in Professor Aubergine's laboratory is mainly dry, but with occasional golden showers!'

Trina falls back on the sofa, convulsed with laughter at her own joke.

Trina has heard about Nanette Aubergine's unusual toilet habit (in strict confidence, of course!) from Dodo and Mayumi, but it seems that word has leaked to others as well, because the nocturnal graffiti artists have left the slogan 'PROFESSOR PISS PUDDLE' on her front door; a commendably alliterative effort which Trina hadn't seen previously because, being at the end of the close, the professor's front door is not visible from number twelve—

but it is visible from Gerald Banbury's house, and that is where they happen to be right now.

And not even Gerald himself has escaped the attentions of the sloganeers, as the legend 'SERIAL GROPER' emblazoned on his front door can attest. And what's more, Trina herself can personally attest to the truth of the accusation: all the back from the restaurant Gerald hasn't been able to keep his paws off her!

This one's in the bag! thinks chicken-counting Trina.

And you can hardly blame her, because very soon Gerald has her in his arms and their mouths are joined together in a frantic kiss. Trina, blissed on wine, horny as hell, writhes in his rough embrace, moaning and moist. And then comes the deft unzipping, unclipping, sliding and discarding of an expert undresser of women going about his work, and Trina is efficiently stripped down to her stockings and suspender belt.

'Oh God, oh Christ,' moans Trina in religious ecstasy. 'Do it now! Take me now!'

'Oh, my darling!' cries Gerald, springing to his feet and fumbling with his belt. 'Oh, my sweet, sweet darling!' He drops his trousers and shorts. 'I'm afraid I can't.'

Trina lets out a scream, horror-stricken eyes fixed on Gerald's crotch. Her first thought is that Gerald is a pre-op transman, but then she realises that what she is looking at are not female genitalia—what she is looking at is no genitalia at all; just a few scrubby patches of his pubic hair and a lot of scar tissue.

Gerald heaves a sigh. 'Yes, my dear; my secret is out. As you can see, although I survived that car crash I told you about, I did not survive intact. My only consolation is that at least it happened after my voice had broken, otherwise I would have been stuck as a treble all my life.'

And with another weary sigh, he pulls his trousers back up.

And poor Trina is crushed. Raised to the unbearable peak

of anticipation, her mind and body and soul imperatively crying out for one thing and one thing only—and then to be abruptly thrown from that peak and to lie stunned upon the jagged rocks of sweet Fanny Adams.

'Well, it's no use lying there with your jaw hanging open, my dear,' says Gerald, expression severe, voice curt. 'You might as well just get your clothes on and skedaddle. There's nothing more for you here. I've wined you and dined you and kissed your fair lips, so now you can clear off, can't you?'

Trina bursts into tears.

Chapter Twenty-One
The Nation's Slayving Grace

'"To Slayve and the tree slut. We've got your goblin sidekick Groob. If you want to see him alive again then come to the Pollutex Chemicals warehouse at three this afternoon. If you don't come, the pointy-eared eunuch gets it. Signed, Vengeance Warrior. P.S. You probably can't read, so get your tree slut to read it out to you."

'"So, this Vengeance Warrior has taken my trusty goblin squire. We must go to his rescue!" says Slayve. "Or, we could just let them kill him and then advertise for a new sidekick for you," says Cassie. Ha, ha, ha! That's Cassie for you! But Slayve's not having any of it. "No! It would be against my barbarian code to do such a thing! We must go!" he says. "Fine, but you know it's a trap, right?" says Cassie. "Have no fear, goddess! For no trap can hold Slayve the Barbarian!"

'Next page. Slayve and Cassie arrive at the Pollutex Chemicals warehouse.

'"What's Pollutex Chemicals?"

'Pollutex? You haven't seen them, but they've been in the comic before. They're this evil corporation who are always polluting the countryside with chemicals cuz they don't care about the environment, they only care about their profits; and the boss of Pollutex is this sleazy guy who's got the whole government in his pocket cuz he gives lots of money to the Tory party.

'Now Slayve and Cassie go inside, and look: there's Groob hanging over a big tank full of bubbling pollution! And see? there's a candle slowly burning through the rope, so if they don't get to him in time, it'll burn through and he'll fall into the pollution!

'"Poor Groob! Doesn't he know how to swim, then?"

'It doesn't matter if he can swim or not! If he falls into that pollution, he'll be dead! It'll turn him into a skeleton in a second!

'"Oh no!"

'"Fear not, Groob! I am here to rescue you!" says Slayve. "Don't just stand there! Look out, you moron!" says Groob. And then WHAM! the Vengeance Warrior comes out of nowhere and slams into Slayve and they go flying across the room! See, that's the Vengeance Warrior; he's wearing this sink-tight costume with a mask cuz he's meant to look like a Marvel Comics villain or something. But he's got to be really strong to send Slayve flying like that; no normal man could do that! And now they're fighting! SLAM! POW! CRACK! BIFF! And Slayve's getting the worst of it!

'"Oh, no! He's stronger than Slayve!"

'And there's Cassie: just look at her face! She's not impressed with how Slayve's fighting! "What's the matter with you? Did you forget to take your vitamins this morning?" she says. Now the Vengeance Warrior's got Slayve pinned down. "My apologies, goddess! But this man possesses unnatural strength! It is as though his limbs are made of tempered steel!" says Slayve. "That's right! You've met your match this time, barbarian! Vengeance will be mine!" says the Vengeance Warrior. "You talk of vengeance, but yet our paths have never crossed before!'

says Slayve. "That's what you think!" says the Vengeance Warrior. "Well, you just keep him busy! I'll go'n rescue Groob!" says Cassie, and she flies across the room to where Groob is.

'"I thought you said Cassie couldn't really fly?"

'Yeah, she doesn't normally. Maybe she can fly this time cuz it's an emergency. "Oh no you don't!" says the Vengeance Warrior, and he leaps after Cassie, grabs her by the hair, swings her around like a lasso, and then lets go so that she goes flying across the room and WHAM! hits the wall! And look, now Slayve is really mad! He doesn't like it when people start bashing his goddess about! "Foul fiend! How dare you lay violent hands on a woman?" he says. "Because this is my vengeance! You will both suffer for what you did to me!" says the Vengeance Warrior. "You speak in riddles, madman! I say again our paths have never crossed before! I would never have forgotten such a powerful adversary!"

'"Then perhaps this will refresh your memory!" and he pulls off his mask. Slayve looks completely blank. "You are a stranger to me!" he says. And there's Cassie, lying in a heap on the floor and she looks confused as well. "Yep. I've never set eyes on you before. You sure you've got the right people?' she says. Ha, ha! Look: the Vengeance Warrior looks really pissed off at them not remembering him! "So, you don't even remember me, you bastards? You don't remember the man you inflicted life-changing injuries on?" he says. "Nope! Can we have some more clues?" says Cassie. Now he's even more pissed off. "It was at the road protest! Remember all those riot police officers, who were only doing their duty trying to break up the protest? And how Slayve went berserk and started chopping off all their arms and legs? Well, *I* was the chief of those riot police!" And see: this panel's a flashback of him when he was just an ordinary riot cop.

'"Oh! So that was back in the week before last's issue!

The first one you showed me!"

'That's right! It was the day we first met, wasn't it? And I made you my apprentice! We've had a lot of fun since then, haven't we?

"'Yeah! We have!"

'Well, back to the comic. "You left me a helpless quadriplegic! But now, as you can see, Pollutex has given me these bionic limbs so that I can take my revenge and also stop you from ever interfering with Pollutex's plans again!" says the Vengeance Warrior. "Very well! Then I will fight you in single combat! Groob: my battleaxe!" says Slayve. "Yeah, I'm kind of tied up at the moment, in case you hadn't noticed!" says Groob, still hanging over the tank.

"'Tied up! Ha, ha, ha! He's tied up! That's a good one!"

'And now TWINKLE! Slayve's battleaxe appears in the air. "Here's your stupid axe! Now hurry up and kill him!" says Cassie. "Yeah, and how about saving me? This rope's gunna break any minute!" says Groob. Now Slayve attacks the Vengeance Warrior with his axe! CLANG! THWACK! CRACK! But it's no good! The axe isn't even making a dent in the Vengeance Warrior's metal arms! And then KERRANG! the Vengeance Warrior swipes the axe out of Slayve's hands and it flies across the room and goes into the wall! And look, here's the Vengeance Warrior looking all gloaty. "Now you're powerless, Slayve! You've lost your weapon!" he says. But look, Slayve hasn't given up! "You are wrong!" he says, and he tears off his bearskin pants! (And look at those cheeks! Hard as fucking rocks!) Turn the page and: "Because I still have this weapon!" and he grabs the Vengeance Warrior by the ears and THRUST! he rams his stonker right through his eye-socket and into his brains!

"'Oooh! Are they allowed to show his willy like that in a children's comic?"

'Normally, they wouldn't be allowed to, but it's okay here cuz it's in what they call a "non-sexual context." And anyway, you can't see the bell-end, and that's the really rude bit. So, the Vengeance Warrior falls to the ground stone dead and Slayve stands victoriously over him, and does his warcry: "RRRAAAAARRRRHHH!" But look: the rope's burnt through and Groob's falling into the tank full of pollution! "Help!" he cries. There's no way Slayve can get to him in time! But Cassie's on the case! "Wind magic!" she says, pointing her magic staff! WHAM! a gust of wind hits Groob just in the nick of time! And he goes flying across the room, hits the wall and ends up hanging by his collar from the handle of Slayve's axe! And now the last page, another splash, and there's Slayve, on top of Cassie, worshipping the tits off her and at the front here's Groob, still hanging from the end of the axe, and shaking his fists and he says: "Hey, what about me? You just gunna leave me hanging around?"

'"Hanging around! That's funny! He's hanging around! Ha ha ha!"

'Yeah, this has gotta be the best issue ever! The first time ever that they've shown us Slayve's cock!'

And Fat Tulip closes the comic and puts it down beside her. Fat Tulip is sitting under her usual tree at the edge of the glade, and she is alone. As you ought to have worked out from the punctuation, Fat Tulip herself has been supplying Abigail's portion of the dialogue during the reading of the comic.

The reason for Abigail's absence is simple: for several days the girl had not been coming to the glade as usual, and so yesterday Fat Tulip had gone to Silver Street in search of her. She had found Abigail playing skipping rope with some of her friends. At first Abigail had pretended to ignore Fat Tulip, but when Fat Tulip had forced her to answer, the girl had turned on her and said she didn't want to play with Fat Tulip anymore. Fat Tulip was a weirdo, because everybody said she was. That's why she hadn't got any friends and hung around in the woods on her own. Abigail didn't want anything to do with a weirdo like Fat Tulip was and who wasn't a proper witch anyway.

And when Fat Tulip had accused Abigail of breaking her promise about not telling and for doing that told her she was going to put a spell on her, Abigail had just said no she wouldn't put a spell on her because she wasn't a proper witch so she couldn't really do spells and she didn't even have a broomstick because she was too fat to even ride on one. And then the other girls had joined in with the jeering, calling her Fat Tulip the phony witch, and Fat Tulip had just turned and walked away.

So now Fat Tulip is without an apprentice. Well, good. Fat Tulip doesn't need an apprentice. Especially not stupid little girl who can't keep secrets and who listens to what other people say about people and thinks that witches have cauldrons and fly around on broomsticks. Yes, Fat Tulip doesn't need a girl like that. She had made a useful servant for Fat Tulip, but Fat Tulip can survive without a servant, especially one as stupid and unreliable as Abigail was.

Pulling off her trainers and socks, Fat Tulip starts to dance around the glade, the hot August sun blazing down on her. Yes, she's totally happy on her own, she doesn't need Abigail and she doesn't need anybody else either. And if, as she dances her dance tears can be seen streaming down her face, then it's probably only because the pollen-count is high today.

Chapter Twenty-Two
Do the Evolution, Baby!

'...remains found in the Tsing-Tao province of two contemporaneous anthropoids. The brain pan of the ugh! female was substantially larger than that of the male, indicating a much higher level of intelligence. The ugh! generally accepted theory is that the fossils were examples of two distinct species that existed at the same time, and that the less intellectually developed species would ugh!

ultimately have become extinct, erased from the gene pool by their more highly-evolved cousins.

'My intention ugh! is to dispute this conclusion, and posit the theory that the two fossils were in fact the male and ugh! female examples of the same species. In support of this belief, I ugh! refer to the fact according to the known pattern of evolution, that it is the larger brain-capacity of the female fossil that is ugh! anomalous for the time-period, while the skull formation of the ugh! male corresponds with that of other remains from the same era, for example, the fossils discovered in Borneo and Mesopotamia.

'It is my contention ugh! that at this time there existed a race whose females had evolved a far greater level of ugh! intelligence than the males, and that the race was matriarchal, with the intellectually-superior females holding authority over ugh! the physically stronger males. This may sound like the stuff of b-movie science fiction, but I believe it to be quite possible that such a society could ugh! once have existed.

'We have always ugh! believed that even since our ancestors ugh! became social creatures that they always evolved ugh! patriarchal societies in which the physically stronger males dominated ugh! through that very physical supremacy—because ugh! for our ancestors as with the animal kingdom, physical ugh! strength was the only true power. That the society of intellectually superior females I am ugh! positing obviously did not survive, we know by the fact that it does not exist today. While the ugh! brains of the modern male and female Homo Sapiens may operate differently when it comes to certain specific functions, they are essentially the same. Therefore my theoretical ugh! matriarchal society must have existed alongside patriarchal societies in which ugh! male and female brain capacity were on the same level—and that this level of brain ugh! capacity would be the same ugh! level of the Tsing-Tao Man, and not the Tsing-Tao Woman.

'This brings us to ugh! the argument that if the less ugh! aggressive matriarchal society was overwhelmed by their ugh! more aggressive patriarchal rivals, are we to assume that ugh! patriarchy is therefore the "natural order of things"? I would argue not.

'First we have ugh! to ask the question, why ugh! would evolution have followed a path in which ugh! the brains of the females of one particular ugh! species evolved more rapidly than those of the males? What would be ugh! the practical benefits of such a discrepancy in ugh! aptitude? The obvious answer would be ugh! that a ruling female elite would have ugh! placed a restraint upon the inherent ugh! aggressiveness of the males. And ugh! how would the women exert this calming ugh! influence? If we ugh! look at the b-movie science fiction, the ugh! females would ugh! generally keep the males in check by ugh! degrading ugh! them, limiting their ugh! personal freedoms, and/or the use of ugh! superior technology or ugh! By extra-sensory mental ugh! control. In these speculative scenarios ugh! the males would be surly and ugh! resentful, forever on the verge of rebellion; but then ugh! we have to remember ugh! that the intention behind these fictions was usually ugh! reactionary in nature. But in the case of ugh! this theoretical prehistoric matriarchy, I would suggest a harmonious society, one in which the ugh! males willingly acquiesced to the ugh! females, whom they would have looked ugh! to as the tribe's natural ugh! administrators and decision makers. Having weaker ugh! mental skills themselves, they would naturally ugh! defer to the wiser females.

'But we have ugh! to acknowledge that ugh! even if a race such as ugh! I am here describing did ugh! indeed exist that ugh! they were in ugh! the minority, and that the ugh! warlike patriarchal tribes ugh!—by whom they must have been ugh! eventually annihilated—were vastly ugh! the majority. Then ugh! why was this ugh! so? Why ugh! did our ancestors evolve such aggressive ugh! natures? Ugh!

Was this a natural ugh! occurrence? Was it ugh! ugh! inevitable? We ugh! talk of ugh! much-abused ugh! terms like ugh! natural ugh! selection and ugh! survival of ugh! the fittest; ugh! is the ugh! course that ugh! evolution ugh! has taken ugh! on the ugh! surface of ugh! this ugh! planet the ugh! only course ugh! it *could* have taken? Is a peaceful ugh! society only ugh! something that ugh! can be ugh! arrived at ugh! after eons of ugh! bloodshed and ugh! extermination? If UGH! we look ugh! at contemporary UGH! society where ugh! we call ugh! ourselves ugh! civilised and ugh! pride ourselves ugh! on equality, UGH! war is still ugh! carried on ugh! wholesale? Is UGH! peace still UGH! to be looked UGH! upon UGH! UGH! as a distant UGH! goal? That UGH! UGH! we UGH! have not UGH! arrived at UGH! UGH! that state of UGH! evolution in UGH! which peace UGH! can be UGH! achieved? Or has UGH! human UGH! evolution UGH! been UGH! following UGH! a wrong UGH! path UGH! all UGH! along? UGH! could UGH! things UGH! UGH! have UGH! UGH! UGH! been UGH! UGH! differ-UGH!ent? If UGH! the UGH! UGH! matri-UGH!archy UGH! had UGH! UGH! survived, UGH! had UGH! become UGH! UGH! the UGH! norm, UGH! the UGH! UGH! whole UGH! of human UGH! evolution UGH! of UGH! UGH! human UGH! history UGH! UGH! UGH! would UGH! UGH! have UGH! UGH! followed *UGH! UGH! UGH! UGH! UUUUUUGGGGHHHHHAAAAAAAAHHHHHH...!*

'...a very different course...'

Chapter Twenty-Three
Drums Across the Suburbs

Orb, the implacable deity, gazes down on Bellend Close, annihilating it, crushing it under the weight of the prostrating humid air. The untended front lawns are a starved yellow, like transplanted fragments of African savannah.

Nothing moves, nothing stirs under that awful burden of light and heat. It has been like this for some time now, each day an empty void, the regular nine-to-five abandoned and forgotten. Beyond the precincts of the close life soldiers on as best it can under the oppressive heatwave, but here the street belongs to the birds and the insects, and only their voices can be heard. During the daylight hours, no human being is seen to set foot out of doors.

After dark, though, it is a different story—because after dark the drums start to sound.

There's something she needs to be doing.

Dodo and Mayumi, panting and post-coital, naked bodies drenched with sweat, lie side-by-side on storm-tossed sheets. The bedroom curtains, an ineffectual barrier against the heat, are closed, and an electric fan on the dressing table blows a sirocco of heated air around the room.

Brushing dripping bangs from her forehead with a movement of her hand, Dodo stares up the ceiling. She knows there is something she needs to be doing. Something, some information received that needs to be acted upon, some inquiry that needs to be made, some task that needs to be performed... But the details elude her...

What could it be? What could it be that is so important? So important that it should tear her away from Mayumi? How can *anything* be more important than the physical expression of their undying, unquenchable love for one another, endlessly, deliriously, reaffirmed?

Good question!

She tries to search her mind, to track down the elusive thought, but her dear, her cherished Mayumi keeps intruding herself between Dodo and other thoughts that are not of Mayumi; the smell of her sweat-soaked hair; the taste of the soles of her feet; the crease of skin that appears between her eyebrows when she comes; her dry, sleepy voice when she first wakes up and calls Dodo 'my master'... These thoughts, snapshots, recollected sensations of her darling Mayumi, keep coming between her and... and...

...*what* was it she was trying to think of...?

Across the landing, in another bedroom in which another electric fan blows hot around like a hair-dryer, lies Trina Truelove, also naked on a naked mattress, similarly drenched and exhausted from a surfeit of sexual pleasure.

Trina is the third wheel. For the past few days while Dodo and Mayumi have been locked in an endless cycle of passion, Trina has been frantically dildoing herself to the soundtrack of their lovemaking. Clitoris stimulation just hasn't been enough for her of late; she wants to be filled; she craves full vaginal orgasms.

Whether this craving has anything to do with her recent experience with Gerald Banbury, Trina couldn't tell you. She has been doing her best to erase the events that evening from her memory, so far without success.

Half the time it's like they forget she's even here, Dodo and Mayumi. When they're not going at it, they're either sleeping it off, or downstairs eating food, reenergising themselves for the next bout. That's all they do: an endless cycle of eating, sleeping and fucking.

They could at least have invited her to join them for a threesome. Every now and then at least. But do they? Not likely. Those two: they're so wrapped up in each other they forget she even exists.

And now darkness has fallen and the nocturnal denizens of the close emerge from their lairs in response to its summons of the tribal drums.

The drums seem to be coming from somewhere further down the street and on the other side of the road. The sound intrudes itself through the open windows of number twelve, urgent and visceral. The sound of the drums does not tempt Dodo and Mayumi to leave their nest and join whatever revelries are going on out there; but it imposes itself on them nonetheless; their lovemaking, slow and languorous during the heat of the day, aligns itself to the beat of the drums, becomes frantic, frenetic, a dervish-dance.

It is during a pause in this fervid lovemaking that Trina appears in the doorway, announcing her presence with a noisy clearing of the throat.

'Oh, hello there,' says Dodo, surprised. 'What's up? We didn't expect to see you back so soon.'

'I haven't *been* anywhere!' snaps Trina. 'I've been here all the time! All day every day.
And I'm feeling *lonely!*' plaintively. 'You could at least... you could...'

'What could we do? Just tell us and it's done!'

'You could... invite me to join you... you know... in bed... Just every now and then...'

Dodo looks at Mayumi. 'She's right. We've been neglecting her, haven't we?'

'We have,' confirms Mayumi.

'We're sorry, sweetheart,' says Dodo to Trina. 'Of course you can join us!' (Instantly, Trina is at the foot of the bed, panting with anticipation.) 'It's just that I'm finding it sort of hard to keep hold of thoughts at the moment...' continued Dodo. 'Things keep slipping away from me... Ah! That reminds me! There's something you told me... I think it was after your date with... whatsisname...? Gerald Banbury. Yes! It was something really important that you told me; I'm sure it was! But I just can't remember... Can *you* remember?

What was it you told me?'

'Well… I told you about him not having a cock…' offers Trina.

'No, not that! It was something *important!*'

'You don't call that important?'

'Well, yes, it is important—especially to him. But I meant it was something important that's to do with what's going on around here… I think it was something Gerald told you that night….'

'Oh, you mean about that Mhambi whatshername not really being a Zulu witchdoctor? That she'd been having you on about that?'

'Yes! That was it!' Dodo's eyes light up. She thumps the palm of her hand. The prompt being given, it all comes flooding back. 'She's not really a witchdoctor, and that hut in their garden was just part of some Allan Quatermain role-playing thing she had going on with her husband…! So, if she's not a witchdoctor, then she's not the one who conjured up those cavemen… She pretty much said so that night at the clearing, didn't she? She told her husband she wasn't the one who'd summoned them…'

'If she's not a witchdoctor then what are those drums all about?' asks Mayumi, practical as always.

'Yeah!' agrees Trina. 'And from my room you can see a light coming up from behind where her house is.' (Trina's bedroom faces the street; Dodo and Mayumi's the back garden.)

'True,' concedes Dodo. 'But then, tribal drumming doesn't necessarily mean any kind of ritual magic ceremony's going on… Oh!'

Trina feels something sharp poke her in the back. She turns to discover that the culprit is the point of a Zulu assegai, and the person wielding the assegai is Ramona Ghai, their neighbour from across the street. Ramona is naked, her face and body daubed with warpaint in colourful stripes and curlicues; but her warlike appearance and possession of a lethal weapon is pleasantly offset by the affable smile on her face. Flanking Ramona are two other women, likewise naked and bedaubed: Mary Marigold, a financier from number twenty-two, and Paula Preston from number five, a landscape gardener.

'Hello, ladies,' says Dodo. 'To what do we owe the pleasure of this visit?'

'We are here to invite you to join our queen at her revelries,' says Ramona.

'And who's your queen?' asks Dodo.

'Mhambi Khoza is our queen.'

'And is that spear you're carrying just a fashion accessory, or is it to let us know that our acceptance of this information is mandatory?'

'Your acceptance is mandatory, yes.'

'Well, that's fine with me. I wanted to have a word with Mhambi, anyway.'

'*Queen* Mhambi.'

Dressed just as they are, our three heroines are escorted down the street to Mhambi Khoza's house. Not a light shows in the windows of any house, and if it wasn't for the drums and the haze of firelight rising from behind Mhambi's house, the close would have seemed as deserted by night as it does during the day. They walk up the driveway, past the front door still emblazoned with the words 'BLACK BITCH' (that's *Queen* Black Bitch to you, buster!) and round to the back garden.

A surprise awaits them. Mhambi Khoza's back garden has become a lot bigger than it was the last time Dodo and Mayumi saw it. By the removal of the partition fences, the gardens of the four neighbouring properties (the nearest two on each side) have been incorporated into her own, and with the destruction of some flower borders and the felling of a tree or two, the whole has been levelled out into one vast open arena. Those felled trees are now doing good service as freestanding flaming torches, which placed at intervals around the edge of the open area, provide the lighting; while the dismantled fences have provided the source material for a wooden platform on which stands a throne, which has been constructed at the back of garden, commanding the whole prospect. Seated on this throne is the reigning queen of Bellend Close, Mhambi Khoza, who, like everyone else, is brightly bedaubed with warpaint; but the addition of her African jewellery and the plumed headdress adorning her head set her apart from her subjects. These subjects form the throng she looks down upon with satisfaction, watching as they dance, laugh, eat, drink and make love to one another. Conspicuous amongst the revellers is Patricia Pinecone who at first glance appears to be performing a mad dance with her husband's framed photograph as her dancing partner—but upon closer inspection she is actually swatting at a swarm of midges who seem to have singled her out for special attention.

    The sound of drums and the smell of cooking meat fill the air—and it is here that two aspects of modernity intrude themselves on the scene, for contrary to Dodo's expectations, the tribal drumming is not being performed live at all, but pre-recorded, is being piped through speakers attached to the rear wall of Mhambi's house; while the meat is not being cooked on a spit over an open fire, but on the modern charcoal grill standing on the patio; the same one that had provided the food on the occasion of Mhambi's afternoon garden party. And just as on that occasion, Gerald Banbury presides over the barbecue; a differently dressed Gerald, however: completely naked save for a loin cloth discreetly concealing his lack of manhood.

    The new arrivals are brought to a stop on the patio.

    'Wait here and I will advise our queen of your arrival,' says Ramona, and heads towards the platform.

    'Evening, ladies,' greets Gerald. 'I'm afraid I can't offer you any food, Dodo and Mayumi; no vegetarian option tonight. No demand for it anymore. So, unless you want to go with the flow and change your eating habits...?'

'No thanks, we're fine,' Dodo assures him.

'Can I tempt you, Trina? You're not a veggie, are you?'

Trina looks away, pointing her nose at the starry firmament.

'Oh, dear. Still in your bad books, I see. Well, if it makes you feel any better, I've played that same little trick on just about every woman you can see here tonight.'

'It doesn't!' declares Trina.

'I thought that might have been your little game,' says Dodo. And then: 'Wait a minute!' A sudden thought has struck Dodo, an alarming one. 'What exactly have you got cooking here?' scrutinising the meat spitting and crackling on the grill.

'Let me see... We've got pork ribs, hamburgers—oh, *I* get it! You thought we might have had something else on the menu, didn't you?' chuckles Banbury. 'Something a tad unorthodox? Well, you can relax: what you see before you are all just from animal carcasses; they haven't started eating their husbands. Not yet, anyway.'

'Then where *are* the husbands? I don't see them here...'

'I believe they're hiding out in some of the houses across the street, feeling sorry for themselves and licking their wounds. Well, no, not actually licking them,' chuckling again; 'that would be rather difficult, considering where the wounds are located. Rubbing ointment into them, shall we say...?'

'And meanwhile you're here playing court jester,' says Dodo.

'I'm not even that anymore,' counters Gerald, affecting a sorrowful tone. 'I'm just the kitchen staff. They've got themselves a new court jester. Look over there.'

Dodo looks. She sees Hom, Ploy and Dao, the three Thai brides, and with them, squatting like a monkey, a collar round his neck attached to a rope lead held by one of the women, is Mike Grimsby, wearing a grass skirt and a lei around his neck. The giggling women are teasing him with a banana, holding it out and then snatching it away when he jumps up to grab it.

'Mike Grimsby!' exclaims Dodo. 'What have they done to him?'

'They've hired him,' answers Gerald. 'I should explain: I'm afraid I told you a bit of fib when I said he was a newspaper journalist—'

'I know. He's a private detective.'

'Ah, you know that, do you? Well, it was the husbands of those fair ladies who originally retained his services. They suspected their wives of infidelity for some strange reason, and hired Grimsby to find out the who, when and where; but somehow the wives got wise to it all and they made Grimsby a counteroffer he just couldn't refuse, so now he's working for them instead.'

'He looks more like a pet than a court jester.'

Gerald shrugs. 'Well, whichever you want to call what he's doing, he's much better at it than he was at being a private investigator.'

At this juncture Ramona returns and announces that Mhambi requests Dodo's presence.

Turning to Mayumi and Trina: 'You two stay here,' says Dodo. '*Don't* get involved in the festivities, no matter how tempted you might be.'

'Can't we even dance for a bit?' asks Trina.

'No. *Especially* no dancing. Dancing is off. Got it?'

Mayumi and Trina make noises of acquiescence and Dodo follows Ramona to the wooden dais and up the steps to the throne where Mhambi Khoza sits in state, dignified and naked, the swirls and stripes of warpaint stark against her ebony body. She greets Dodo with a smile which, friendly enough, seems somehow more distant than any Dodo has received from the woman in the past.

'You may leave us,' she says to Ramona.

'Yes, your highness.' Bowing, Ramona departs

'A pleasure to see you, Dodo,' says Mhambi graciously. 'It's been a while now, hasn't it? Not since the evening you dropped by my hut, I think.'

'Yes, and speaking of that hut,' says Dodo. (She can see the hut in question now, still there at the back of the garden, but overshadowed by the structure of the throne and its platform.) 'Your so-called "Zulu witchdoctor's hut," which I've since found out is nothing of the sort, but is really just a bloody *King Solomon's Mines* sexual role-playing hut!'

'Not *King Solomon's Mines* actually, but one of the other Allan Quatermain books—'

'Never mind which book it's from. The point is, you were leading me up the garden path when you told me all that bullcrap about your being a practicing Zulu witchdoctor, weren't you?'

'I'm afraid I was,' confesses Mhambi.

'Which means you've known all along why I'm really here, don't you? I *thought* you might have, but I wasn't... So that idiot husband of yours went and told you, did he?'

'In fairness to my idiot husband, he didn't intentionally blow your cover; it was just that he'd told me a long time ago about the association between his boss Mark Hunter and the TV psychologist Dodo Dupont; so when that same celebrity suddenly decided to move to the neighbourhood I didn't have much trouble putting two and two together.'

Dodo sighs. 'Brilliant. So thanks to him my cover was blown before I even got here... I *thought* you might be onto me, but I still believed your witchdoctor story... I thought that explained everything; that you'd used your magic to make those caveman lovers of yours appear; but then you said you weren't the one that summoned them...'

Mhambi looks at her. 'Did I? I don't recall ever telling you that.'

'Not directly, you didn't; but Yumi and me were there at the clearing in the woods the night you got abducted.'

'Really? You were there?'

'Yes, but we cleared off when your rescue party arrived.'

'Then you missed the best part!' smiles Mhambi.

'Yeah, me and Yumi aren't really into watching the guy-on-guy action. But, question: if you didn't summon those beasts, then who *did?*'

'I *can* summon them, of course; we all can. But no, I'm not the one who made them appear in the first instance, and I've no idea who did.'

'What?' exclaims Dodo. 'You don't know? Seriously?'

'I don't know. Seriously. Perhaps it wasn't anyone. Perhaps it was something that just… *happened*…'

'No…' says Dodo. 'No, somebody's got to be behind all of this…' Her eyes range across the firelit garden, seeking a particular face and body amongst the throng… She doesn't find what she's looking for but she spots one woman, small and obese, her face hidden behind an African mask. She stands by herself, this woman, at the very edge of the lighted area, an observer of the festivities rather than a participant…

'Erm, if I could have your attention, please?' Dodo turns back to Mhambi's sardonically smiling face. 'I've yet to explain why I invited you here tonight. It wasn't just for the chat we've just had: I have a proposition to make to you.'

'Oh, yes?'

'Yes. I want you to join our ranks. You and your two friends.'

'Yumi is more than just my friend, she's my partner, and I don't want any others, thank you. Look, you know why I came here; I'm trying to stop what's going on around here—and I'll admit I haven't done a very good job of it, because all that's happened is that things have spiralled completely out of control. Surely you can see that, can't you? That this has gone way too far? I mean look at you: sitting on a throne and calling yourself a queen!'

'I *am* a queen,' says Mhambi, her expression hardening.

Dodo looks at her. 'You really are far gone, aren't you?

And what are you doing in this little queendom of yours? You're just fucking. Fucking, fucking and more fucking. All day every day, a nonstop fuck-fest.'

'And what have you been doing the past few days?' challenges Mhambi.

'Well, I—that's not—!' splutters Dodo. 'Look: that's because of you lot, polluting the air with your vibes! You've got us all permanently on heat. And what's more, there's more to life than just fucking!'

'No there isn't,' is the calm reply. 'Fucking is all there is; fucking is everything there needs to be. And with our Friends we have found our perfect sexual partners. They are physically perfect, generously endowed, possessed of tremendous stamina; almost zero recovery time. They obey us, they excite us to a frenzy and fuck us like we've never been fucked before—*and they don't talk*. What more could a woman ask for?'

'I could think of quite a few things, actually,' responds Dodo. 'For one thing: you say they're physically perfect, but not everyone goes for that kind of overdeveloped musclebound physique.'

'If you didn't before, you soon will come to prefer that type of physique,' Mhambi tells her. 'It may be an acquired taste, but it's very quickly acquired.'

'I have no intention of acquiring it. And what is it about their faces? It's like you can never really see them properly.'

'That's because their faces don't matter. Faces are for distinguishing individuals, and our Friends have no individuality, no personality; they are just fucking machines, creatures of instinct that exist for our pleasure.'

'So, they're all exactly the same, then?'

'Well, yes, but there are too types: the regular and the extra-large. I'm talking about penis size here. The extra-large are for external use only; they are too big for penetrative sex.'

'And why would nature create a male whose genitalia

was too large to safely penetrate the female?'

'That's just my point. They were not created by nature for penetrative sex; they were created for our pleasure.'

'Well, I must say it's very generous of nature to start thinking outside the box like that,' remarks Dodo.

'Quite so. But now, it's time for me to really kick things off,' says Mhambi. She rises from her throne and stamps an imperative foot on the platform, three times: one! two! three! At this signal the music ceases, and the assembled women become still and silent. All eyes are turned to Queen Mhambi.

'My sisters!' she booms. 'The night belongs to us! We will now commence the festivities!'

The drums recommence, but now with a different rhythm, even more powerful, even more erotically charged. The women quickly form a human chain, each with her hands around the waist of the person in front. And now they begin to chant.

'Fuck! Cock! Cunt!
Fuck! Cock! Cunt!
Fuck! Cock! Cunt!
Fuck! Cock! Cunt!'

The human chain becomes a sinuous dance, the women repeating their mantra over and over in time to the beat of the drums. At the head of the line Patricia Pinecone holds her husband's picture aloft as she leads the dance.

'Fuck! Cock! Cunt!
Fuck! Cock! Cunt!
Fuck! Cock! Cunt!
Fuck! Cock! Cunt!'

'Catchy little number, isn't it?' says Queen Mhambi. 'This is it. This is how we summon our Friends. They will be here very soon, and tonight you and your friends will have your initiation; you will join the festivities and you will become like us; and after tonight you will all belong with us, body and soul.'

'No thanks,' says Dodo. 'We're not interested in joining your club.'

'I'd speak for yourself, if I were you,' says Mhambi. 'Look.'

Dodo looks: and there at the end of the dancing human chain are Mayumi and Trina, both of them vigorously kicking out with their legs and chanting along!

'Oh, those stupid—!'

And Dodo, practically leaping from the platform, makes a beeline for Mayumi and Trina. Not one minute! She can't leave them alone for one single minute! Queen Mhambi has completely lost it, those hairy studs are about to turn up, and if they end up getting caught up in the ensuing orgy, that will be it! They have to get out of here, and they have to get out right now!

'What did I tell you two about not dancing?' she grates, pulling Mayumi and Trina out of the human chain, and giving them a shaking for good measure.

'Sorry!' apologises Mayumi, contritely. 'We kind of got caught up in the moment.'

'Well, we're all going to get "caught up in the moment" for good if we don't get out of here pretty quickly!' avers Dodo. And then: 'If it's not already too late.'

Mayumi looks where Dodo is looking. Large, hulking forms are starting to appear out of the darkness, lumbering towards the dancing throng.

'Come on!'

Dodo grabs Mayumi's hand and starts running towards the house. She then realises Trina is not with them. She stops, turns and sees that Trina has rejoined the dancing human chain. Muttering words not at all complimentary to Trina, Dodo runs back, grabs the errant photographic assistant, spins her round, and punches her under the jaw. Throwing the stunned girl over her shoulder, she runs back to Mayumi. By now, the creatures are closing in fast on all sides.

Just in time, they make it out of the garden and round the side of the house.

'Phew!' says Dodo, as they emerge onto the lamplit street. 'Come on, sweetheart; don't stop running! Let's get home and make sure we lock all the doors. I think we're safe enough for the rest of tonight, but we won't take any chances. And then tomorrow, tomorrow we have a very important call to make—and I don't intend to forget about my priorities this time!'

Chapter Twenty-Four
The Unlimited Cream Company

There's something she needs to be doing.

Dodo, Mayumi and Trina, panting and post-coital, naked bodies drenched with sweat, lie side-by-side on storm-tossed sheets. The bedroom curtains, an ineffectual barrier against the heat, are closed, and an electric fan on the dressing table blows a sirocco of heated air around the room.

Brushing dripping bangs from her forehead with a movement of her hand, Dodo stares up at the ceiling. She knows there is something she needs to be doing. Something, some information received that needs to be acted upon, some inquiry that needs to be made, some task that needs to be performed... But the details elude her...

She also has the distinct feeling that she has been here before, that history is repeating itself...

She looks at Trina, and wonders how the girl has come to be there with them... Her memories are of just Yumi and herself endlessly making love; but now suddenly, out of nowhere it seems, Trina has joined them, becoming a third participant... Dodo has nothing against Trina; a lovely girl; and she has nothing against threesomes either, not too often, but just every now and then... But...

Her eyes wonder down to Trina's crotch, where strap-on Mark points proudly in the air. Yes, Trina has grown rather attached to Mark, since having been introduced. Yes, she's always had the hots for Mark Hunter, so of course she was thrilled to meet his penis, if only in life-sized effigy; but that being the case, you'd have thought she would have relished more being the recipient of Mark, rather than the operator. And at first that was just what she *did* like; but now, since having taken over the controls, she seems to be getting more of a kick out of *being* Mark than being done by him...

Maybe it's not Mark at all. Maybe she's still hung up on her Gerald Banbury experience, and now she is as it were compensating for *his* lack of manhood. Now, this may sound bizarre to the layperson, but an expert like Dodo can tell you that when it comes to the twists and turns of the human mind, *nothing* is too bizarre.

And if that is what she's doing, it suggests Trina has more sympathy for poor Gerald than she realises herself... Gerald. Gerald Banbury. Gerald Banbury who'd told Trina the truth about Mhambi Khoza's Zulu hut, about how it wasn't a witchdoctor's hut at all, because Mhambi Khoza wasn't really a witch doctor, and because she wasn't really a witch doctor, she wasn't the one responsible for making the Beasts of Bellend appear, and if it wasn't Mhambi then logically there's only one other person it could be, and that's why Dodo needed to get over there as soon as possible and why she mustn't let this important task slip from her mind and end up spending all day fucking in bed instead of—

Shit!

'Now listen, you two! This is important! We've got to get our shit together and stay focused. I know it's bloody hot out there, but we've got to go right *now*. It's only during daylight we can be sure of getting where we're going to without being stopped by Mhambi and her gang of painted ladies. We can't let the daylight slip past us, because if we put this off till nightfall we are going to be in serious danger—!'

Nightfall.

Dodo and Mayumi step out through the front door. The music of the drums, the nightly muster call from Queen Mhambi to her subjects, has begun. There is no sign of activity in the street. Dodo locks the front door and then goes to place the key in—in what? She looks first down at her naked pelvis, and then at Mayumi.

'Didn't we used to have… have…?'

'Clothes,' supplies Mayumi.

'I was going to say "pockets" actually. But yes, it was the clothes that had the pockets in them, wasn't it?' She holds up the key. 'So, what are we going to do with this? I don't want to be carrying it around all evening.'

They think about this.

'I know!' says Mayumi. 'Under the doormat! You always put the spare key under the doormat!'

'Great, except that we haven't got a doormat,' says Dodo, indicating the unadorned threshold.

Some more thinking.

'I know!' says Mayumi again. Grinning, she takes the key from Dodo's hand and, emphasising every gesture in the manner of someone giving a demonstration, she opens the letterbox and drops the key through it. Expecting a look of smiling admiration from her lover, she is disappointed to see instead an expression that can only be described as pained.

'Why did you just do that, Yumi?'

'Simple!' declares Mayumi. 'We don't need to take the key with us! We just ring the doorbell when we come back and Trina can let us in!'

'Sweetheart,' says Dodo, laying a hand on Mayumi's shoulder, 'we just left Trina completely tied up. You tied her up yourself, remember? She *can't* let us in.'

'Whoops,' says Mayumi.

They had been left with no choice but to tie up Trina, or

they would never have set off. Refusing to relinquish strap-on Mark, Trina seemed to have become possessed by her acquired manhood, and like Burt Kwouk in a Pink Panther film, had taken to leaping out from unexpected places and attacking Dodo and Mayumi. In the end they had had to overpower her, securely bind her and remove strap-on Mark from around her loins. (Trina had more strenuously objected to the latter operation than the former.)

'Never mind,' says Dodo. 'We'll just have to break in when we get back, that's all. But for now, let's get a move on.'

Mayumi salutes. 'Agent Mayumi, ready for duty!' she says.

Dodo returns the salute. 'Good show, Agent Mayumi. With any luck this will be the final stage of our assignment.'

And hand in hand, the two women set off along the lamplit close, the pavement warm beneath their feet. Not a light shows in the window in any of the houses, a fact which does not mean that none of the houses are occupied; but electric light seems to have gone out of fashion of late; even at number twelve they haven't been using the lights at all.

The drum music grows louder as they draw closer to Mhambi Khoza's house.

'We should be alright,' murmurs Dodo. 'It's not as though they'll have lookouts posted or anything, and they'll be busy stuffing their faces and warming up for the evening fuck-fest. If anyone *does* see us it'll just be bad luck—which we do seem to have been having more than our fair share of today.'

However, they pass the Khoza residence without incident and very soon the curve of the road conceals the house from view.

'That's that, then,' says Dodo, expressing the relief they both feel. 'Looks like we're home free now. We can relax.'

And if any further proof was needed that Dodo, under the influence of the prevailing atmosphere of Bellend Close, is 'off her game' at the moment, then this is it; because under normal circumstances, Dodo, with her ample experience of the espionage business, really ought to have known better than to so recklessly tempt fate by saying something like that.

For behold: from the shadows three gaunt, ragged men appear, blocking their path; three of the abused and neglected husbands, saddle-sore and sullen, fast reverting to a state of misogynistic savagery. Each of the three men is armed: the first with a driver, the second with a 5-iron, the third with a 9-iron. Clothes in tatters, hair unkempt and chins unshaven, the men glare hollow-eyed at Dodo and Mayumi with faces bitter and resentful.

'Look guys, we're not your enemies,' says Dodo. 'We're not with Queen Mhambi and her crowd. See? No warpaint,' indicating hers and Mayumi's unadorned selves. 'We're the newcomers to the neighbourhood, remember? And we're here to try and sort this mess out; and in fact we're on our way now to where we can hopefully do just that. So if you'll just let us—'

'The enemy...' intones one of the men.

'The enemy...' intone the second and third men.

'No, we're not your enemy,' repeats Dodo patiently. 'I have no wish to harm you, but you have to let us pass or—'

The leading man swings at them with the driver. Dodo's response is rapid and decisive: and with a whirl of naked limbs, she flies at the assailants, and in a trice they are all lying on the ground, stunned, bloody-nosed and broken-ribbed.

Dodo's face assumes a look of displeasure as she looks down at the results of her violence. 'I enjoyed doing that a bit too much...' she says.

'I enjoyed watching you!' grins Mayumi.

Dodo takes her hand, smiles. 'Then we're both in the wrong, aren't we? Come on, let's hurry up and try and sort this mess out once and for all, while we're still capable of cognitive thought.'

They set off running and soon reach their destination, the house at the end of the close whose front door is bears the graffitied legend 'PROFESSOR PISS PUDDLE.' The house, like all its neighbours, is in darkness. Dodo and Mayumi, slowing to a brisk walk, make their way around the back and head straight across the lawn to the laboratory.

It has to be Nanette Aubergine. Dodo is sure of it. The geneticist who has been searching for the missing link; it's too much of a coincidence. On the last occasion she had seen her, Dodo had joked with the Professor about discovering caveman DNA and making use of it to clone cavemen and open a caveman theme park. Yes, she'd joked about it, but now it looks like that is exactly what Nanette has been doing all along.

Except for the bit about opening a theme park.

Dodo and Mayumi approach the bunker-like building at the end of the garden; being windowless, its outer aspect gives no indication as to whether or not anyone's home.

'You think she'll be there?' asks Mayumi.

'I'm hoping she will be,' says Dodo.

'She might have gone to the party.'

'I don't think so. She wasn't there last night, anyway. I looked for her and I didn't see her. The only woman in the close who wasn't there.'

'What if she won't let us in?'

This proves not to be an issue as, the moment they reach the entrance, the door slides open to admit them.

'Looks like we were expected,' says Dodo.

They step inside. The normally brightly-lit laboratory is this time in near-darkness. Its one source of light the display of the desktop computer, the room is silent and at first glance, unoccupied.

'Hello?' calls out Dodo. 'Nanette? Are you here? It's Dodo and Mayumi.'

There is no response.

'Okay; maybe we *weren't* expected. Come on: let's take advantage of the professor's absence and have a nose around.'

They cross the room. Bleeping sounds alert them to the arrival of Darwin and Huxley, the cleaning robots. The robots are following close at their heels, cleaning up the trail of dirty footprints they are leaving on the tiles. Drawing level with them the little robots begin butting against their feet, bleeping at them with what sounds very like petulance.

'Are they ticking us off for walking in with dirty bare feet?' wonders Dodo.

'Maybe they just want to clean them,' suggests Mayumi. She presents the sole of one foot and sure enough Darwin (or is it Huxley?) moves in and Mayumi feels her foot being energetically sponged by a spinning brush. She giggles. 'It works!'

Dodo lifts her own foot and now receives the same service from the other robot. 'Actually, considering her unorthodox toilet habits, it makes sense that Nanette would program these things to do feet,' she observes.

Their feet washed and blow-dried, they resume their course across the vacant portion of the room.

'What the hell…?' says Dodo, suddenly stopping in her tracks. 'Look at the walls!'

Mayumi looks. The walls of the laboratory it will be remembered, are panelled floor-to-ceiling with whiteboards. Although only dimly visible in the uncertain light, it can be seen that the calculations, equations, graphs and charts that had previously filled those boards have been erased, and in their place now stands a gallery of penises; larger-than-life marker-pen penises. Penises in portrait, penises in profile; penises pissing, penises ejaculating. Penis after penis after penis, all lovingly rendered, perfect in every detail.

'Someone's got cock on the brain,' says Mayumi.

'Well, technically *everyone's* got cock on the brain around here,' says Dodo. 'Therein lies the problem; and it's looking more and more like I was right about who we've got to thank for it. But where is she...?'

The computer screen, when they reach it, they discover to be displaying the image of yet another phallus: this one a bronze statuette of a penis, standing on a base formed by the testicles.

'I know what that is,' says Dodo. 'That's the penis statue Nanette told us about; the one she went and lost. Funny... I'd swear I've never seen this statue before, not even a picture of it, but somehow it looks familiar...' Dodo hunkers down to inspect the image more closely. 'It's the shape of the thing... Where have I seen something like this...? I know! Oh, Christ!'

'What's wrong?' asks Mayumi, leaning forward to look at the screen.

'Don't you see? The shape of the statuette, the outline: it's identical to the one in the satellite photos! The one in the clearing in the woods! Look at it, Yumi! It's just the same! Every single detail; I'd swear it is!'

'You're right,' confirms Mayumi, peering over her shoulder. 'It's the same cock.'

Dodo looks at her. 'You know what this might mean? It might mean I've got it all wrong *again*. I thought Nanette must be making caveman clones, but now I'm thinking we've come to the wrong place, and maybe it *is* magic that's behind all this after all, and not science... Come on, let's just check the lab equipment first.'

They move over to the equipment bench. Dodo peers through the viewer of the DNA analyser, the device Nanette had been operating on the occasion of her last visit. The machine is inactive. They walk along the bench, Dodo inspecting each piece of equipment.

'No...' she says. 'There's no cloning machine amongst this lot...'

'You know what a cloning machine looks like?' challenges Mayumi.

'Of course I know what a cloning machine looks like! Plus, a cloning machine has to be at least as big as whatever it is you want to clone, and I don't see any caveman sized piece of equipment here; do you?'

Mayumi admits that she does not. 'So you don't think Professor Aubergine's the bad guy?'

'No, I do think it *is* her, but I don't think she's been using cloning to create the beasts; I think she's using magic and I think the place where it's all happening is not here but at that clearing in the woods.'

'Erm, are you sure about that…?' says Mayumi in a strange tone.

It is the smell that alerts them to the situation: that same overpowering masculine aroma they have experienced before; it quickly permeates the lab. And then, shapes begin to take form; a ring of shadows, humanoid shadows, visible against the whiteboard walls of the room; shadows that soon begin to solidify.

'Come on!'

Dodo grabs Mayumi's hand and they run for the door—but creatures have appeared there as well, one of them manifesting itself between the two women and the exit. They skid to a halt in the middle of the vacant floorspace. They are surrounded; they are at the centre of a ring of fast-materialising beast-men.

Dodo hugs Mayumi tightly against her chest.

'Just keep still, sweetheart…'

And now they have fully materialised, those musclebound hirsute bodies, each one identical to the one beside it—and they stand motionless; they make no threatening gesture. As always, the heads of the creatures remain shadows, no details allow themselves to be discerned; but even so Dodo can feel that they are watching, that all of them have their attention fixed upon Mayumi and herself. A soft growling sound emanates from the creatures, slow relaxed, more like respiration than anything else, and no more threatening than the purring of a cat.

'It's okay,' breathes Dodo. 'I'm pretty sure they're not going to hurt us…'

'Yeah, but they might fuck us,' says Mayumi, all in a whisper. 'And didn't you say if the beasts fuck us, we'll be like all the other women?'

'I don't think they plan to fuck us,' replies Dodo. 'Mhambi Khoza told me something last night: she said that these creatures come in two varieties; regular and extra-large. And the extra-large are for external use only. I think these gentlemen are all extra-largers.'

'You sure?'

'Well look at them, sweetheart: their cocks are practically knee-length. They're much more well-hung than the ones we saw in the woods that night; and apparently these extra-largers don't even try to fuck you; they know they're too big for that.'

While speaking, Dodo and Mayumi have both been staring at the same one creature, and as if in response to their gaze, its penis comes to life, swiftly filling out, thickening, lengthening, rising, until it is fully tumescent.

'No way…' breathes Mayumi.

'Jesus fucking Christ…' breathes Dodo.

They contemplate the spectacle in silence for a while.

'Yumi?' says Dodo.

'Yes?' says Mayumi.

'Do you get the feeling that cock wants us to come over there and introduce ourselves?' asks Dodo.

'For sure,' answers Mayumi.

'And do you think we should?' asks Dodo.

'I think we should,' answers Mayumi.

Hand in hand, they walk up to the aroused creature and drop to their knees before the rampant extra-large. With exploring hands caress the velvet-glove surface of the shaft, then with gripping fingers, grasp the iron fist.

'This is like cock times a thousand,' says Mayumi.

'Yes, I think we may be looking at the Ideal Cock; the cock of which all other cocks are just mere reflections,' says Dodo.

'The Ideal Cock?' says Mayumi, repeating the capital letters.

'It's from Plato. He believed that everything had an Ideal template that mere mortals were never privileged to see,' says Dodo.

'Including cocks?' says Mayumi.

'Including cocks. So yes, this must be the Platonic cock,' says Dodo.

'I thought platonic meant when you're just friends with someone and don't fuck them,' says Mayumi.

'I meant Platonic in the sense that comes from Plato's writings. Mind you, I suppose you *could* say it's a Platonic cock in the platonic relationship sense, as well. It's too big to actually have sex with,' says Dodo.

'External us only,' says Mayumi.

'Yes, so really we can only be good friends with it,' says Dodo.

'Let's make our friend come,' says Mayumi.

'Yes, let's,' agrees Dodo.

And this they do (platonically of course!), manipulating the cock until it ejaculates, sending a three-stage geyser of semen across the room, splashing onto the tiles. The creature, the appendage to the penis, has remained standing passively throughout this operation.

'Impressive range,' says Dodo. And then: 'Hello!'

The next penis along, unbidden, is now awakening into tumescence; and then, the moment it achieves this happy state, the next penis after that starts to rise; and then the next, and then the next, until the whole circle of cocks has become fine upstanding citizens.

'You have to admire the choreography that went into that,' says Dodo, impressed.

'Let's jerk off all of them,' says Mayumi, straight to

practicalities as always.

They move on to the next cock. This one Dodo caps with her hand at the moment of orgasm. She feels the geyser jetting against her palm, sending the eruption of semen back along the shaft of the cock and spraying into the air between her fingers. The two women lick the cock clean, lapping up the warm semen, from root to fruit, one on each side. Their creamy lips meet and they fall into an embrace, and the embrace becomes a tussle, and rolling along the floor they arrive at the next cock.

'I'm gunna do this one with my feet!' says Mayumi, and raising her legs, she grips the penis between the balls of her feet.

Dodo helps her out manually, and when the moment of crisis comes, Mayumi receives the blast full against the soles of her feet, and it streams down her legs in a torrent. Dodo hungrily licks them clean.

And then: 'I know!' says Mayumi, taking hold of the next cock. 'You go over there and we see if we can hit each other!'

'A cock shootout?' says Dodo, grinning. 'Why not?'

She sets off across the room.

'Hey!' calls out Mayumi.

Dodo stops, turns and receives a spray of semen right in her face! Mayumi, triumphant, howls with laughter!

'You... *bitch!*' cries Dodo, cum-drenched. And then, making a rapid decision: 'Right! This is war!'

She runs to the next cock, pumps it fast and hard, and locking onto her target, fires a broadside. Mayumi, a willing target, takes the full blast.

This is just the start. Running from cock to cock, the two women fire salvo after salvo at each other, giggling like schoolgirls in a pillow fight, until they have discharged every weapon in the arsenal.

And now they are skidding sliding across slippery semen

floor, tumbling they are in frantic embrace and writhing and squirming with creamy frothy bodies rolling and rolling under ivory rainfall, rainfall of cocks gripped in hairy hands, slippery sliding, licking lips sticking, back to front and front to back, rubbing groins, lubricated loins firing piss-streams of lady-love slippy fingers sliding into creamy caverns deep deep sloppy licking and laughing coming and cumming twisting and writhing and floating up high in toss tossed warm spermy ocean rising fast foaming and swirling and whirling and cum after cum in dizzy dizzy whirlpool of love love love higher and higher oh my darling my master faster faster *faster—!*

The laboratory door bursts open, and a tidal wave of semen rushes out into the moonlit garden, and with it comes Dodo and Mayumi, the ivory tide carrying them right across the lawn until it leaves lying prone on the grass, side by side, panting and exhausted, delirious in the afterglow of satisfied bliss.

And they start to laugh. They laugh and they laugh and it's the pure innocent laughter that they laugh, the childlike laughter of unadulterated *joie de vivre*, of blissful, ecstatic happiness.

Chapter Twenty-Five
Finished – Or, We'll Never Be Oopart

Several buckets of water later, and Dodo and Mayumi have rinsed themselves squeaky clean, both hair and bodies cleansed; the venue for these ablutions being the paving of the patio. By now the semen spill from the lab is starting to be absorbed into the lawn, and whether the parched grass will be any the better for this inundation I am not enough of a botanist to be able to say. Also ejected from the laboratory along with the two women were Darwin and Huxley, the cleaning robots, who now lie inert on the lawn. Poor things! They just couldn't cope with the workload and they've blown their circuits!

(They have already checked inside the lab and the beasts have disappeared.

Dodo: 'D'you think our audience enjoyed the show?'

Mayumi: 'They were all pulling for us.')

'Before we go to the woods,' says Dodo now, 'I just want to check inside the house and make sure that nobody's home.'

Downstairs there *is* nobody home, but ascending to the first floor, the sound of snoring reaches their ears: that softer, more delicate female version of snoring. Tracing this sound to an open bedroom door, they look inside and discover within Professor Nanette Aubergine, sprawled naked on her own bed, sleeping the sleep of the exhausted.

Impatient of any ceremony, Dodo just switches on the light. The result is instantaneous: Nanette shoots up as though galvanised into a sitting position. Voicing the obligatory 'who? what? where?' noises, she blinks groggily at the women standing in the doorway, and then reaches for her glasses reposing on the bedside cabinet. She puts them on and has another go at looking.

'Oh, it's Dodo and Mayumi!' she exclaims, face lighting up. 'How lovely to see you both! How have you been keeping?'

'Never mind how we've been keeping,' replies Dodo tersely. 'Where's your penis?'

'My penis?' confused.

'The Bronze Penis; your statuette.'

'Oh, that! I'm sorry, but I still haven't found it.'

'Rubbish. You never lost it. You've had it all along. And you've been using it, haven't you?'

'No, I have not! That would be very unhygienic!'

'I don't mean using it for that. Now stop playing around and tell me *where is it?*'

'But I tell you I *don't know* where the wretched thing is!' insists Nanette. 'And why are you being so hostile all of a sudden?

'Because we're onto you, that's why. You're the one responsible for everything that's been going on around here. You've been using that penis statue to summon those cavemen or whatever they are. Don't deny it.'

'Summoning the cave—?' Nanette rubs her disordered hair. 'What are you talking about, Dodo? I wasn't the one who caused those brutes to start turning up; how could I have? And with the penis statue…? It's just a lump of bronze!'

'It's not just a lump of bronze; it's a powerful magic object, and you've been using that magic to summon the creatures. Now where is it? Is it here, or have you got it hidden somewhere in the glade in the woods?'

'But I haven't got the thing, I tell you! I'm a scientist and I don't know anything about magic and I don't know anything about any glade in the woods, and I wish you'd stop bullying me!'

She bursts into tears, burying her face in her hands.

Mayumi squeezes Dodo's arm. 'Go easy on her,' she admonishes. 'I think she's telling the truth.'

Dodo sighs. 'Yes, I think you're right…'

Followed by Mayumi, Dodo walks over to the bed and sits down on it beside Nanette, who, with a renewed outbreak of tears, falls into Dodo's arms.

'I'm sorry,' says Dodo, hugging her. 'I thought you were the culprit because I just couldn't see how it could be anyone else. But it looks like I'm wrong, and I'm sorry. If the statue really is missing, then that means somebody else must have got hold of it… I just can't think who it could be…'

'Mhambi Khoza,' says Mayumi.

'Yes, she's the obvious suspect,' agrees Dodo. 'Except

that she denies being the one who summoned the beasts in the first place, and I just can't see any reason why she'd feel the need to lie about that… So, if it *isn't* her…'

'My daughter…' sniffles Nanette.

'Your *daughter?*' Dodo looks at Nanette, who nods her head in tearful confirmation.

'Yes, she's into magic… You know, Wicca and all that neopagan business… And if anyone could have got hold of my statue, it would be her, wouldn't it?'

'Your daughter… Christ, I never even considered her; but then I've even seen her… Where is she now? Do you know?'

'No idea. I never know what that child's up to; in and out the house as much as she pleases…'

'Where's her bedroom? Let's check there first.'

Nanette leads them across the landing.

'This is her room.' She knocks on the door. 'Tulip? Tulip, darling? Are you in there?'

'Tulip?' echoes Dodo, frowning. 'Is that her name?'

'Yes. Haven't I told you that before?'

'I thought you *hadn't* ever told me your daughter's name, but Tulip rings a bell, so maybe you did…'

Nanette opens the bedroom door and switches on the light.

'No, she's not here…'

A poster on the wall facing the door immediately catches Dodo's eye. A colourful, giant-sized poster of a comic book barbarian wielding a battleaxe. She recognises the character at once: Slayve the Barbarian.

Slayve the Barbarian…

Slayve the Barbarian!

Now Dodo remembers. 'Is your daughter a girl with glasses and sort of bobbed hair and is a bit on the stocky side?' she demands urgently.

'Yes, that's her. You've met her then, have you?'

'I have! And it was at that clearing in the woods; the place that has to be the epicentre of all this! I didn't know she was your daughter, though, because she lied to me. She was with another girl she said was her sister…!'

'No, she hasn't got a sister; she's my only child.'

'Oh, that lying little—! Come on; we've got to get to that clearing!'

Yes! To the clearing! Clearly they have got to get to the clearing! They set off forthwith, our two valiant heroines and the absent-minded geneticist, into the precincts of Bellend Wood, first following the footpath and then striking off into the trees, keeping up what is known as a 'brisk pace.'

Dodo explains the situation to Nanette as they go along.

'It occurs to me that she might not even be there in the woods,' says Dodo. 'I was at one of Queen Mhambi's orgies last night and I think I caught sight of her there. She was wearing a mask though, some I'm not certain.'

'What?' exclaims Nanette. 'At one of those bacchanalias? Then I shall have to have words with that young lady; she's way too young to be going to places like that!'

Dodo smiles. 'Well, if it will set your mind at rest, I think she was only there as a spectator. That's what it looked like, anyway.'

They reach the glade, and they see at once that they have come to the right place, because there, out in the open, dancing under the light of moon is Fat Tulip, naked except for her face an African mask concealing her face; the same one Dodo had seen her wearing the night before. So wrapped up in her dance is Fat Tulip that she completely fails to spot the three newcomers until they are within throat-clearing distance.

Hearing the sound of approaching newcomers, she freezes to the spot mid-pirouette in a position that makes Mayumi think of the Karate Kid.

'You've got a lot of explaining to do, young woman,' declares Nanette, hands on hips, fixing the ceremonial headgear with a severe expression.

A pause, and then: 'Infidels! How do you violate this holy place! Begone, or you shall face the wrath of Quetzalcoatl!'

'Don't you Quetzalcoatl me, Tulip Aubergine. Since when did you start worshipping Quetzalcoatl? And what's more, Quetzalcoatl is an Aztec god, and that's a Zulu mask you're wearing, which makes what you are doing a blatant act of cultural misappropriation!'

'I know not of any Tulip Aubergine! I am Quet—!'

'Look, I think I know my own daughter when I see her, Zulu mask or no Zulu mask!'

'Well, I'm surprised you even recognize me at all!' humphs Fat Tulip, throwing the mask aside and fixing her mother with a sulky pout. 'Seeing as you hardly ever even set eyes on me!'

'Well, I've been busy in the lab, recently...' replies Nanette, discomfited by the sudden accusation.

'You're always busy in the lab!' retorts Fat Tulip. 'You've never got any time for me, have you? I might as well not exist as far as you're concerned!'

'But... but darling, I thought I was just giving you your space! I didn't want to be one of those controlling parents! Because I know you're at that age—'

'Excuse me,' interjects Dodo firmly. 'I hate to cut in and I appreciate that the two of you have got some outstanding mother/daughter relationship issues that need ironing out, but please, first things first!' To Fat Tulip: 'Where's the penis statue?'

Fat Tulip's face goes blank. 'What penis statue?'

'The penis statue you've been using to summon those cavemen who have been spreading marital discord across Bellend Close. *That* penis statue.'

'Yes, and what's more, it's *my* penis statue, as well!' adds Nanette. 'You had no right to take it, young lady!'

'What's yours is mine, isn't it?' says Fat Tulip innocently.

'No, what's mine is *not* yours! And especially not

something like that! Give it back!'

'And I haven't got it.'

'Don't you tell lies to your mother!' snaps Nanette. 'You don't seem to realise how much trouble you've got yourself into! Do you know who these people are?' indicating Dodo and Mayumi.

'Yeah, they're the people who moved into number twelve.'

'Yes, but they didn't just move here by accident. These ladies are officials. They were sent here to investigate what's been going on around here! And their investigations have led them to *you*. *Now* do you see? This isn't a game, young lady; this is serious!'

Judging by the look on her face, Fat Tulip *does* see. She looks at Dodo and Mayumi with alarm in her eyes. 'Are you going to arrest me?'

'*Not* if you cooperate,' says Dodo, seizing the opportunity. 'And the first thing you have to do is hand over that statue. Where is it?'

'It's over here,' sighs Fat Tulip.

Much to Dodo's lack of surprise, she leads them over to the stone slab in the middle of the glade. Squatting down beside the elevated end of the stone, she reaches an arm under the overhanging section.

'So, you've got it hidden under the stone?' says Dodo.

'Not *under* it; *in* it,' replies Fat Tulip. 'There's this sort of gap in the rock… Ah!'

The bronze penis statuette! That bronze age relic discovered in the stone age rock strata, and dismissed as a fake by the leading experts. But the leading experts were wrong, and Professor Aubergine, having more faith in her palaeontologist colleague, was right: a genuine oopart, and out of place artifact! And a great deal more besides…

Fat Tulip holds the statue aloft, where catching the moonlight, it seems to glow from within. This impressive effect is abruptly terminated when Dodo snatches the statue from her hand.

'So this is the culprit!' she says, examining it. 'At least I hope it is; I'm getting very tired of making the wrong guesses...'

'There's got to be a connection,' declares Nanette, peering at the statuette. 'Look at the shape of it: identical to the penises the cavemen have; the same in every detail!'

'A bit smaller, though...'

'No, not those really big ones! I mean the brutes with the smaller, just reasonably huge penises; the ones you can actually fit inside you.'

'Too much detail, Mum,' growls Fat Tulip.

'Sorry, darling. But yes, if you ask me, I'd say this statue was taken from a cast of one of those penises; that would certainly explain the detail. Normally you expect primitive art to be more, well, primitive...'

'Yes, and it's also the same shape as the one in satellite photos...' says Dodo.

'What satellite photos?' asks Fat Tulip.

Her mother turns to her. 'Yes, young lady, since you brought *my* penis statue to this place, this great big image of the thing has appeared on the ground. No, you can't see it from here, but they can see it up in space alright! Yes, it's been caught by a CIA spy satellite! The CIA! Think about it! What would you have done if the CIA had shown up here instead of a couple of nice, understanding ladies like Dodo and Mayumi? You would've vanished into thin air most likely!'

'Getting back to the point,' says Dodo. 'What did you do, Tulip? When you first brought this thing here; what did you do to summon the cave creatures?'

'Well, I just cast a spell with the... whatsit...'

'The penis? Okay, but what did you actually *do* with it while you were casting your spell? Were you holding it, or...?'

'No, I wasn't holding it. I just put it down here on the

rock.'

'And what sort of spell did you cast? Was it one you got from a book…?'

'No! It wasn't from a book! It was a spell I just sort of made up myself…'

'You mean you improvised it?'

'And how do we undo the spell?' wonders Nanette. 'Darling, maybe you should try reciting the spell backwards…? You know, the same way Satanists recite the lord's prayer backwards…'

'Mum, I can't remember the whole spell! I can't remember it *forwards*, never mind *backwards*! And I'm not a Satanist, either. A lot of people confuse—'

'I don't think you'll need to undo the spell you cast,' interrupts Dodo. 'I think it might have been your placing the statue on the rock that did it, not so much the words you said. You've been keeping it hidden in that cavity ever since then, have you?'

'Yeah, 'cept from when I've taken it out to have a look at it…'

'But basically, the statue has been here in physical contact with the stone all the time, yes? So, maybe that's what did it. And maybe now we've broken the spell just by taking it away from the rock; like we've broken the circuit or something…'

'You think the beasties might have disappeared for good?' asks Nanette.

'They might have. Or maybe we need to take the statue further away first; maybe the further away it is from this particular spot the more its power weakens…' She looks at Nanette. 'I know! Why don't we see if we can find out? Why doesn't one of us try and summon one of the creatures? Yumi and me never got the knack of it, but you can do it, can't you, Professor?'

'Well, yes…' says Nanette, twisting a stray lock of hair and looking very uncomfortable. 'But do I have to…? I mean, I don't really want to start... um... you know, *pleasuring* myself in front of my daughter...'

'Oh, *Mum*!' cries Fat Tulip, disgusted. 'That is totally *gross*! You don't have to do *that* to make the things appear! Least, I don't, anyway. You can just sort of *want* one to appear...'

'Then can you do it now, Tulip?' requests Dodo. 'Can you try and make one of them appear now?'

'Okay...' She points across the clearing. 'There,' she says. 'I'll make one appear over there...'

They look, and Fat Tulip concentrates. Sure enough the by-now familiar outline of one of the creatures begins to appear... But something is wrong: instead of taking solid form the figure remains diaphanous, ghost-like, fading in and out of existence...

And then it vanishes entirely.

'It's not working,' Fat Tulip tells them. 'I'm only doing what I always do, and it started to come, but now it's gone, and it's not there anymore; it's like I can't make any contact with it...'

'Well, that's good, then,' says Dodo, relieved. 'That's the result we were looking for.'

'Speak for yourself,' sulks Fat Tulip. 'They weren't doing any harm...'

'Look, Tulip, do you realise how much trouble you've caused by doing what you did? Look what's happened to the people in the close! The whole street has reverted to a... shall we say an undeveloped state?' (deftly avoiding loaded words like 'primitive' or 'savage.') 'The women have turned into a tribe of penis-worshipping nymphomaniacs, while their discarded husbands are slowly withering away to nothing... I'm not sure how, but it's like just by being here the beasts were somehow cancelling the men out... Well, hopefully the insanity will be starting to wear off now. And I think we need to take *this*,' holding up the penis statuette, 'much further away from here, just to make good and sure.

So I'm afraid that means you can't have it back, Nanette. You live way too close to the danger zone.'

'Oh dear! I was rather fond of the thing; it made such a lovely paperweight. What are you going to do with it, then? You're not going to destroy it, are you?'

'I think I'll just give it to Mark Hunter and let him decide. Mark's the man Yumi and me are acting for. Mark's the real spy; Yumi and me are just friends of his; we help him out from time to time…' She turns to Fat Tulip. 'So, young lady, you're off the hook. Mark is a very understanding sort of guy so he's not going to send you to gaol or anything. But tell me: why were you so keen on seeing some real live cavemen that you started casting spells to magic them into existence? Was it because of your mum's line of work?'

'I didn't want stupid cavemen!' explodes Fat Tulip. 'They weren't what I was wishing for at all! But the spell went wrong, didn't it? Probably cuz of that stupid penis thing!' pointing at the offending object.

'Then what *were* you trying to conjure up?'

'I wanted my own barbarian, didn't I? I wanted a man like Slayve the Barbarian!'

'Oh, so *that's* what it was!' understanding.

'Yeah. Cassie the New Age Dryad brought Slayve forward from the past by doing a spell, so I wanted to see if I could do the same…'

'I see. And did Cassie use a bronze penis when she cast her spell, then?'

'Of course she didn't! She used her magic staff, didn't she? I thought you said you knew about the Slayve comic!'

'Yes, I know *about* it; I never said I subscribed to it.'

'Well, it was in issue fifteen: "The Origin of Slayve." Cassie needed a champion to help her fight the government and the chemical companies, and so she cast this spell with her staff that caused a time storm, and brought Slayve the Barbarian from Celtic times to the present day.'

'I see. And not having a magic staff of your own, you

thought a bronze penis statuette would be a suitable substitute.'

'Well, I knew there was something special about that thing; I could feel it!' retorts Fat Tulip defensively. 'First time I held the thing, I could feel there was something magic about it.'

'And as it happens you were right: except that what it conjured up for you was something from a lot farther back than Celtic times.'

'Tell me about it,' mutters Fat Tulip. 'Major disappointment.'

'But then why didn't you just send them back, darling?' asks her mother. 'Why did you pass them on to the neighbours like that and end up causing all this trouble?'

'I didn't mean to do that! I didn't do anything, really… It was just that once they were here, they were here, I suppose… And that's why the other women in the close started being able to make them appear for them…'

'Wait a minute,' says Dodo. 'There was an incident that occurred here a few nights back: the men had kidnapped Mhambi Khoza and brought her here to question her; but then the beasts turned up and… Was that *your* doing?'

'Well, yeah…' admits Fat Tulip, shamefaced. 'The husbands were using this place for their secret meetings, and I heard them planning to kidnap Dr Khoza… So I thought I'd help… you know….? rescue her…'

'And couldn't you have got your friends to effect that rescue without raping all the men?'

'I didn't know they were going to do that!' hotly. 'I thought they'd just beat them up a bit or something…'

And now Tulip's mother steps forward and takes the girl in her arms. 'There, there. Your intentions were pure and that's what really counts… Oh dear… What a dreadful muddle you've caused…! Well, at least you got some good out of all this, didn't you? Eh? Yes; my sweet little girl is not quite such a little girl anymore, is she? She's a woman now!'

Nanette now holds her daughter at arm's length, the better to admire her with maternal pride.

But Fat Tulip is only confused at this show of affection. 'What do you mean by "I'm a woman now"?'

'Well, darling, I mean you have experienced physical intimacy, haven't you? You have experienced physical love. You have relinquished your virgin status—'

'WHAT?' protests Fat Tulip, full volume. 'You don't seriously think I actually shagged any of those things? You've got to be kidding! Yeurgh!'

'Why, whatever's wrong, Tulip, darling? I thought you liked men with those well-developed muscular physiques?'

'Yeah, but not with all that body hair on them! Gross! I want my first time to be with someone who's smooth all over, like Slayve is! He can have hair on his head and over his wedding tackle, but that's it!'

Mayumi howls with laughter, while Dodo, controlling her own mirth with an effort says: 'Well, if the body hair was the only problem, why didn't you just get hold of one of those gentlemen and shaved him?'

'You think I didn't think of that?' retorts Fat Tulip. 'I *tried*! Right here it was! I gave one of those things the full-body depilation treatment! And the moment I'd finished doing it *Bam!* it all grew back again! And I mean all of it, and in an instant!'

Even Nanette bursts out laughing at this; and while she's trying to explain to her daughter between giggles that they are laughing with her and not at her, and Fat Tulip is arguing that for this to be the case she would need to be an active participant in the general mirth herself, the sound of an aeroengine diverts Dodo's eyes upwards. Searching the sky for the moving lights that would indicate the position of this nightflying aircraft, she locates them and, even as she watches, sees an object, white against the starry sky, separate itself from the moving lights, and start falling towards them.

'What's wrong?' inquires Mayumi.

'Someone's just jumped from that plane with a parachute,' reports Dodo. 'Funny thing to be doing at this time of night.'

All four of them are now watching the descending parachute. As it grows larger, they can see it is one of the rectangular-canopied variety.

'Why, it's coming this way!' exclaims Nanette. 'Do you think they're going to land in this clearing?'

'Well, it's a steerable parachute, but even so they'd still have to be a very good parachutist to land on a small target like this in the dark,' says Dodo. 'Come on; let's move to the edge of the clearing.'

They hurry to the perimeter of the clearing, and it soon becomes clear that the parachutist does indeed intend to touch down right here in the glade.

Watching it come in, a smile slowly spreads across Dodo's face. 'You know, I've got an idea I might know who our nocturnal visitor could be…'

The parachutist makes a perfect landing. Touching down at the far end of the glade, the observers see him touch down, roll and recover. Releasing himself from his harness, the parachutist springs to his feet, and then, moving cautiously, he advances across the glade. The observers, still unobserved themselves, see a handsome man with neat, side-parted hair, and dressed in a smart brown suit.

Two of those observers know him very well.

Dodo steps out from beneath the shadows, and the man, reacting with lightning speed, draws a gun from his shoulder holster. (And right at the very end of what was shaping up to be a blessedly firearm-free novel, someone has to come along and spoilt it!)

Dodo raises her hands. 'Don't shoot; it's only me!'

'Dodo!'

'Hello, Mark, sweetheart.'

Yes, it is Mark Hunter himself! The Spy in the Brown Suit, The Thinking Woman's James Bond; to quote but two of the many titles with which he has been regaled.

The others now step forward, and introductions are exchanged, bashfully on Fat Tulip's part, concealed behind her mother.

'And is there any particular reason why you're all naked?' inquires Mark, with the casual air of a man who takes these things in his stride.

'Well, speaking for myself, sweetheart,' says Dodo; 'naked is how I always seem to end up when I'm working on one of your cases. What made you decide to drop in on us like this?'

'Well, I was worried about you, wasn't I? I hadn't heard from you for days, and then I started hearing these vague but bizarre reports as to what was going on in Bellend Close, and—so what *is* going on? What's the present situation, and why did you break off contact?'

'The present situation, Mark—and I know you're not going to like this—the present situation is that there is no situation at all, that the situation has only now just been successfully resolved and therefore your dramatic entrance has been in vain—not that we're not very glad to see you, I hasten to add. We are glad to see him, aren't we, Yumi?'

Mayumi energetically nods her head in confirmation of this fact.

'So in other words, I have once again arrived just after it's all over,' summarises Mark, reholstering his automatic.

'Basically, yes. Although actually, there is something you can do: you can take charge of this,' and she hands him the bronze penis.

'Thank you,' says Mark, eyeing the gift dubiously. 'Just what I've always wanted. By the way, where's Trina? Is she alright?'

'Oh yes, Trina's fine; she's back at the house. Ah! That reminds me: you're quite handy at picking locks, aren't you…?'

Epilogue

And so, with the situation resolved, peace and harmony were restored (more or less) to Bellend Close, and just for once nobody got killed in the process.

After the removal of the bronze penis from the vicinity, the Beasts of Bellend vanished from whence they came—and just where that whence might be is something that even Professor Aubergine couldn't tell you; the beasts were an evolutionary anomaly, an out of place lifeform.

And with the beasts removed from the equation, the husbands regained their vigour, the wives regained their sanity, and with many a tear and many more apologies, a number of severely mutilated marriages were successfully patched up. Not all of them, though. Just a few of the aggrieved husbands were unable to find it in their hearts to forgive their spouses, and so they packed their bags and vacated Bellend Close for pastures new. The reader will perhaps not be surprised to hear that Jubin Ghai was one of those husbands who did not forgive; but you might be more surprised to hear that David Jarman was one of the husbands who did! (Although I understand that the Zulu hut has been dismantled and the Allan Quatermain safari suit consigned to a charity shop.)

I would love to be able to report that in a final magical act, the bronze penis was placed upon Gerald Banbury's vacant crotch, whereupon it attached itself and transformed into a flesh and blood set of genitalia—I would love to be able to report this, but if I did I would be lying. As far as I know the experiment was never even attempted, and Gerald Banbury remains Bellend Close's resident eunuch.

As to what finally became of the bronze penis, I don't know. Dodo Dupont gave the statuette to Mark Hunter, and he passed it on to his superiors and that is the last he heard about it. But I can add that Fat Tulip went to the clearing in

Bellend Wood one day to find that the altar stone had mysteriously disappeared; and she was not best pleased about this, having come to consider the glade along with all its fixtures and fittings to be her own personal property.

Another thing that disappeared shortly after the events narrated above was the *Slayve the Barbarian* comic series. It was decreed that in that last issue, with Slayve using his erect penis to dispatch an enemy, that this heretofore wholesome children's comic had finally gone too far, that a line had been crossed—and the fact that Slayve's stonker was depicted in an entirely nonsexual context was just not enough of a mitigating factor. Such was the outcry that the following week's issue, already at the printers, had to be pulped and the series was discontinued.

(And if any of you were expecting it turn out that the mystery author of *Slayve the Barbarian* was actually a resident of Bellend Close, perhaps even Fat Tulip herself, you're going to be disappointed—it wasn't any of them, and the identity of the author-artist is still unknown.)

I'm sure you are all anxious to know what became of Mike Grimsby, P.I. Well, he relinquished his collar and lead, resumed his Hawaiian shirt and baseball cap and returned to London amply remunerated for his services. (Although he's still a long way off from being able to afford that Ferrari.)

And as for Mark Hunter, Dodo Dupont, Mayumi Takahashi and Trina Truelove: their stories cannot be neatly rounded off; their stories are endless.

Last but not least, naturally, all the women of Bellend Close soon discovered they were pregnant. According to the scans, the developing foetuses are all perfectly normal and healthy—but just what those babies will grow up into, only time will tell.

written March-May, 2023

Samurai West

disappearer007@gmail.com

Printed in Dunstable, United Kingdom